The moment her hands skimmed his flesh, Rory could feel the changes.

When her strong fingers began massaging his shoulder, his heartbeat became erratic. His breathing accelerated. His mind was swept clean of all thought save one. He wanted more. He was desperate to feel her hands touching him everywhere.

He clenched his teeth to keep from crying out. Clenched his hands into fists to keep from dragging her into his arms and taking what he wanted.

"You haven't been moving your arm as you should," AnnaClaire said.

"And how would you know that?"

"Because I can feel a knot of tension here." She kneaded his flesh, and he bent his head forward slightly to give her easier access. "And here." She pressed her thumbs over his stiff shoulder, working the flesh in firm but gentle strokes.

"Perhaps the tension is from something other than pain."

"And what would that be?"

He sighed, as much in pleasure as frustration. "I'll leave you to figure that one for yourself, my lady...."

Dear Reader,

Entertainment. Escape. Fantasy. These three words describe the heart of Harlequin Historicals. If you want compelling, emotional stories by some of the best writers in the field, look no further.

Ruth Langan is one of those writers. With over forty-five books to her credit, this bestselling author has made a name for herself in the world of romance fiction. We are thrilled to bring you *Rory,* the first book in her new medieval series, THE O'NEIL SAGA. Legendary Irish rebel Rory O'Neil has a price on his head for his attacks on English soldiers. When he is wounded in battle, he is nursed by an English noblewoman who eventually must choose between her love for Rory or her loyalty to the Queen of England. Don't miss this heart-wrenching story!

A Father for Keeps is a heartwarming reunion romance by the talented Ana Seymour. A wealthy miner returns to Nevada to win back the woman who secretly had his child. In *Robber Bride* by Deborah Simmons, the third de Burgh brother, Simon, finds his true love in a runaway bride who is hiding from her despicable would-be husband.

And be sure to look for *The Tender Stranger* by Carolyn Davidson. In this gripping tale, a pregnant widow flees from her conniving in-laws to an isolated Colorado cabin, and later falls in love with the bounty hunter hired to bring her back East.

Whatever your tastes in reading, you'll be sure to find a romantic journey back to the past between the covers of a Harlequin Historical.®

Sincerely,

Tracy Farrell
Senior Editor

Please address questions and book requests to:
Harlequin Reader Service
U.S.: 3010 Walden Ave., P.O. Box 1325, Buffalo, NY 14269
Canadian: P.O. Box 609, Fort Erie, Ont. L2A 5X3

RUTH
LANGAN
RORY

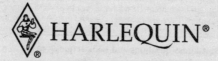

HARLEQUIN®

TORONTO • NEW YORK • LONDON
AMSTERDAM • PARIS • SYDNEY • HAMBURG
STOCKHOLM • ATHENS • TOKYO • MILAN • MADRID
PRAGUE • WARSAW • BUDAPEST • AUCKLAND

ISBN 0-373-29057-8

RORY

Copyright © 1999 by Ruth Ryan Langan

This edition published by arrangement with Harlequin Books S.A.

® and TM are trademarks of the publisher. Trademarks indicated with ® are registered in the United States Patent and Trademark Office, the Canadian Trade Marks Office and in other countries.

Printed in U.S.A.

Books by Ruth Langan

Harlequin Historicals

Mistress of the Seas #10
†*Texas Heart* #31
Highland Barbarian #41
Highland Heather #65
Highland Fire #91
Highland Heart #111
†*Texas Healer* #131
Christmas Miracle #147
†*Texas Hero* #180
Deception #196
The Highlander #228
Angel #245
Highland Heaven #269
‡*Diamond* #305
Dulcie's Gift #324
‡*Pearl* #329
‡*Jade* #352
‡*Ruby* #384
Malachite #407
The Courtship of Izzy McCree #425
Blackthorne #435
Rory #457

Harlequin Books

Outlaw Brides
"Maverick Hearts"

*Harlequin Historicals
  Christmas Stories* 1990
"Christmas at Bitter Creek"

†Texas Series
*The Highland Series
‡The Jewels of Texas

RUTH LANGAN

traces her ancestry to Scotland and Ireland. It is no surprise, then, that she feels a kinship with the characters in her historical novels.

Married to her childhood sweetheart, she has raised five children and lives in Michigan, the state where she was born and raised.

For sweet little Macey Langan Bissonnette
And her big sisters, Aubrey, Haley and Kelsey
And her proud parents, Carol and Bryon

And to Tom
Always

Prologue

Ireland, 1560

The chapel at Ballinarin, the ancestral home of the clan O'Neil, was filled to overflowing with family and friends who had come from as far as Malahide Castle in Dublin, and Bunratty Castle in Clare. The mood was festive as they prepared to witness the union of Rory O'Neil, eldest son of Gavin and Moira, and his beloved Caitlin Maguire.

In a small room at the back of the chapel Rory paced while his brother, Conor, stood by the door and watched as the last of the guests filed into pews.

"What's keeping her?" Rory paused. Sunlight speared through a high window, turning his dark hair blue-black. He was resplendent in black breeches and shirt, with his cloak bearing the O'Neil crest tossed rakishly over his shoulder.

"You needn't worry that she's changed her mind, Rory. The lass has loved you since she was old enough to know her own mind. Just be patient."

"Damn your patience."

Conor grinned. "Aye, that was never one of your virtues, Rory. But give the lass time to make herself beautiful for her husband."

"Nothing could make Caitlin more beautiful than she already is. And why should I be patient? I've waited a lifetime for this day."

"Aye. It seems like you've been in love with her forever."

"Since I was ten and two." He flashed the smile that had caused maidens from Derry to Cork to dream of snagging his attention. But Rory O'Neil had eyes for only one maiden. "I was born for her alone. I tell you, Conor, this day my life will be complete." He lowered his voice. "Did I tell you that I slipped over to see her last night? I told her I couldn't wait until today. I wanted to lie with her."

Conor threw back his head and roared. "Don't let Friar Malone hear of this."

"It wouldn't matter. She refused. She said she wanted to wait for her wedding night. It was to be her special gift to her husband." He grinned. "Husband. I like the sound of that."

"And with all this love stored up, I'm sure your wedding night will be one to remember."

Both brothers turned as the door was thrust in and a slender lass in a gown of pink gossamer hurried inside.

"I was afraid I'd be too late."

"Too late for what, Briana?" Rory couldn't help grinning at the sight of his little sister. Her waist-length hair, the color of flame, was wind-tossed. Her cheeks were bright with color. From the sound of her breathing, he could tell she'd just run the entire distance from the keep to the chapel. All her young life she'd been running to keep up with her two older brothers.

"Too late to kiss my brother before he left me for good."

"You talk as though I'm going away. Caitlin and I will be living right here on the grounds of Ballinarin."

"Aye. But you'll be a husband." She dimpled, and the two brothers knew she'd overheard at least some of their conversation. But it would go no further. Briana could always be counted on to keep a secret. "And in no time, seeing the way you two look at each other, you'll be a father as well. And you'll have no time for a sister."

Rory drew her close and pressed a kiss to the top of her head. "I'll always have time for you, Briana. And you can come over every day and help Caitlin with the wee ones."

"Just how many are you planning to have?"

"At least a dozen. All the lads will be handsome like their father, and all the lasses will have dark hair like their mother, and skin as fair as the crystal water in the River Shannon, and so beautiful that I'll have to lock them up to keep the local lads from stealing them all away."

Conor and Briana burst into gales of laughter.

"That's what I like about you, Rory. When you dream," his brother said with a laugh, "they're always such grand dreams. Let's just hope it isn't the other way around. After all, your sons could be small and delicate like their mother, and your daughters could all be giants like you."

"Not a chance. They'll…" He paused at the sound of a commotion in the chapel and gave a smile of relief.

"Finally. I was beginning to think—" At the sudden chorus of shouting voices his smile dissolved.

He hurried from the room, followed by his brother and sister.

A lad of six or seven, clothes torn and bloodied, stood gesturing wildly. "English soldiers. More than a dozen of them."

Rory's heart nearly stopped as he shouldered his way through the guests. He recognized the lad as a son of Caitlin's eldest brother. He knelt down, caught him by the shoulders. "Where are the others, Innis?"

"By the bend in the road." The boy's eyes were wide with pain and shock. "My da fell on top of me, pinning me to the ground. All I could do was watch. They're all dead, Rory."

"No!" Rory's voice echoed through the chapel as he released the boy and jumped to his feet, pushing and shoving through the stunned crowd.

Outside he grasped the reins of the first horse he spotted and leapt onto its back, urging it into a gallop. He could hear the sounds of other horses following behind, but he never looked back.

He followed the bog road until he came to the bend. Even before he got there, he could hear the strange, eerie silence. No birds sang. No creatures moved. It was as though the entire land was holding its breath.

And then he saw them. The mass of bodies. Animal as well as human. The ground ran red with their blood. The horses had died where they'd fallen, with lances through the neck or heart. The men had fought a fierce battle. Many lay, face up, still holding their swords. But the worst savagery had been inflicted upon the women.

Rory saw the flutter of white. Caitlin's bridal gown.

It was the only way he could identify her. He picked his way through the carnage and knelt beside her. The gown had been cut away, except for one sleeve that still clung to her wrist. From the marks on her body he could see that she'd been brutalized before her throat had been cut so violently her head had nearly been severed from her body.

With a cry of pain and rage he gathered her against him and buried his face in her bloody hair. His body shook with great, wrenching sobs that spoke of a heart shattered beyond repair.

"Rory. God in heaven, Rory." Conor was the first to find him. He could do no more than weep as he stood, watching his brother silently rage against the horror of it.

As the others arrived, Gavin O'Neil strode through the carnage to stand over his firstborn son. His voice shook with raw emotion. "The lad, Innis, says the leader was called Tilden by the others. Tall, brawny, with yellow hair and a face disfigured by a scar that ran from his left eye to his jaw. 'Twill not be an easy face to hide."

"I'll find him." Rory unfastened his cloak and used it to cover Caitlin's nakedness. He staggered to his feet, cradling the broken body of the woman who had been his reason for living. This night she would have lain in his arms, in their bed. Instead she would lie forever in the cold, hard earth. He looked up to stare at his family and friends. All were weeping uncontrollably.

His own tears had dried. His eyes, hard as stone, stared beyond the bloodstained ground. "I give you my word. I'll not rest until I find the English bastard who did this."

His father laid a hand on his shoulder. "We'll fetch a wagon to take her and the others to be buried."

Rory shook off the hand. "No one will touch Caitlin. I'll carry her. It's all I can give her now."

It was a somber, silent procession that made its way back to the chapel. The guests in their wedding finery were a sharp contrast to the bloody bodies being hauled in hay wagons. At the head of the column walked Rory O'Neil, his tunic and breeches clotted with blood. The body in his arms was completely covered with his cloak, except for a spill of raven hair matted with blood and grass.

At the chapel he continued to stand and hold Caitlin cradled to his chest as a hole was dug and Friar Malone began the words that would consign the body to holy ground.

For hours, while the holes were dug and the bodies buried, Rory continued to kneel silently at the mound of earth that covered his beloved. And when the last body had been disposed of, he looked around the grave site, then fixed his gaze on the distance.

As his family gathered around, he embraced his mother and father, and kissed his sister's cheek.

Briana's cries became great, wracking sobs that shook her slender frame. "You musn't go, Rory. Please, don't go. If you do, I'll never see you again."

"Hush now." He held her close for a moment, whispering against her forehead, "I'll return. Trust me."

Conor clamped a hand on his shoulder. "Will you let me come with you?"

Rory gave a firm shake of his head. "It's something I must do alone. You'll be needed here." He turned to his mother, who stood behind Innis, her arms wrapped around his thin shoulders. "You'll see to the lad?"

She nodded. "He'll be a son to me, until my own returns."

Rory strapped on a sword and tucked a knife at his waist and in his boot.

His father removed his own cloak, which bore the O'Neil crest, and wrapped it around his son's shoulders. Lifting his hand in benediction he said, "May God ride with you, Rory, and bring you home to those who love you."

Without a word, Rory pulled himself onto the back of his horse. He turned for one last look at Ballinarin. In the distance Croagh Patrick stood guard over the land. The mountain changed color so rapidly it was never the same. Earlier, it had been a harsh gray-green in the misty rain. Now it had softened to a peach hue in the warmth of the fading sun. Its sides were cloaked with stunted, twisted shrubs and trees and at the base, tall conifers and clumps of rhododendron. Waterfalls tossed themselves over the side, spilling down until they reached the river. Torn shreds of clouds drifted overhead. This lonely, savage piece of land held his heart. It was the only place he'd ever wanted to be. But now, the deceptively gentle scene mocked him. Because of the violence that had occurred here, he would begin an odyssey. An odyssey that could take him far away for years, or even a lifetime, until this thing was finished.

Chapter One

County Dublin, 1562

"So many of them, Rory." The voice was little more than a whisper on the breeze.

Half a dozen figures crouched by the banks of the Liffey, watching the English soldiers frolic in the brown water.

"Aye. I'd hoped for only a dozen or more. There must be close to fifty." Rory turned to the weathered farmer kneeling beside him. "Why so many?"

"Now that the English have discovered the healing properties of the boiling spring, this river has become a favorite place for them to congregate." He wrinkled his nose at the strong odor of sulphur. "It helps them relax after they've had the fun of killing a few of us."

Rory watched from his place of concealment. "You're certain the one with the scar is among them?"

The farmer's eyes narrowed as he scanned the distant figures. "I haven't spotted him yet. But he was with this group of bastards yesterday when they caught my little daughter in the fields and made sport of her."

His voice betrayed his pain. "She's only ten and one,
Rory. And the things they did to her. The one with the
scar demanded to be first. She told me he taunted those
who refused to join in." In a fierce whisper he added,
"I want to be the one to kill him."

Rory touched a hand to his arm. "I know how you
feel, Seamus. But you've done enough. Go home to
your family now."

"I need to see him dead." The farmer fingered his
only weapon, a small crude knife.

"Your family can't afford to lose you, Seamus. Go
now. Leave the killing to us."

"You'll kill him, Rory? For my Fiona? For me?"

"Aye. If he's here, I'll see the bastard dead." For
Caitlin, he thought, especially for Caitlin.

Seeing the hatred that glittered in Rory O'Neil's
eyes, the farmer had no doubt that his family's honor
would be avenged. In the past two years, all of Ireland
had heard of the quest for vengeance that drove this
fierce Irish warrior. Wherever there was a battle between his countrymen and the hated English, Rory
O'Neil could be found in the thick of it. He had killed
so many soldiers, there was now a price on his head.
He was the most hunted man in the land. And the man
most despised by his enemy. He was known throughout
England and Ireland as the Blackhearted O'Neil. Despite the fact that his likeness was posted throughout
the country, Rory O'Neil was so loved by the people,
he could count on being safely hidden in any town or
village throughout the land. Everywhere he went, men
joined his ragged band in its quest for vengeance.

"Can we take them now, Rory?" one of his men
whispered when the farmer was safely gone.

"Patience, Colin." How odd that he now counseled patience, when he'd had so little of it in his life.

He watched as the last of the soldiers stripped off their tunics and walked into the water. Only a handful of men remained as lookouts, while the others swam and bathed and splashed each other like boys.

"Ready, lads?" he asked as he stood and unsheathed his sword.

His men nodded and did the same.

A ripple of anticipation passed through them, charging each man with almost supernatural fervor. The very air around them seemed somehow changed. No one spoke. No one moved as they waited for the signal from their leader.

"Now," Rory called in a fierce whisper.

They scrambled down the banks of the river, screaming like banshees. The hapless guards didn't even have a chance to unsheath their swords before they fell in their own blood.

The English soldiers, who had only moments earlier been laughing and calling to one another, now struggled feverishly to retrieve their weapons. Though they outnumbered the Irish warriors almost ten to one, they had the disadvantage of being caught unawares.

Rory plowed into the water, using his sword with an economy of movement. With each thrust of his blade, another man stiffened, gasped, tumbled headlong into the river. In no time the brown waters of the Liffey ran red with blood. And still the killing went on.

Each time he encountered another soldier, Rory stared into his opponent's face, searching for the telltale scar. And each time, he experienced the sting of disappointment when he realized this wasn't the one he sought.

He had long ago stopped feeling the shock along his arm when his sword encountered muscle and bone. And was able to block out the muffled sobs and high-pitched shrieks of the dying. What he couldn't erase from his mind was the sight of his beloved Caitlin, her body bloodied and battered beyond recognition. This was what drove him. This was what gave him the will to go on, no matter what the odds.

As he stepped over yet another body, he caught a glimpse of a soldier with yellow hair plucking a sword from one of his fallen comrades.

At last, Rory thought. At long last, his quest would be ended. With a cry of pain and rage he lunged through the water lapping at his hips and stumbled forward.

Hearing his voice, the soldier momentarily dropped the sword.

"Pick it up, you coward." Rory's voice was thick with passion. "Pick it up and face your death like a man."

Rory saw the soldier grasp the sword as he lifted his own. The thought of victory sang through his blood and misted his vision.

"Now," he shouted. "Now, Tilden, will you taste the vengeance of Rory O'Neil."

He could no more stop the thrust of his blade than he could still the waters churning beneath his feet. And yet, in that last moment, he realized his mistake. This man had no scar. His face was unlined. It was the face of a youth. The eyes wide with terror. The mouth round in surprise.

The force of the thrust sent his blade through the lad's chest and out the other side. The young soldier was dead before his body hit the water.

With a feeling of horror and revulsion, Rory pulled his sword free and watched as the water around the body turned blood red.

For the first time he stared around at the scene of carnage. Not a single soldier remained. The Liffey and its banks were littered with bodies. Three of his own men were sitting in the shallows, looking dazed. One was tying a tourniquet around his bloody leg. Another was leaning against a tree, retching.

How long had this killing lasted? Minutes? Hours? Time was nothing but a blur.

Had he really been on this quest for two years now? Two years of blood and violence and death. Two years of being hunted, and hiding out in hay barns and accepting food from strangers.

And yet, how could he stop the carnage? In every village he heard the stories of cottages burned and crops destroyed and women and children violated.

He was weary beyond belief. The thought of Ballinarin taunted him, tempted him. At times all he could think of was turning his back on this quest and returning to his home and family.

But then, he would see again in his mind his beloved Caitlin. And he knew, no matter how weary, no matter what the Fates meted out to him, he could never stop until he found the English bastard who had brutalized and murdered his future bride and her entire family. Tilden had to pay.

"Will we stop awhile, Rory?" one of his men called.

"We'll move on." He forced the weariness aside as he allowed the water to wash the blood from his sword. Then he sheathed it and stepped from the river. "If we move quickly, we can sleep tonight in Dublin."

* * *

"I'm sorry I must leave you, AnnaClaire."

"I understand, Father. You have your duties."

"But it's so soon since Margaret…"

The young woman touched a hand to her father's lips to still his words. "I'll not deny I miss Mother. As do you. Every day of our lives we'll miss her. But I can't ask you to forsake everything and spend the rest of your life holding my hand."

"The grief is still so raw."

"Aye. I expect a year from now I'll still be grieving. But I'll find ways to stay busy. I promise."

"I wish you'd change your mind and come with me."

"We've gone over this before, Father. I'm just not ready to leave Mother's home, her grave."

"I know. And I understand, my dear. I've asked Charles Lord Davis to look in on you. And Lady Alice Thornly is planning a lovely dinner party. She hinted that there would be several interesting men recently arrived who might snag your interest."

AnnaClaire managed a smile. "You just can't help yourself, can you, Father?"

"Do you blame me? You need a husband, a family. You're far from home, without the comfort of your mother, and now your father abandons you as well."

"You aren't abandoning me. You said yourself you'll be back in time for my birthday."

"And I shall. But I'd feel better if I knew you had a young man looking out for you while I was gone."

"I'll have an old one. Lord Davis is a dear."

"But not quite what I had in mind. No matter." He turned to see his trunks being unloaded from the lorry and deposited on the docks. "I don't want you to remain until my ship sails. I'd just as soon you not mingle with the locals.''

He could see that she was about to voice an objection so he gave her shoulders a squeeze. "Go now. Tavis is waiting with the carriage. Stay well, my dear. Stay busy. And do be careful. These are dangerous times."

"Goodbye, Father. God speed."

AnnaClaire turned away and began to move slowly through the crowd.

It was market day, and the docks teemed with life. Gnarled, ruddy fishermen sat mending their nets while children, no older than nine or ten, pushed carts piled with cockles and mussels. Old women in faded gowns held up striped sea bass and cod to entice buyers. Chickens squawked in crude wooden pens. Farmers displayed the bounty from their land. Potatoes, carrots, peas.

The air was ripe with the scent of sea and earth and humanity. Wealthy landowners mingled with the poorest of the poor as vendors vied with one another to sell their wares. AnnaClaire felt a tug at her heartstrings. From her earliest childhood she had always loved the sights and sounds and smells of Dublin.

English soldiers, fresh from their journey across the Channel, disembarked from Her Majesty's ship, the *Greenley,* and shouldered their way through the throng, escorting half a dozen of the queen's own emissaries. Each month, Elizabeth dispatched more titled English to deal with what was being called "the Irish problem."

"Out of the way, you fools." One of the soldiers raised his sword menacingly, and the crowd fell back.

From her vantage point, AnnaClaire felt a wave of

disgust. Every time another boatload of soldiers arrived on these shores, the discontent grew. And not without good reason. Some of these crude louts could neither read nor write, yet they seemed determined to prove to the locals that they were superior in every way.

As the soldiers approached, AnnaClaire saw a young woman, heavy with child, grasp the hand of a toddler and try to snatch her out of the way. At the last moment the child pulled free and stepped directly into the path of the marching men.

"Oh, no. Someone please stop her," the woman cried.

AnnaClaire couldn't believe what she was seeing. The soldiers continued pressing forward. With the surge of the crowd, the little one would surely be trampled.

Without a thought to her own safety she dashed forward and snatched up the child, sidestepping out of danger only a second before the soldiers marched past.

"Oh, thank you, miss. Bless you. Bless you." With tears of gratitude the young woman kissed Anna-Claire's hands before taking the little girl from her arms and hugging her to her heart.

"You're welcome. I can't believe they didn't see what was happening."

"They saw." The young woman's eyes narrowed. "They just don't care. Our lives mean nothing to them." Her voice lowered. "But soon, very soon, they'll feel the sting of the Blackhearted O'Neil."

"I don't understand."

"He's here." Now the young woman's voice was little more than a whisper. "They say he's here in the crowd."

"Who is here?"

"Rory O'Neil. The Blackhearted O'Neil. Praise heaven. Come to put an end to the injustice." Her eyes suddenly widened. "God in heaven. There he is now. Come, miss. We mustn't tarry. It's begun."

AnnaClaire was aware of a murmur going through the crowd. "What's begun?"

"There's no time." Before AnnaClaire could argue, the young woman tugged her out of the way of a band of ragged men wielding swords. Moments later she shoved AnnaClaire down behind a cart heaped with stinking fish. From there AnnaClaire watched in wide-eyed wonder as that small band engaged more than a dozen soldiers in battle.

The scene was one of complete chaos. The soldiers, honor-bound to protect the queen's emissaries, stood in a tight line, swords raised against the intruders. But instead of falling back, these Irish confounded them by charging directly at them, swords flashing, voices screaming.

Several of the young soldiers, who were engaging the enemy for the first time, looked absolutely terrified. Instead of standing their ground, they turned and fled, ignoring the shouted commands of their sergeant-at-arms.

To add to the confusion, many of the cages were upended, releasing squawking chickens and quacking ducks. From her position behind a cart, an old woman began tossing her supply of fish at the English soldiers. Others soon joined in, until the docks were littered with the slimy remains of seafood.

AnnaClaire watched as the leader of the Irish warriors leapt between one of his own men, who was bleeding profusely, and a soldier who was about to run him through with his sword.

"That's Rory O'Neil," the young woman beside her said with a trace of awe. "Our Blackhearted O'Neil."

AnnaClaire couldn't take her eyes off him. She'd never seen anyone like him. This man looked like the devil himself, leaping, dancing, his sword singing through the air and landing fatal blows with uncanny accuracy. He was everywhere. Deflecting an English sword. Taking a blow meant for one of his men, then retaliating with a powerful thrust of his own blade. When one of his men was wounded, he shouldered him aside and saved him from certain death, before returning to the fray.

As the battle wore on, only three English soldiers remained standing. But when the queen's emissaries began to flee, Rory's voice stopped them.

"We have not come to harm you. The one we were seeking is not here. We wish only that you carry this message to your queen. All we desire is to live in peace. But know this. We will not lay down our arms until those soldiers who have harmed our innocent women and children have paid. Beginning with the one called Tilden. He is the one we seek. He brings shame to his queen and country. Do you understand?"

The titled men glanced nervously at one another before nodding their heads.

Satisfied, Rory lowered his sword. "Now tell your soldiers to lower their weapons, and we will take our leave of this place."

As the three soldiers began to comply, a voice from behind them shouted, "Cowards. You will not surrender to these barbarians."

A burly soldier stepped into their midst. His yellow hair hung nearly to his shoulders. A wide, puckered scar ran from his left eye to his jaw. At the sight of him the crowd of Irish onlookers gave a collective gasp before falling eerily silent.

AnnaClaire turned to the young woman beside her. "What is wrong? Who is that?"

"He is the soldier they came seeking. His name is Tilden. But most call him Lucifer. Especially those who have tasted his cruelty."

"What sort of cruelty?"

"Beyond anything you can imagine. He enjoys torturing our men before finally taking their lives. He despoils our women and children, and often forces husbands and fathers to watch the brutality before killing them. And he has vowed to be the one to stop our Blackhearted O'Neil." The woman's lips trembled. "But if there is a God in heaven, Rory O'Neil will prevail. Else, all in this fair land are lost."

AnnaClaire decided it was best to keep her thoughts to herself. But she wondered what possible chance one exhausted, bloody, wounded Irish warrior could have against a soldier who had just stepped afresh into battle.

"He is mine," Rory shouted as he charged toward the laughing soldier.

The throb of passion in his voice sent shivers through the crowd. But before he could confront Tilden, more than a dozen soldiers stepped from their places of concealment and brandished swords. Rory found himself fighting for his life.

Once again the crowd fell back and watched in silence as Rory and his small, wounded band fought valiantly. It was an amazing sight to see men leaping, lunging, the blades of their swords running red with blood. And though the ragged band of Irish warriors was now beyond exhaustion, they never gave up, never fell back.

Amazingly, they fought until the last of the soldiers fell to the ground. Then, bleeding from half a dozen wounds, Rory looked around for the one he'd come seeking. Though his right arm hung limply at his side, and his clothes were soaked with blood, the blaze of fury was still in his eyes.

"You cannot hide, Tilden. Show yourself, coward."

One of his men threw an arm around his shoulders. "Come, Rory. We must flee. There are more soldiers aboard the English ship. You can be certain a coward like Tilden wouldn't fight alone. He's surely gone for reinforcements."

"I want him. I've come too far to turn away now."

"Nay, friend. Come. You've lost too much blood. We must flee now, while we can still walk. Thus will we live to fight another day."

As Rory was led away he stumbled, righted himself, then moved numbly through the crowd.

AnnaClaire watched as the people surged forward, forming a protective wall of humanity so that their hero and his ragged band could melt away in the crowd.

"Well. That was quite a spectacle." She got to her feet, dusting off her skirts. "I can see why Rory O'Neil is called the Blackhearted O'Neil. But I…" She turned toward the place where the young woman had been kneeling beside her. But she and her child were gone.

AnnaClaire frowned. All these people, it would seem, had a habit of simply disappearing into thin air.

"Thank you, Tavis." AnnaClaire watched as her driver hung the pen holding the chicken at the rear of her open carriage.

It had taken more than an hour to make her way through the milling throngs, especially since she'd been forced to wait until one of the vendors retrieved his scattered chickens.

"I hope Bridget is sufficiently grateful for all we went through to bring home supper."

"Aye, my lady. But when you taste what my Bridget can do with one little chicken, 'tis you who'll be grateful."

She laughed as Tavis Murphy gave her a hand up. She settled herself comfortably, arranging her skirts as the carriage jolted ahead. She gave a glance around. "I believe we've lost my lap robe."

"Nay, my lady. The day is warm. I set it in back, out of the way."

"Thank you, Tavis."

He nodded in acknowledgment. "'Twill be slow going, my lady." He pulled back on the reins and brought the horse and carriage to a walk.

"I don't mind. After all I've seen today, I'll just sit here and catch my breath."

"You saw the battle then?" He steered around a cluster of men and women who were still talking and gesturing.

"It was right before my eyes."

He half turned. "You saw our Blackhearted O'Neil?"

She nodded. "I saw him."

"Handsome devil, I'm told."

"Some might say that. The devil part at least. I'd call him dangerous. And violent."

"Aye, he's violent. A man of deep passion, I've heard. But with good reason. His bride-to-be was brutalized and murdered on their wedding day."

She felt a quick jolt, then swept it aside. "From what I saw today, he's more than made up for one woman's death. Do you know how many English women will weep and mourn the loss of husbands and sons this day?"

Tavis held his silence, and concentrated on urging the horse through the maze of carts and wagons and people.

AnnaClaire recognized his silence as disapproval. She studied her driver's profile. Though Tavis and his wife Bridget were paid handsomely for their services to her father, she had no illusions about their loyalty. This was their land; these were their people. And though her mother had been born and raised in Dublin, AnnaClaire was considered an outsider. Her mother, Margaret Doyle, had married an English nobleman, and had educated her own daughter in London.

"Here we are, my lady." Tavis brought the carriage to a halt and helped her down. "I'll see that Bridget gets the chicken right away."

"Thank you, Tavis." She turned toward the door, then turned back as the carriage jolted ahead. "Oh, wait. My lap robe."

"I'll bring it in after I've rubbed down the horse and cleaned the carriage," he called over his shoulder.

"But I…"

The carriage was already rounding the corner of the drive. She stood a moment, watching the way her robe, mounded on the back platform, fluttered in the breeze. With a shrug of resignation, she turned away and entered the lovely manor house, Clay Court, that had been in her mother's family for six generations.

Her first order of business would be to wash away the stench of fish that clung to her skin and clothes.

Then she would make herself presentable for her visit with her father's oldest friend.

"Bridget, the dinner was lovely."

"Thank you, miss. Will you have more tea?"

"No. Lord Davis? More tea? Or perhaps a bit more ale?"

The old man patted his stomach. "Not another drop, my dear. I fear I'll explode."

"It was kind of you to come by tonight and keep me company."

"I knew you'd be feeling lonely with your father gone. And I was concerned when I heard about the fighting that went on at the docks today." He wiped his mouth, set his napkin aside. "If I'd known you were anywhere near those barbarians, I'd have been there to personally escort you home."

"I was never in any danger. The only one they really wanted was an English soldier named Tilden."

"Don't be fooled, my dear. No one is safe around desperate men such as those. An innocent like yourself has no idea what they're capable of doing. Why, the stories I've heard about the fate of fair English maidens at the hands of those animals would make a grown man cringe."

The dishes in Bridget's hands clattered.

AnnaClaire glanced at her housekeeper. "You look pale, Bridget. Are you feeling all right?"

The housekeeper backed away. "Aye, miss. Just a bit tired is all." She turned, clutching the dishes to her chest, and fled the room.

"How about a game of chess, my dear?"

AnnaClaire shook her head. "I'm sorry, Lord Davis.

Like Bridget, I'm afraid I'm too tired to offer you much of a challenge tonight.''

''All right.'' He stood, then held her chair as she got to her feet. ''Perhaps another night.''

''I'd like that.'' She led the way from the ornate dining hall, then tucked her arm through his as they walked together along the corridor toward the front door. ''Will you be going to Lady Thornly's dinner party?''

The old man nodded. ''Wouldn't miss it. Though in truth, the food won't be nearly as tasty as what we enjoyed tonight.''

Outside, his carriage and driver were silhouetted against the night sky. The old man leaned close and brushed a kiss over her cheek. ''I bid you good night, my dear. And tell Bridget those were the best fruit tarts I've ever tasted.''

''I believe you told her. Three times.''

He chuckled. ''That's so she would return three times to offer me more. If you aren't careful, I'll steal her from you.''

He was helped up to the carriage. When he was settled he doffed his hat. ''Sleep well, AnnaClaire.''

''And you, Lord Davis.''

She waved until the carriage pulled away. Then she went inside and made her way up the wide staircase to her suite of rooms on the second floor. Within minutes she had shed her clothes.

''Would you be wanting anything else, miss?'' Bridget hovered by the door to AnnaClaire's bedchamber. The little maid, Glinna, was busy turning down the bed linens and gathering up assorted skirts and petticoats. By morning they would be washed and ironed and carefully returned to the wardrobe.

"No, thank you, Bridget." AnnaClaire yawned behind her hand. "As I'm sure you've heard, it's been quite a tiring day."

"Aye, miss."

AnnaClaire looked at her a little more closely. A worried little frown furrowed the housekeeper's brow. Her skin seemed to have lost all its color. "Are you certain you're feeling all right?"

"Aye, miss. I'll be fine after a bit of sleep. If there's nothing you need, I'll say good night now."

"Good night, Bridget."

AnnaClaire waited until the housekeeper and maid had departed, then blew out her candle and climbed into bed. But sleep wouldn't come. She rolled from one side to the other, unable to find a comfortable position. She was simply too stimulated by all she'd seen and heard this day. Determined to sleep, she closed her eyes. At once she was assaulted by the image of the darkly handsome Rory O'Neil. She had never seen a man quite like him. Such a commanding presence. So fearless in the face of almost certain death. He was either the bravest man she'd ever seen or the most foolhardy.

And that voice. Just the thought of all that rage and passion had her trembling again. She sat up, shoving a tangle of honey curls from her eyes. There was no point in trying to sleep. Instead, she would make herself a cup of tea and then write a letter to her father.

Slipping out of bed, she caught up a warm shawl and tossed it over her nightshift, then padded barefoot from the room. Candles in sconces along the hallway sputtered in pools of wax, casting eerie shadows along the walls.

She made her way to the kitchen and placed a kettle

of water over the glowing coals of the fire. As she waited for the water to boil, she noticed her lap robe tossed carelessly over a bench. Odd. It wasn't like Tavis to be so casual with her things. As she picked it up, she felt something damp and sticky. Lifting her hand to the firelight, she frowned. It appeared to be red as blood. It must be the glow from the coals fooling the eye.

She held a candle to the flame until the wick caught fire, then lifted it high and studied the cloth more closely. Dear heaven. It was blood. Not just a drop or two, but great wet rivers of it staining the entire robe. She dropped it as though the touch of it burned her.

At the sound of a footfall behind her she spun around. And went deadly still at the sight that greeted her.

Rory O'Neil had pulled himself from the shadows and was leaning heavily against the table. ''I'm sorry about that fine robe. I seem to have ruined it.''

Blood still oozed from his neck, his chest, his arm, soaking the front of his tunic, staining his breeches and boots. In his right hand he held his sword aloft.

His eyes narrowed as he studied the vision before him. A vision that seemed to shimmer and shift. In the glow of firelight the woman appeared to be bathed in a halo of light.

He slowly lowered his sword. ''So. That's it then. I'm dying.'' His voice, still rich and deep and passionate, seemed to warm as he smiled.

At that moment his sword clattered to the floor, and he gripped the edge of the table with both hands. The blood drained from his face. He slowly sank to his knees, then slid bonelessly to the floor.

As AnnaClaire stood over him he muttered, "I feared I'd be damned to hell for the path I'd chosen. It's happy I am to give up my life, now that I've met one of heaven's angels come to escort me home."

Chapter Two

"My lady." Bridget, carrying a basin of water from the well outside, stopped dead in her tracks. "I thought you were abed."

Tavis, holding aloft a candle, came to an abrupt halt behind her.

Guilt stained their cheeks.

"I know what you thought." Anger made Anna-Claire's color equally high. "You thought to hide this murderer right here in my home. Behind my back." When she pointed to the figure on the floor Bridget dropped the basin, splashing water everywhere. In quick strides she and Tavis were kneeling beside Rory, searching for a pulse.

Despite her anger, AnnaClaire found herself touched by their concern.

"Is he dead?" Tavis asked.

There was a moment of silence, and AnnaClaire held her breath.

"Nay. He lives. Praise heaven." Bridget crossed herself.

AnnaClaire stared at the ever-widening pool of

blood. "If you care about this man, why did no one see to his wounds?"

Tavis looked up. "He wouldn't permit it until all his men were cared for. I've been scouring the city for safe shelter for them."

"I should think that would be no problem, considering how highly everyone seems to regard their..." AnnaClaire wrinkled her nose. "...Blackhearted O'Neil."

"Aye, my lady. But after that confrontation on the docks today the queen's emissaries have issued a proclamation. Anyone found harboring Rory O'Neil or his men will be considered an enemy of the Crown, and will be hanged."

"Hanged?" AnnaClaire's outrage grew. "And knowing that, you brought him to my home?"

"He is dying, my lady." Tavis paused. "We had no way of taking him elsewhere. It was dangerous enough getting him away from the docks. Had it not been for your carriage, and your lap robe, even that couldn't have been accomplished." He brightened. "Besides, since you are considered English, my lady, the law would not apply to you. You could always claim rightly that you knew nothing about this."

AnnaClaire found herself studying these two people with new respect. She had known them all her life. Had spent an occasional summer here, escaping the noise and crowds of London. Yet she had never thought of these two quiet, humble people as particularly courageous. Until this moment.

"You would be able to make no such claim for yourselves. Yet you would risk your lives for this stranger?"

Tavis nodded. "Rory O'Neil risks his life every day

for his people, my lady. We can do no less for him. With your permission we'd like to bind his wounds."

"And then what?" AnnaClaire folded her arms. "He is mortally wounded. But even if he should live, how could you possibly smuggle him out of Dublin?"

The old man scratched his chin. "We haven't thought that far, my lady. First we must keep him alive."

"And where do you propose to hide him for the night?"

Tavis got to his feet. "In the stables, with your permission."

AnnaClaire shook her head. "That will involve too many people. The stable master. The lads who muck the stalls. The less people who know, the better chance you have of keeping your secret." She tapped a foot, her mind working feverishly. She wasn't even aware that she was becoming caught up in a deadly game. To her, this was merely a chance to use her wits and her cunning, to help these two old people who had been with her family for so many years. "Your best course of action is to hide him where no one has any chance of coming upon him by accident." She suddenly smiled, pointed. "I know. The little attic room above mine."

Tavis and Bridget exchanged surprised glances. Did the lady know what she was saying?

"No one can get in or out of that room without going through your bedchamber, my lady."

"Exactly. Not even Glinna will be aware of our secret guest."

"But how will we be able to care for him up there?"

AnnaClaire shrugged. "I hadn't thought of that. I

suppose it will fall to me. But considering how long I cared for my mother, it will be nothing new.''

Before she could change her mind, Tavis bent and struggled to lift the unconscious Rory. ''It is a grand plan, my lady. But I fear not even the three of us could get him up those stairs.''

''He must walk.'' She caught up the skirt of her nightshift, careful to avoid his blood, and knelt beside the still figure. ''Rory. Rory O'Neil.''

At her commanding tone he opened his eyes and stared vacantly.

''We're going to take you up now. But you must help us.''

''Take...me...up.'' He smiled. ''Aye. Will I... finally see my Caitlin?''

AnnaClaire turned to Bridget. ''What is he babbling about?''

''He thinks he has died, my lady.''

''I see.'' She bent close. ''Rory O'Neil. Take my hand.''

''With...pleasure.''

Despite his injuries, his grip was surprisingly strong. As his fingers closed around AnnaClaire's she felt a rush of heat that left her thoroughly shaken.

''Here, Tavis.'' She sought to ignore the tingling along her spine. ''Take his other hand.''

The two of them managed to haul him to his feet. Then, draping his arms about their shoulders, they began moving ever so slowly up the stairs. When they reached AnnaClaire's room, they opened a door that led to a narrow staircase. By the time they reached the little attic room all of them were out of breath and Rory's wounds were bleeding profusely. They eased him onto the bed, then AnnaClaire stepped back and watched as Bridget and Tavis began cutting away his bloody clothes. The extent of his wounds sickened her, and she found herself wondering how he could bear the pain.

Bridget speared her with a glance. "Perhaps you should leave now, my lady. This won't be pleasant."

It was all AnnaClaire needed to stiffen her spine. "I don't expect it to be any more pleasant than was the care of my mother. But if I could care for her all those long months, I can certainly help bind this man's wounds." At once she took charge. "We'll need clean linens, Bridget. And some opiates."

"Aye, my lady." The housekeeper beckoned to her husband. "We'll need hot water, Tavis."

When the two were gone, AnnaClaire stared down at the still figure on the bed. Until this moment she hadn't given a thought to what she was getting herself into. Now, suddenly, she had to question her sanity. How had she agreed to hide a murderer in her own home? A man considered an enemy of the Crown. If he were found here, all of them could be hanged.

Sweet heaven. What would her father have to say about all this if he should learn the truth?

She pushed the worrisome thoughts from her mind and set to work cutting away the rest of his clothes. She would simply have to see that her father never learned of this. By this time tomorrow Rory O'Neil would most probably be dead. If by some miracle he survived, she would send him on his way and look back on this as a momentary madness.

"There now. We've done all we can. The rest is in God's hands, my lady." Bridget smoothed the covers

over the still figure of Rory O'Neil and got to her feet.
"Now you'd best get some sleep."

"I will. Now remember. Trust no one. Not even
Glinna."

"Aye." Tavis held the door, then trailed behind the
two women as they descended the stairs. "The little
chambermaid would never be able to keep such a secret. She'd have to boast to all her friends that she
knew the whereabouts of the Blackhearted O'Neil. And
in no time all of Dublin would know, as well."

When they reached AnnaClaire's room, Bridget
caught her hand and brought it to her lips. "Bless you,
my lady, for your compassion. I'll not soon forget what
you did this night."

"Nor I, my lady." Tavis did the same, bowing over
her hand. "You are an angel of mercy."

Or a fool, AnnaClaire thought as she secured the
door behind them. What had she been thinking? She
crossed to her bed and, ignoring the bloodstains on her
nightclothes, climbed between the covers. But she was
far too agitated to sleep. Instead she lay, watching the
stars and thinking about the man asleep one floor above
her.

If she were caught harboring this criminal, she
couldn't plead ignorance. She knew exactly what she
was doing. And, if she wanted to be completely honest
with herself, she knew why.

One look at him and she'd been hopelessly lost. This
Irish warrior who had leapt into battle and had fought
so fearlessly, had kindled a flame in her silly, romantic
heart. In her life she'd never seen anyone quite like
him. The titled Englishmen she'd met at Court were
bland by comparison.

When she had cut away his tunic she'd been amazed

by the muscles of his arms and chest. And horrified by the scars of battle. There was something so touching about this man and his dedication. The story that Tavis had told her lingered in her mind. Love such as that experienced by Rory O'Neil for his intended bride was rare indeed.

She closed her eyes, willing herself to sleep. But the enormity of what she had done had her twitching with nerves. When she suddenly heard a loud thud above her head, she bounded from bed and raced up the stairs.

Rory was on the floor, thrashing around in the bed linens.

AnnaClaire knelt beside him and caught his hands to still his movements.

"Rory O'Neil. Can you hear me?"

His movements stilled. His eyes opened. "My...sword. Need...weapon."

"Have no fear. There is no one here who will harm you."

"My...sword."

She sighed. "I'll fetch it. But first you have to get back into bed." She urged him upward, but her strength was no match for his. When he tugged on her hands, she was forced back to her knees.

"Where...am...I?"

"You're in my home. Clay Court. In Dublin."

"Dublin." He closed his eyes. "Not heaven." A moment later they snapped open. "Who...are...you?"

"My name is AnnaClaire."

He struggled to focus on her face. Then for a moment the pain lifted and his eyes were lit with a smile. "Ah. My...angel."

"Come now, Rory. You have to get back into bed."

She tugged on his hands, and this time he managed to lever himself back to the edge of the mattress.

As he slowly sank back against the pillows, his face revealed his pain. "Need…weapons."

"You have no need…"

"Weapons." His voice was little more than a croak. But the passion, the fervor, still rang.

"Very well." She crossed the room and picked up his sword, surprised at how heavy it was. The hilt was an intricately carved coat of arms, encrusted with jewels. "Here is your sword."

She placed it beside him in the bed and noted how his hand curled around the hilt.

"More."

"More weapons?"

He nodded.

She searched among his things and discovered two knives. It would seem this warrior took nothing for granted. When she handed them to him, he positioned one beneath each hand. Only then did he give in to the weariness and close his eyes.

She realized that this was what he'd been seeking when he slipped from his bed. Despite the seriousness of his wounds, he had fought through the pain to search for his weapons. He would be a warrior, she supposed, until death claimed him.

"I'll leave you now," she whispered.

"Stay."

She dropped to her knees beside the bed. "Why? What is it? Are you afraid?"

"Of…dying?" He shook his head. "I welcome…death. But stay, angel. Be my guide…as I leave this world."

"You aren't going to die, Rory O'Neil." Though

she spoke fiercely enough, the very thought of it had her trembling.

"Did He…tell you?"

"He? Oh, you mean God." She nearly laughed. "I'm afraid He doesn't speak to me directly. But I have it on good authority that your wounds, though painful, are not fatal." She hoped she would be forgiven for her lie. But she desperately wanted to offer him hope.

"Then why…are you here?"

She touched a hand to his lips to silence him. "No more questions. You must sleep if you're to heal."

When she started to remove her hand he surprised her by placing his fingers over hers and holding them to his mouth. The press of his lips against her flesh caused a rush of feelings that were so startling, all she could do was stare at him.

"Just stay. A little…while longer."

Each word he whispered against her hand sent another jolt surging through her already charged system. Had he asked for the moon, she'd have tried to get it. As long as he continued touching her just so.

"All right, Rory O'Neil." She smoothed the bed linens as she had seen Bridget do, then settled herself into a chaise beside the bed. "Just a little while longer."

She watched the uneven rise and fall of his chest, willing each breath, praying to hold off his death for a few moments longer, until sleep claimed her.

The opiates had long ago worn off, and Rory's body was engulfed in fire. Pain, a burning, blazing pain, radiated from his shoulder and his back to the very tips of his fingers and toes. His closed eyes felt hot and gritty. His temples throbbed as though they would burst at any moment.

Because the simplest movement added to his pain, he forced himself to lie perfectly still. Sweat beaded his forehead and upper lip, but he had not the strength to lift a hand.

It occurred to him that, although his own breathing was shallow and unsteady, there was another sound close by. A soft, rhythmic sound. Like the whisper of an angel.

His eyes opened. He beheld a most wondrous sight. A chaise had been pulled close beside him. In it was a woman asleep. Her feet were tucked under her, her cheek resting on her clasped hands. Hair the color of spun gold drifted around her face and shoulders.

He had thought he'd only dreamed her. But she was real. As if to prove it to himself, he reached out a hand and touched a strand of her hair. It was as soft as angel down.

In her sleep she brushed aside his hand, then lifted her head and opened her eyes. For a moment he could read her confusion. Then those eyes, the color of the sea after a storm, suddenly cleared.

She shifted, swinging her feet to the floor. "You're alive, Rory O'Neil."

"Am I?"

"How do you feel?"

"Like I've been run through by a score of English swords."

"From the looks of the scars on your body, you have been." She motioned toward the table against the far wall. "I can give you a potion to ease the pain."

"And I'll gladly take it. In a moment. Right now I'd like to keep a clear head."

"Why is that?"

"Because I need to know where I am." He glanced

around at the sloped ceilings, the stone of a chimney that soared through the roof. Except for a tiny opening that allowed a glimpse of dawn light, there were no other windows.

"You're in an attic room of my home, Clay Court, in Dublin."

"Your home, is it?"

"It's been in my mother's family for generations."

"And what might her name be?"

"It was Margaret Doyle."

Was. He heard the pain in that one word and decided not to press further. "And what might your name be?"

"My name is AnnaClaire."

"Well, AnnaClaire, if you don't mind, I'll take that potion now." The pain was raging out of control, setting his entire body on fire.

She sprinkled some powder into a tumbler of water, then sat on the edge of the bed. Very gently she lifted his head and held the glass to his lips.

"Has anyone ever told you you have a very gentle touch, AnnaClaire?"

"Are you trying to charm me, Rory O'Neil?"

"Is it working?"

"I think you'd better save that charm for another time. Now drink."

He swallowed, wondering if anything could put out the flame that raged through his blood. A flame that had flared higher when she touched him.

"Now I must leave you," she said as she lowered his head to the pillow. Taking a spotless handkerchief from her pocket she mopped the sweat from his face.

He caught her hand. "Aye, a very gentle touch."

She struggled to ignore the feelings of pleasure that he aroused in her. "My bedchamber is directly below here. When it is safe to return, I shall. But you must not call out or make any sound. Is that clear?''

''Why?''

''Because we must keep your presence here a secret. Since that scene at the docks, there is more than a price on your head, Rory O'Neil. It has been decreed that anyone found harboring you or your men shall be hanged.''

''Bloody English,'' he muttered. Then to her he said, ''I understand. Have no fear, lovely AnnaClaire. Even if I find myself dying, I'll see to it that I do so in silence, so as not to call attention to myself.'' A shadow of a smile flickered across his lips, making him even more handsome.

''I'll hold you to that.'' She crossed the room and let herself out without a backward glance.

Rory lay very still, allowing the opiates to weave their magic. As he drifted once more to sleep, he found himself wondering if the lovely AnnaClaire was real, or a product of his befuddled brain. Either way, she was the most beautiful creature he'd either seen or conjured. All tiny and slender and golden, with skin like porcelain and a full, pouty mouth that could trap a man with one kiss.

Her hair wasn't black as a raven's wing, as Caitlin's had been. And her eyes weren't blue. For all of his life, his beloved Caitlin had been the measure of all other women. And not one had ever come close to her beauty. But right now, try as he might, he could no longer hold on to her fading image.

It was the potion, he knew. Not the woman who had just left him. But it worried him all the same.

With Caitlin's name repeated again and again in his mind like a litany, he fell into a fitful sleep.

Chapter Three

"Good morrow, my lady." After a single knock on the door, Glinna, the little chambermaid bustled in, her arms laden with clean clothing.

Caught unawares, AnnaClaire had no choice but to dive beneath the bedlinens, to hide the bloodstains on her nightshift.

"You're up early this morrow, my lady. I heard you stirring and thought you'd be needing these." Glinna began arranging the petticoats atop a nearby night table, then hung a clean gown in the wardrobe. "What would you like me to fetch for you?"

"Nothing just yet. I believe I'll stay abed for awhile."

"Are you unwell, my lady?"

"Well, I…" AnnaClaire smoothed the linens, avoiding the maid's eyes. "I think perhaps I'm coming down with something."

They both looked up at another knock on the door. Bridget entered, carrying a tray covered with a linen cloth.

"Good morrow, my lady." She shot AnnaClaire a knowing look. "I hope your night went undisturbed."

AnnaClaire nodded. "It went fairly well, Bridget."

The housekeeper gave a sigh of relief. "I brought you a bit of porridge and some tea and biscuits."

"My lady won't be needing them," Glinna said with importance. "She is feeling unwell and intends to stay abed."

The housekeeper placed the tray on a bedside table. "Then I shall leave this in the hope that something will appeal to you later on."

"Thank you, Bridget." AnnaClaire turned to Glinna. "Since I won't be needing you today, you may help Bridget below stairs."

"Aye, miss." The little maid walked away looking plainly dejected. A day at Bridget's mercy meant scrubbing floors until they gleamed, then accompanying Tavis to the docks for fresh fish. Chores she would gladly leave for one of the other servants.

When they were alone AnnaClaire slipped out of bed. Glancing down at her nightshift she whispered, "I hope you can find a way to explain these stains to Glinna without arousing suspicion."

"Aye, my lady. I'll think of something." Bridget lowered her voice. "Now about our...guest. Did he survive the night?"

"He did."

The housekeeper blessed herself and whispered a prayer of thanks. "I'd feared..." She brushed aside a tear. "Perhaps we should see to him now."

"I just left him." At the housekeeper's startled look AnnaClaire felt the heat rise to her cheeks. "During the night I heard him fall from his bed and went to see to him. He asked me to stay, and I...fell asleep on the chaise."

"Of course you did, after all you've been through.

Bless you, my lady. And praise heaven the O'Neil is still alive. Is he in much pain?''

"A great deal of it." AnnaClaire nodded for emphasis. "Judging by the scars he bears, I'd say he's accustomed to pain. But I gave him one of the potions. That should make him comfortable for a few hours."

"Then you think he will live?"

AnnaClaire shrugged. "Only God knows. But he's strong. A fighter. And he's already survived the worst hours."

Bridget pointed to the covered tray. "I thought, if you were going to see to his needs, you wouldn't care to take breakfast below stairs in the dining hall."

"Quite right, Bridget. Just see that the servants are warned not to disturb me."

"Aye, my lady. And if the O'Neil is strong enough to eat, there's food for him, as well." The housekeeper took her leave, closing the door behind her.

When she was alone AnnaClaire peeled off her nightshift and crossed to a basin of water. When she had scrubbed away all trace of Rory's blood from her skin, she slipped into a delicately embroidered chemise and petticoat, then pulled on a gown of pale pink. She secured her hair with jeweled combs and slid her feet into soft kid boots. Picking up the tray she made her way up the narrow stairs to the attic room.

Rory was lying so still she thought he was asleep. But when she drew nearer she realized that his eyes were wide and glazed with pain. The bed linens were damp with his sweat. Still, he neither tossed nor turned nor gave any indication that he was in distress.

She set down the tray and knelt beside him, touching a hand to his forehead. His skin was on fire.

"Ah." A soft sigh escaped his lips. "My angel has come back. I did as you asked, and made not a sound."

She was touched by his courage. "I'm sorry it took so long." She dampened a cloth with water from a basin and began to bathe his face and neck, his chest and shoulders. "It appears the potion didn't work."

"It did. For a while. I had a lovely visit in heaven, before the fire of hell came back to claim me."

She mixed another packet of powder and held the glass to his lips. "Drink this. Maybe it can hold back your pain."

"I'm feeling better already, now that you're here." He drained the glass, then lay back weakly, breathing in the scent of crushed roses that seemed to cling to her.

"You're a charming liar, Rory O'Neil." She sat down in the chaise beside his bed, then dipped a spoon into a steaming bowl and held the spoon to his lips.

He turned his head. "What's this now?"

"Porridge."

He shook his head. "My mother used to insist that we eat it. I'd have rather eaten mud."

"I'll remember to bring some of that tomorrow. But for now, you'll eat your porridge. My housekeeper, Bridget Murphy, made this for you, to build up your strength. And you're going to eat at least a few bites."

"God in heaven, you sound just like my mother." He opened his mouth and accepted a taste. When he'd managed to swallow it he shot her a look of surprise. "Bridget Murphy must be a sorceress. This tastes unlike any porridge I've ever eaten."

"I'll tell her you approve. That just might spare you having to eat mud tomorrow." She held out another bite, and he accepted willingly.

It occurred to AnnaClaire that feeding this man was not at all like feeding her sick mother. Each time he opened his mouth, she found herself fighting a strange yearning to taste those lips. When he swallowed and closed his eyes in appreciation, she felt a sudden tug deep inside.

AnnaClaire felt completely out of her element with this raw, earthy man, who seemed to delight in the simple pleasure of eating. She had never known a man such as this. It didn't seem to bother Rory O'Neil in the least that he was naked beneath those covers. Yet she was bothered more than she cared to admit. She simply couldn't get the thought out of her mind.

He managed to devour nearly half the bowl of porridge before he lifted a hand in refusal.

"No more. It's too much effort."

She returned the bowl to the tray and poured a cup of tea. "Could you manage a few sips?"

He shook his head. "Not even one."

"Then we'll sit a while and wait for the opiates to ease your pain."

As she settled herself on the chaise he managed a smile. "Just looking at you does me more good than your potions."

She felt the heat rise to her cheeks. "You're too charming for your own good, Rory O'Neil."

He passed a hand over his eyes. "You should meet my brother, Conor. He's the charmer."

"Really? And what are you?"

"The fighter. Always the fighter."

She sipped her tea. "Tell me about your family."

"Conor, at a score and one, is two years younger than I. He was educated abroad, and our mother hoped he would be a priest. But our father has other ideas."

"What ideas?"

"With Conor's good looks and fine mind, Father hopes to use his connections in England to see that Conor represents our people at the Court of Elizabeth."

AnnaClaire smiled. "It would seem to me a far better way to effect change than your way with the sword."

"Ah. I hear a note of disapproval from my angel."

"I don't hold with fighting."

He shot her a look that made her blush. She decided to change the subject. "Do you have any more brothers?"

He shook his head. "There's just our little sister, Briana."

"Does she take after Conor? Or does she favor her eldest brother?"

"The lass was my shadow since she was born." His tone warmed with affection and pride. "She can wield a sword better than most men. And no one is better with a knife."

AnnaClaire couldn't help laughing. "Heaven help us. Another O'Neil warrior."

"Aye. She is the despair of our parents."

"Tell me about them."

"My father, Gavin, is from a noble line. Descended from King Brian himself. My mother, Moira, can trace her own lineage to the ancient Druids, then later to the Celts. After all these years, their love still blazes brighter than all the stars in heaven. It's a lovely thing to see."

She thought of her own parents' love. Of her father, who had suffered so gravely during his wife's long illness. No one would ever take the place of his beloved Margaret. "They're very lucky to have each other."

"Aye. That sort of love is rare indeed. And even more wondrous when the two lovers have so many years together." He fell silent, and AnnaClaire wondered if he was thinking about the woman who had almost been his bride. What sort of bitter taste would it leave to have a lover snatched away without the chance to say and do all the things locked in one's heart?

She set the tea aside. "I think you'd better try to sleep now."

"I believe I will." He closed his eyes. When he heard her getting to her feet he clamped a hand around her wrist. "Thank you, lovely AnnaClaire."

"For what?"

"For allowing me to forget my pain for a few minutes."

"That wasn't me. It was the potion."

He merely smiled. "And thank Bridget Murphy for the porridge. I do believe I'd prefer it again tomorrow, instead of the mud."

"I'll tell her."

She watched him a moment, then let herself out, knowing he was already asleep.

At noon, Bridget returned to AnnaClaire's room with another tray.

"How much longer do you wish to feign illness, my lady?"

AnnaClaire shrugged. "I suppose sometime late this afternoon I must make an amazing recovery, for I have to attend Lady Thornly's dinner party tonight."

"Very well. I'll check with you before sending Glinna up to help you dress."

"Thank you, Bridget." As she picked up the tray

and headed toward the narrow staircase she paused,
turned. "By the way, Rory O'Neil sends his compliments on your porridge. He found it far superior to his
mother's."

The housekeeper was beaming with pride as she
scurried away. AnnaClaire marvelled that such a simple remark from a hardened warrior could elicit such
feelings in the old woman.

In the little attic room, AnnaClaire found Rory
sweating profusely as he struggled to lift his sword
from the floor where it had fallen. It took both his
hands to retrieve it, and the effort left him lying weakly
against the pillows.

The wound to his shoulder, she noted, had opened
and was oozing blood.

"Now look what you've done." With a hiss of anger
she set down the tray and bent over him, touching a
square of linen to the wound. "And all for a foolish
weapon."

"Foolish?" He clamped a hand around her wrist and
stared up into her startled eyes. "Woman, you
wouldn't think that if you found yourself facing a line
of soldiers brandishing swords. Then it would be worth
any price to have a weapon with which to defend yourself."

"But there are no soldiers here, Rory O'Neil. You're
safely hidden away."

He gave her a long, thoughtful look. "So you say.
But how can I be sure?"

"You have my word. Isn't that enough?"

He nodded. "Aye. It is. If you say it is."

"You'd be wise to save your strength and give your
wounds a chance to heal."

"So I would." He relaxed his grip and allowed her

to mop up the fresh flow of blood. But he didn't completely let go of her, instead keeping his fingers wrapped lightly around her wrist. "Old habits are hard to break."

While she bent to her task, she could feel him boldly studying her. It brought a flush to her cheeks. Worse, she knew her pulse was racing. Knew, too, that he could feel it at her wrist.

To cover her confusion she poured a liberal amount of spirits on the wound. "This will hurt a bit." She heard his quick intake of breath. "Hold still now while I tie this clean linen." She glanced down and realized that he was still staring at her. Only now his gaze was fixed on her mouth. Her throat went dry. Their lips were so close they were almost touching. She need only make the slightest move to taste him.

As if reading her mind he drew her fractionally closer. "You smell like my mother's rose garden."

She swallowed, and it sounded overloud in her ears. She knew he could hear the tremor in her voice. "I'm not your mother, Rory O'Neil."

"I never had a minute's doubt of that." His lips curved in a dangerous smile. "I never wanted to kiss my mother the way I want to kiss you."

She braced a hand against his chest, intending to push away. "Don't…"

Her protest was swallowed as his mouth covered hers.

His lips were warm and firm and practiced. They moved over hers, tasting, teasing.

At the first contact her breath backed up in her throat. She would have pulled back but he had anticipated her move and now held her firmly against him. He pressed a palm to the back of her head while his other hand slid across her shoulder and along her back. And all the while his lips moved over hers until she could no longer hold back a sigh of pleasure.

"Let this be a lesson to you, AnnaClaire. Never tell me what to do," he muttered against her mouth. "There's just something in my nature that refuses to accept orders."

She took in a deep breath, feeling her head swimming. "I'll remember that in the future. Now release me, Rory O'Neil."

He flashed that dangerous smile, and she realized, too late, her mistake.

"You see?" He framed her face with his hands. "You've done it again." With no effort at all he drew her head down for another drugging kiss. This time his fingers tangled in her hair, and, while her senses were still reeling, he kissed her until she was breathless.

He knew the exact moment when her resistance gradually turned into acquiescence. Her hands, which had been pressed firmly against his chest, now lifted to encircle his neck. Her breasts were flattened against him in a most enticing manner. She lay, warm and pliant, in his arms.

Arousal was swift, insistent. He felt the rush of desire pulse through him before he carefully banked it.

In one smooth motion he caught her firmly by the shoulders and held her a little away. It was all the time he needed to clear his head and calm his pounding heart.

"I hope you've learned your lesson. Never tell me what to do."

Her eyes darkened with anger. Though it was difficult to speak, when her heart was still tumbling helplessly inside her chest, she managed a note of sarcasm.

"You mean, in order to keep this from happening again, I ought to order you to kiss me?"

He threw back his head and laughed. What a delight she was. "Do you take me for a complete fool? Whether you told me to kiss you or not, you're too lovely to resist. I'd simply have to kiss you."

"And I simply have to leave you."

"Now? Before you've properly tended my needs?"

"Your needs." She tossed down the square of linen and indicated the tray on the night table. "Last night I feared you would die in your bed. But you're far from dead, Rory O'Neil. Any man strong enough to hold a woman can surely hold his own bowl of broth. I hope you find Bridget's soup as appetizing as her porridge."

"I'm sure I will."

When she yanked open the door he added, "But it won't be nearly as pleasant without you feeding it to me."

In reply she pulled the door firmly shut behind her.

When she reached her own room, she sank down onto the edge of the bed and pressed a hand to her lips. They were still tingling from the touch of his mouth. And his dark, dangerous taste still clung to them.

This was a foolish game she was playing. All because she had allowed this Irish warrior to touch some romantic chord in her heart. She wouldn't be the first maiden to have her heart broken by a rogue. But, she reminded herself, there was more than her heart at stake here. She was playing a game with people's lives. And the consequences could be deadly.

Chapter Four

"How are you finding your first visit to Ireland, Lord Dunstan?" Since her hostess had insisted upon seating AnnaClaire beside the handsome young visitor, she had no choice but to attempt pleasant conversation with this dour, brooding man. Apparently she was the only female in the room who hadn't fallen under the spell of his chilling smile and icy gray eyes.

"Fascinating. From what I've seen, a savage land. And savage people." He acknowledged the nods of agreement around the table. "Were it not for meeting you, my lady, I would have returned to England without a single good thing to say for my time spent here."

She felt his knee nudge hers beneath the table cover. When she moved aside, he shifted closer, so that she couldn't escape his touch.

"I've had the good fortune of meeting your father several times in London, my lady." He laid a hand over hers, pressing firmly when she tried to pull it away. It was obvious that he enjoyed being the center of attention. Knowing that the others were watching and listening, he began to play to his audience. "Had I known that Lord Thompson's daughter was so lovely,

I would have made the journey across the Channel much sooner.'' If he felt her cringe, he took no notice of it.

"I wish we could persuade you to stay a while longer, Lord Dunstan.'' Lady Thornly sipped her wine, thoroughly enjoying the company of her countrymen. "I grow so weary of this local dialect, and do so yearn to be among my own kind and hear the language spoken as it was meant to be.''

The young man gave her his most charming smile. "Perhaps you should sell your estates to me, Lady Thornly. Then you could return to England to live out your years among your own kind.''

"As if you need more land.'' She waved a hand in dismissal and laughed like a coquette.

The others joined her laughter. It was common knowledge that Lynley Lord Dunstan was quickly becoming one of the richest men in England.

A gentleman across the table said, "You were recently at Court with Her Majesty, Dunstan. How does Elizabeth intend to deal with this Irish problem?''

The young man puffed up his chest. His father and grandfather had held important positions with Elizabeth's father, Henry VIII. A grateful king had granted them generous sections of land, and several of the most beautiful homes in England. The current Lord Dunstan had learned well from his ancestors, using his loyalty to his queen to add to his own fortune.

"The Queen values my opinion. In fact, I am here at Her Majesty's request, to see for myself if there is a problem.''

"Rest assured there is a problem.'' The elderly Lord Davis, seated beside their hostess, spoke in hushed tones. "And it grows more serious with each day.'' He glanced around. "Any word on that wounded Irish warrior? The one they call the Blackhearted O'Neil?"

AnnaClaire went perfectly still, hardly daring to breathe.

Dunstan snorted with disdain. "Warrior? Court jester would be a better name. As far as I can determine, he is nothing more than a peasant leading a small band of ruffians, hoping to become a hero to the locals."

"I saw with my own eyes how that 'peasant' and a few of his swordsmen could rout an entire battery of English soldiers." Lord Davis drained his goblet and paused while a hovering servant filled it. "There is nothing more dangerous than a zealot who appeals to the heart of the masses. Mark my word, Dunstan. The man is stirring a cauldron of simmering passions. Very soon now, they'll come to a boil. And Her Majesty might find herself with the one thing she has sworn to resist."

"And what might that be, Lord Davis?"

"A war that drains England's coffers."

"War?" Dunstan gave a snort of disdain. "With these peasants?" He threw back his head and chuckled, and one by one the others around the table followed suit. "Queen Elizabeth is no fool. If this so-called Blackhearted O'Neil should begin to take himself seriously, our queen will simply send over a company of her finest soldiers. Believe me, Lord Davis, our swordsmen could put down any rebellion led by an illiterate peasant and his band of lackeys."

He turned to AnnaClaire. "You've grown quiet, my lady. Does all this talk of war upset your delicate sensibilities?"

"Aye." AnnaClaire swallowed, uneasy at having the attention shifted to her.

"Forgive me, my dear." Lord Davis pushed from the table and walked to her side. With a hand on her shoulder he said gently, "How inconsiderate of me to have forgotten. AnnaClaire was forced to witness that bloodletting at the docks yesterday. I'm sure it was most upsetting for her." He leaned close. "Would you care to take your leave, my dear?"

It was the excuse she'd been hoping for. She placed her hand in his. "Thank you. I would indeed."

"Oh dear." Lady Thornly touched a fine lace cloth to her lips. "I had so hoped we could keep you here a while longer, AnnaClaire. Lord Dunstan has so little time before he returns to London."

"I'd be happy to accompany Charles and Anna-Claire to their homes," the handsome Englishman said gallantly.

It was on the tip of AnnaClaire's tongue to refuse. But there was no way she could do so gracefully. And so she found herself bidding her hostess good-night and climbing into a carriage with her father's old friend and a young man whose arrogance was as unsettling as his ignorance.

"How long do you hope to remain in Ireland?" Lord Davis settled himself comfortably across from the young couple, and their carriage started off through the streets of Dublin.

"I had hoped to be here no more than a few days." Lord Dunstan turned to smile at the young woman beside him, whose face was shrouded in shadow. "But now, I think I might be persuaded to stay a while longer."

AnnaClaire groaned inwardly.

"Excellent." The old man smiled in the darkness. His friend, Lord Thompson, would be delighted to hear that his daughter had caught the interest of someone as important as this young friend of the queen herself.

"Shall I have my driver take you home first, Charles?"

Before AnnaClaire could issue a protest, the old man was nodding vigorously. "I was about to suggest it myself. I'm feeling a bit weary after all that food and stimulating conversation."

AnnaClaire knew exactly what her father's old friend was up to. And though his meddling was galling, there was nothing she could do about it. He was as determined as her father to see that she made a good match.

Dunstan shouted an order to the driver. At once they changed directions and were soon at the old man's door.

"Good night, Lord Dunstan." The older man touched the tip of his hat, then leaned across the seat and brushed his lips over AnnaClaire's cheek. "Good night, my dear. I can rest easy, knowing I've left you in such good hands."

"Good night, Lord Davis." AnnaClaire watched him climb from the carriage and ascend the steps of his mansion.

At a command from her companion, the driver urged the team forward and they were once again making their way through the darkened streets.

When the carriage veered to the right and started up a slight incline AnnaClaire found herself pinned against Dunstan's side. Though his movement was subtle, she felt his hand brush her breast. She stiffened and pushed away. But when she glanced over at him, she could see the smile playing on his lips. His insensitivity was vexing. She experienced a wave of relief when they started up the drive that led to her home.

Lord Dunstan turned to study the graceful curve of courtyard, the warmth of candles glowing in the curtained windows. "So this is where you stay when you are in Ireland. What is it called?"

"Clay Court. It was my mother's ancestral home."

Something about the way she spoke the words had him turning to look at her. "I would be careful if I were you, my lady. Some might think you consider this place more home than England."

At his words AnnaClaire felt the trickle of ice along her spine. He had taken no pains to mask the warning. "I'll remind you, Lord Dunstan, that my father is a respected member of the queen's council. And though I am of mixed heritage, my loyalty has never come into question."

"Nor should it, my lady. But there will always be some who will wonder at your allegiance to your mother's people."

Lord Dunstan climbed down, then turned and offered his hand to help her from the carriage. She had no choice but to accept his assistance.

At the door she managed a smile. "Thank you for seeing me home, Lord Dunstan. I'll say good night now."

When she started to close the door he startled her by stepping inside. "It wouldn't be wise to see you home and not see you safely settled, my lady."

"I have loyal servants to see to my safety."

"Ah. That is reassuring." He glanced around, noting the highly polished stones of the foyer, the crystal chandelier in which blazed dozens of candles. "I would have expected such loyal servants to meet you at the door.''

"They have their chores to see to. Tavis will be above stairs, no doubt, laying a fire to warm my bed-chamber.''

"Tavis, is it? If you but asked, lovely lady, I could do the same. And I would need no wood nor torch. The touch of your hand on mine would be enough to set the blaze between us.''

She hated the smirk on his lips. Hated more the heat that rose to her cheeks at his insinuation.

She kept her voice even, as though dismissing him. "My little housemaid, Glinna, will be waiting to help me undress.''

"A most pleasant chore, I would think. And one I would be most pleased to undertake in her stead.''

She itched to slap him and knew that she had to tread very carefully around this man. She would, instead, ignore him. Something he'd seldom experienced, she surmised.

"And Bridget is most probably in the kitchen, pre-paring tea before I retire.'' She lifted a hand to her lips and forced a yawn. "Forgive me, Lord Dunstan. It has been a long day, and I fear I must bid you good night.''

"Of course.'' He caught her hand and lifted it to his lips, lingering until she forcefully withdrew it from his grasp. "I hope I have your permission to pay a call on the morrow.''

"I...'' She struggled to think of a polite way to de-cline. "I fear I will not be home.''

"I see. A pity. But there will be other times.'' He gave her a lazy smile, to let her know that he had already seen through her little charade. His voice low-ered, as though sharing an intimate secret. "You are unlike so many of your gender who smile and flutter their lashes in invitation. This feigned reluctance on your part is most intriguing. I must admit, you have aroused my curiosity, as well as…other things. Now I simply must get to know you better, my lady. It is my good fortune that Lord Davis and I will be spending a great deal of time together. Perhaps, when he is paying a call, I shall accompany him.''

"Yes." She kept her tone carefully bland. "Of course."

In the glow of the candles he studied her more closely. "You are really quite lovely. And more than a little mysterious." His smile grew as he reached out a hand and stroked her cheek. Her startled reaction made him chuckle. "And now that I have made your acquaintance I have already forgotten whatever objections I had to visiting this damnable land. Good night, my dear AnnaClaire. Until we meet again.''

She watched as he stepped outside and climbed to the seat of his carriage. As the image of horse and carriage disappeared into the darkness she let out the breath she hadn't even known she was holding.

"So. The vain English peacock makes you sigh, does he?''

AnnaClaire whirled. Rory stepped from the shadows, wearing nothing more than the bloody breeches he had hastily slipped into. On his face was a look of absolute fury.

"What are you doing below stairs?''

"Watching you make a fool of yourself. Is this what our women have come to? Playing coy with our enemy?''

Her chin came up as she fixed him with a hateful look. "Ireland cannot lay claim to me.''

"What are you saying, woman? You're Irish. You said your mother was Margaret Doyle."

"Aye. And my father is Lord James Thompson."

For a moment all he could do was stare at her. When he found his voice he said, "Your father is chief counsel to the bloody Queen of England?"

When she nodded, he shook his head in wonder. "What do you think he would say if he knew you were aiding the Blackhearted O'Neil?"

"It would break his heart. He must never know."

"So, despite your father's position and title, you consider yourself Irish."

She stiffened her spine. "I am neither English nor Irish, Rory O'Neil. I answer to myself. As for playing coy, you are as mistaken as Lord Dunstan was."

He took a step closer. "So. That was Dunstan? I've heard of him. All his titles bought and paid for with the blood of innocent farmers. He'll say and do whatever it takes to please his queen, so long as she continues to repay his loyalty with more wealth and power." He gave AnnaClaire a long, measuring look. "And your denial rings hollow, my lady. I heard with my own ears how you allowed him to speak to you." His tone lowered with feeling. "And saw with my own eyes how you allowed him to touch you."

The intensity of AnnaClaire's temper surprised her. Rory's words brought fury bubbling dangerously close to the surface. She lifted her skirts and started to flounce past him. "I'll not stand here and argue with the likes of you, Rory O'Neil."

"Nay. Especially since you'd lose the argument. Nor will I allow you to dismiss me like some groveling servant." Without taking time to think he caught her roughly by the shoulder and dragged her into his arms, hauling her against his chest.

His temper had always been his undoing. And there had been plenty of time for it to grow as he'd watched the handsome stranger put his hands on AnnaClaire. As if that hadn't been enough, the mention of her father's name had caught him by surprise. Now fury propelled him into acting without thinking. His big rough hands closed around her upper arms, lifting her nearly off her feet as he covered her mouth in a savage kiss.

Temper met temper as their lips mated with the heat of the moment. The effect was so potent he felt as if he'd taken a blow from an enemy's broadsword. He reared back, lifting his head to study her as though he couldn't quite believe what he was feeling. Even now his head was spinning, and the blood was roaring in his temples.

AnnaClaire was so startled she was frozen into momentary silence. It wasn't only the rush of heat from his bold kiss. That would have been unsettling enough. But this man was naked to the waist, and the feel of his flesh against her palms had her thoughts scrambling, her fingertips tingling. It was one thing to touch him when he was unconscious and burning with fever. It was quite another to touch a man whose flesh rippled with muscle, and who burned with heat from a very different source.

When she'd gathered her thoughts, she pushed against him. "How dare you, Rory O'Neil! Unhand me at once."

He thought about it. Briefly. Then just as quickly decided to ignore her protest. In that one stunning moment all the anger had drained from him. In its place

was something very different. Desire curled hotly
through his loins.

He felt the warmth of her breath against his cheek.
Saw the way her eyes darkened with the gathering
storm. Breathed in the fragrance of roses that drifted
around her.

He lowered his face and claimed her mouth again.
This time his hands softened, as did his lips. But
though the kiss was less savage, it was no less potent.
The taste of her was unlike anything he'd ever sam-
pled. Sweet as a summer garden. As gentle as rain.
Innocent. Untouched. And yet, he sensed in her a slum-
bering passion. A passion that excited him.

He kissed her with a thoroughness that had her heart
pounding, her palms sweating as they slipped around
his waist and pressed against his lower back. She
wasn't even aware that she was clutching him franti-
cally, holding on for fear of falling.

AnnaClaire had been kissed before. There had been
many a lad who had hoped to stake a claim on the
daughter of the wealthy, powerful Lord Thompson.
And many more, like Dunstan, who thought their title
and privilege gave them the right to take liberties with
the women at Court. But AnnaClaire had been equally
adept at avoiding all entanglements of the heart. Until
now.

The feelings being awakened by this man were unlike anything she'd ever experienced. The hands that
held her were so strong they could easily break her in
two. Yet their touch was so unexpectedly gentle, she
couldn't help but melt against him. His lips, so warm,
so firm and practiced, moved over hers with a gentleness that did strange things to her heart, causing it to

pound inside her chest until she feared he would surely hear.

Rory loved the way she became lost in the kiss. A soft sigh escaped her lips and her arms lifted, encircling his neck. He slid his hands down her arms, along her sides, until his thumbs encountered the soft swell of her breasts. When she started to pull away he moved his hands across her back, soothing, calming, while his lips continued to feast.

She was a delightful surprise. Innocent yet sultry. Both shy and bold. Despite her hesitance, there was an underlying strength of will that Rory found deeply arousing.

Desire, swift and fierce, caught him by surprise. The thought of taking her, here and now, had the blood pulsing hotly through his veins. He knew if he didn't soon end this, he would find himself stepping over the line of reason. Still he lingered over the kiss, loving the taste of her, the feel of her in his arms.

When at last he gathered the courage to lift his head, he was rewarded by her little moan of frustration.

"Just doing your bidding, my lady." He shot her a wicked smile. "You did tell me to unhand you."

"I did." The words nearly stuck in her throat. She took a step back, breaking contact. Still, the taste of him, dark, mysterious, remained on her tongue. Her breathing was shallow and ragged. She had to swallow several times before she managed to say, "And since you're well enough to force yourself on me, Rory O'Neil, I suggest you're well enough to take your leave of my home at once."

"Aye, my lady. As you wish." His smile widened. "But if you wish to be perfectly honest, you'll have to admit that it required no force on my part to involve you in that kiss.''

She felt her cheeks flame as his words found their mark. It was true. She had been more than willing to shamelessly indulge herself. For if truth be told, ever since that first kiss in his room, she had wanted him to kiss her again. And the feel of his lips on hers had been every bit as wondrous as the first time.

She turned away to hide her shame. ''I'll expect you to be gone before the first light. That way there will be no chance of the servants spotting you.''

She expected some sort of argument. Relished the thought of another duel of words.

When he didn't respond she turned back, eager to attack.

Rory was gripping the edge of a table. His face had lost all its color. Blood was seeping from his wounded shoulder to snake along his back in a thin line of dark red.

Rushing to his side she examined his wound, then draped his arm around her shoulder and began to lead him toward the stairs. ''Now look what you've done.'' Anger was a much safer emotion than what she'd been feeling just moments before. With anger there would be no guilt, no recriminations. With anger she could force herself into immediate action.

''Where…are you taking me?'' he asked through gritted teeth.

''Up to bed.''

''You just ordered me to go.''

''That was before. Now, I'll have to tend that wound again.''

He didn't argue. Couldn't. He'd just been given a reprieve of sorts. But as he moved along beside her up the stairs, he wasn't certain whether to curse the Fates or bless them.

Chapter Five

"You wish to break your fast in your chambers again, my lady?" Glinna was looking at AnnaClaire in a strange way as she moved around the room. "Could it be something you ate at Lady Thornly's last night?"

"Of course not. I'm not ill, Glinna. Just a bit tired. Leave the tray now, and go help Bridget below stairs."

"Aye, my lady."

As soon as the door closed behind her, AnnaClaire bounded out of bed and completed her toilette, slipping into the clothes Glinna had laid out. Then, balancing the covered tray in her hands, she climbed the cramped stairs to the little attic room. No doubt, she thought with a sigh, the little maid was still fretting over what might have caused this sudden malaise.

In truth, AnnaClaire would have gladly remained in her room rather than face Rory O'Neil this morning. She'd had enough of him throughout the long night. Even after she'd dressed his wound and put him to sleep with one of Bridget's opiates, he had remained with her. Dark thoughts and images of him holding her, kissing her, had tormented her, robbing her of precious sleep. The handsome rogue had her thinking of things that were better left alone.

She sighed. Another day or two and he would be out of her life. As she nudged the door open and swept inside, she wondered why that knowledge didn't cheer her. In fact, it only added another layer of tension.

"Good morrow, Rory O'Neil." She set the tray on the night table with a flourish, then turned.

His features were ashen. He was holding his left hand firmly against his right shoulder.

She was beside him instantly. "What is it? What's wrong?"

"I can't...make this damnable arm work."

She sat on the edge of the bed. "I'm sure it's nothing more than the strain of the fresh wound."

"Nay. My sword slipped from my grasp during the night. I couldn't retrieve it."

Up close she could see the sweat beading his brow and upper lip. "You're much too hard on yourself, Rory. I'm sure by tomorrow..."

"You don't understand." His left hand clamped around her wrist. As always, the strength in his grip caught her off guard. "I've been coddling myself too long. Lying abed when I should have been leading my men into fresh battles. And now, as punishment, I've lost my strength."

"As punishment?"

"Aye."

"For the sin of laziness, no doubt."

He glowered at her. "Do you mock me, woman?"

She tried not to smile, though her lips quirked. "I? You think I would dare to mock Ireland's fierce Black-hearted O'Neil?"

His eyes narrowed. She looked far too fetching, in a

gown the color of heather, and the bloom of youth and innocence on her cheeks. Her eyes danced with a teasing light that only made her all the more desirable. Her low, breathy voice whispered over his senses, teasing him, taunting him, even through the pain.

"You're having fun with me, AnnaClaire. And all the while I'm lying here weak and helpless."

She glanced at the hand gripping her with such strength. "If this is how you are when you're helpless, I'd hate to see you when you're feeling strong."

At once he realized what he was doing and released her, hoping his touch hadn't left bruises on that fair skin. He struggled into a sitting position.

AnnaClaire could see the pain even that small movement caused him. She busied herself plumping pillows behind him, smoothing the blankets, before removing a bowl of porridge from the tray.

"Perhaps some food will help. Bridget made this especially for you."

When she offered him a spoonful, he glowered at her. "I'm not an infant to be coddled. I can see to my own feeding."

"Suit yourself." She handed him the bowl and proceeded to pour tea into two cups.

When he'd managed to empty the bowl, she took it from him and replaced it with a plate of biscuits and a steaming cup of tea. Though he ate in silence she could see that his spirits were slowly being restored.

"Now, about your arm…" She saw the sudden frown as he glanced at her. "You'll need to begin using it, a little at first, until the strength returns, and then a little more, and in no time it'll be as good as it ever was."

"It's easy for you to offer such advice. You aren't the one in pain."

"But you must work through your pain."

"Is that so?" He shot her a dark look. "And how is it that you know about such things?"

"I took care of my mother for several years before she died."

Though she wasn't aware of it, a hint of pain had crept into her voice. Rory watched and listened, sensing that this was a recent loss.

"The longer my mother remained in bed, the weaker she became. Her limbs began to shrivel from lack of use. I discovered that by moving her arms and legs many times each day I could slow the process."

He was watching her in that quiet, measured way that always left her feeling so uncomfortable. To avoid looking at him, she turned away, setting aside her empty cup, placing his dishes on the tray.

"We'll have to go slowly at first so we don't open the wound again. You've lost too much blood as it is. But if we're careful, I think we can manage to build your strength without straining that shoulder."

"*We* can, can *we?*" His tone was rougher than he'd intended. But the wrenching pain, and the weakness that was so foreign to him, put his teeth on edge. Besides, watching the ease with which she moved about the room while he was forced to lie perfectly still made him want to lash out at someone, anyone. "It would seem that I'll be doing all the work, building my strength and restoring my arm. What will the other half of 'we' be doing?"

"I'll be helping you."

"If it's all the same to you, I can do without your

help." To prove his point, he gripped his right arm with his left hand and forced it upward.

Pain ripped through him, leaving him gasping. His arm dropped limply at his side and he found, to his amazement, that he didn't even have the strength to flex his fingers.

Seeing the look on his face, AnnaClaire's heart went out to him. But she cautioned herself to hide her feelings. Pity was the last thing this man wanted or needed, especially when he was in such a foul mood.

She picked up the tray and headed toward the door. "Well, if you'd rather do it yourself..."

"AnnaClaire."

The sound of her name on his lips made her pause. She took a moment to compose herself before she turned to him. "Is there something you need?"

"I need..." He hated this. Would have done anything to avoid it. But the truth was, he had no other choice. For the moment. "It would seem I do need your help after all."

She crossed the room and returned the tray to the bedside table. Then she straightened and rolled her sleeves.

The look of her, all crisp and efficient, had him silently cursing.

"Very well. If you're willing, 'we'll' begin at once." At her emphasis on the word, he silently cursed again.

"You'd probably be more comfortable in the chair." She offered a hand and helped him from the bed to the chair. The effort seemed to drain all his strength.

She knelt in front of him and took hold of his right hand.

"Does this hurt?" she asked as she began to massage his fingers.

"Only a little." In truth, having her kneeling between his legs led him to think of things other than pain. Things that would have her blushing if she were to read his mind. He breathed in the fragrance of roses that always seemed to surround her, and decided that he might learn to like this sort of treatment.

"Good." She continued kneading his fingers, pressing them together to make a fist, then slowly straightening them.

With each movement he could feel a tingling that began in his hand and inched along his arm and shoulder. But he wasn't certain if it was caused by the movement, or by the press of her hands on his.

Her fingers were long and graceful, the nails beautifully shaped. The thought of those hands touching other parts of his body made him smile.

"You find this amusing?"

He arched a brow. "Shouldn't I?"

"You'll not be smiling when we get to the more difficult part."

"And what might that be?"

"Using this arm. In no time I'll have you lifting your sword above your head. And swinging it the way you did on the docks, the day you were injured."

"Did I tell you that I saw you there?"

His voice, so close to her ear, had her looking up in surprise. But when she found him staring directly into her eyes, she looked away.

"How could that be?"

"You deny you were there, AnnaClaire?"

"Nay. I was there. And I watched the battle between your men and the English soldiers. But how could you have possibly had the time to see me, when you were busy fighting for your very life?''

''You'd be impossible to overlook, my lady.'' His voice lowered to a caress. ''Of all the women on the docks that day, your face is the only one I remember.''

He was staring at her again. To hide the blush she knew was on her cheeks, she ducked her head. But she couldn't help glancing at him from time to time from beneath lowered lashes.

''You have beautiful eyes, AnnaClaire. Did you know they're the windows to the soul?'' Judging by what he'd seen so far, hers was the most pure and innocent of souls.

''I think you should stop talking and concentrate on the work.''

''Aye. The work,'' he said with a smile. ''If this be work, I'll gladly labor for a lifetime.''

''I'll remind you of your words tomorrow, when we get to the difficult part.''

Just as he began to feel comfortable with the gentle flexing of his fingers, she startled him by slowly raising and lowering his arm. The pain of even that simple movement left him clenching his teeth.

''I'm sorry to have to cause you more pain. But it's necessary if you're to regain the full use of your arm.''

''I understand.'' He sucked in a breath and braced himself as pain hot as fire seared his arm and settled in his stiff shoulder.

She continued the motion several more times, then lowered his arm and heard his sigh of relief.

From the tray she removed the square of linen and rolled it into a ball. ''Whenever you have time, roll this over and over between the fingers of your weak hand. It will help strengthen them.''

She got to her feet and shook down her skirts before turning away.

"That's it? That's how you intend to help me get back my strength?"

She nearly laughed aloud at his look of annoyance. "You're forgetting how severely you were injured, Rory O'Neil. It's a wonder you even survived. If you attempt too much too soon, you'll lose even more strength. Now you need to rest."

He bit back an oath as she helped him to bed and handed him a glass of water into which she'd sprinkled the now familiar opiate. By the time she'd slipped from the room and descended the stairs, he was already sound asleep. With the touch of her hands still upon him. And the fragrance of roses still filling his lungs.

"My lady. I beg permission to enter."

AnnaClaire had no sooner returned to her bedchamber than she heard Glinna's voice from outside her door. She took a moment to compose herself, then opened the door.

"Yes, Glinna? What is so important that you would disturb my rest?"

"Bridget sent me to tell you that Lord Davis is here." She lowered her voice. "And he isn't alone. There's a very handsome man with him."

AnnaClaire's eyes narrowed. "Lord Dunstan?"

"Aye, that's the name, my lady. He and Lord Davis are awaiting your company in the parlor. Shall I help you change into something more elegant?"

AnnaClaire caught sight of herself in the looking glass. Her gown was a bit rumpled, as was her hair. Still, the thought of primping for Dunstan held no appeal to her.

"Thank you, Glinna. This suits me. You may take my tray downstairs."

"Aye, my lady." The girl didn't bother to hide her disapproval. If a man of means like Lord Dunstan ever came calling on her, she would move heaven and earth to look her best. But then, all the servants had speculated for years on AnnaClaire's future. She had wasted too many years caring for her invalid mother. Now she was simply too old, too headstrong, too defiant of convention, to ever snag a husband. What man would offer his name and his fortune to a woman who hadn't the least idea how to use her feminine wiles?

The little housemaid frowned as she followed AnnaClaire down the stairs.

"Lord Davis." AnnaClaire paused a moment on the threshold, then crossed the room and offered her cheek.

"My dear." The old man kissed her lightly. "I hope you don't mind this intrusion."

"You are as much family as my father. You could never intrude."

He gave her a radiant smile. "Lord Dunstan and I are heading to the docks to greet an old friend arriving from London. We thought you might come along and enjoy a bit of fresh air."

"I'm sorry. I have a...prior appointment."

"Then perhaps we could drop you," Dunstan said. "It would be my pleasure to place my carriage and driver at your disposal."

"Thank you, Lord Dunstan." AnnaClaire forced herself to greet him, offering her hand for his kiss. "That's most kind of you. But I have already instructed Tavis to prepare my carriage."

"Perhaps another time then, my lady."

She inclined her head and forced a smile to her lips. "I look forward to it."

"Tomorrow, perhaps?"

"I promised Lady Thornly I would pay a call tomorrow."

"Then Lord Davis and I shall take you there, since we have also agreed to visit the dear lady. Isn't that so, Charles?"

The older man was grinning from ear to ear as he nodded.

AnnaClaire knew she was trapped. The old dear was determined to play matchmaker. And Dunstan was nothing if not persistent. There was naught to do but accept defeat with grace. "I thank you, Lord Dunstan. I will accept your kind offer."

He bowed over her hand. "Until tomorrow, then, my lady."

She walked with them to the door and watched as they climbed into their carriage. Then, to assuage her guilty conscience, she ordered Tavis to prepare her carriage. Perhaps a ride in the fresh air was the very thing she needed to clear her head.

When she entered her room, she was startled to see the door to the attic room open. Rory was leaning weakly against the landing at the foot of the narrow stairs.

"What are you doing?" she demanded.

"Keeping one ear to the door."

"You should have been sound asleep by now."

"Aye. I was. But the sound of a certain voice roused me." He took a step nearer. "What did your Englishman want this time?"

"I told you. He isn't *my* Englishman. He merely offered me the use of his carriage."

"With him in it, I'll wager."

"That's none of your concern, Rory O'Neil."

He caught her by the shoulder. "Damn you, AnnaClaire. Everything that happens in this house is my concern. The man is as much a butcher as is Tilden. And you let him fawn over you and court you…"

Her eyes blazed. "I cannot help his fawning. But no man courts me without my permission. Lord Dunstan is far from home and missing his own kind. He sees in me a kindred spirit."

He caught her by the chin, forcing her to face him. His eyes were as stormy as hers. "If you think that, AnnaClaire, you're only fooling yourself. The man covets you. And why not?" His thumbs traced the fullness of her lips, sending heat curling along her spine. "A fairer lass I've never seen."

She drew back, afraid of the feelings his touch caused. "That's just the opiates, Rory O'Neil."

"The drugs may have weakened me, but they haven't affected my vision. Or my mind. Do you not see in yourself what others see, AnnaClaire?"

"I see…" She trailed off. For in truth, she could see herself reflected in his eyes. And it gave her the strangest feeling.

She was accustomed to flattery from the peacocks at Court. Such words from the lips of one such as Lord Dunstan would merely sound slick and condescending. But when spoken by this man, they took on a whole new meaning.

"Come now." She indicated the stairs. "I'd better help you back to bed before you find yourself unconscious right here in my room."

"Aye." He bit back his temper on a long, deep

breath, then made his way slowly up the stairs, with AnnaClaire trailing behind him.

Minutes later he lay in his bed and listened to the sounds of activity one floor below. Soon he heard the sound of carriage wheels. And then there was only silence.

The pain was forgotten, as was his temper. He lay very still, thinking about AnnaClaire. She was unlike any woman he'd ever known. Bright, educated, articulate, with a sharp wit and a clever mind. A wealthy woman who seemed to shy away from the grand displays of society. Though her home was fashionable, and every bit as grand as his home in Ballinarin, her life-style was simple. She was a woman so beautiful she took his breath away, and yet she seemed completely unaware of her effect on men.

And she was the daughter of Lord James Thompson, a close friend and advisor to the queen.

As he finally drifted into sleep, the image of AnnaClaire's lovely face played through his dreams. He would have been stunned to know that, alone in her carriage, AnnaClaire was experiencing a nearly identical situation. As she had so often lately, she found herself enumerating a certain rogue's fine qualities. And struggling to find a valid reason why she should continue to hold him at arm's length.

Chapter Six

"Lord Dunstan, I understand you met friends at the docks yesterday." Lady Thornly took a seat in her formal parlor and fanned her skirts out around her, while her guests took their places nearby. "What was the news?"

Dunstan looked pleased with himself. "The queen received my first missive, and obliged me by sending a boatload of soldiers. I've ordered them to sweep the city in search of the Irish brigands."

AnnaClaire's heart nearly stopped. "More soldiers?"

"Her Majesty has assured me she will take all of my advice to heart," Dunstan said with importance. "After all, that is why she sent me here."

AnnaClaire took a deep breath. Since she was forced to endure an entire afternoon in the company of Lord Dunstan, she decided she may as well attempt to glean all the information she could. "I would think by now the rebels have left Dublin far behind and have secreted themselves in the countryside. Do you not agree?"

"Nay, my lady. I disagree. We've had soldiers watching every road leading out of Dublin since that day on the docks, and not one of the brigands has been spotted. That tells me they've decided to hide out here in the city.''

''What will you do?'' AnnaClaire visibly tensed. ''Go door to door in search of them?''

''If we must. But there might be an easier way.''

''And what is that?'' Lady Thornly asked.

''Put such a price on their heads, especially on that of their leader, that even their own people will be hard-pressed to ignore it. After all, half these peasants are starving. The thought of a king's ransom should be enough to tempt at least a few of them to come forward. All we need is the hiding place of a couple of these rats. We'll make an example of those who would disregard the orders of their queen. In time, the rest will become so frightened after witnessing a hanging or two, they'll even refuse to give shelter to their own sons and brothers. And this little rebellion will die like a whimpering dog.''

''I do so admire a strong man.'' Lady Thornly sipped her ale and glanced from Dunstan to Anna-Claire. ''Don't you, my dear?''

AnnaClaire chose her words carefully. ''Strength is something we can all admire. But I wonder if you might be underestimating the strength of will of the Irish people.''

''You don't think enough money can persuade them to turn on one of their own?''

''Perhaps. There may be some who have no loyalty.''

''I'm counting on it. I need only one person willing to whisper a secret or two, and the Blackhearted O'Neil will be mine.''

''I hope you're right.'' Lord Davis yawned behind

his hand. They had spent the better part of the day at
Lady Thornly's, and now, with dinner behind them,
dusk was already settling over the city. "If you succeed, Her Majesty will be greatly relieved."

"Who knows?" Lady Thornly said with a trace of
awe. "Perhaps a grateful Elizabeth will reward you
with knighthood. And give you charge over your own
country."

"She could indeed." Lord Davis nodded vigorously.
"I say Ireland would be the logical choice. Despite the
poverty here, there are some exquisite parcels of land
and some really lovely estates."

The old man glanced at AnnaClaire, whose face
looked pale in the candle glow. "You've grown quiet,
my dear. Are you tired?"

"A bit."

"Then I think we must take our leave." He stood
and crossed to her, offering his hand.

She shot him a grateful smile. And kept the smile
frozen in place while she bade her hostess good-night
and endured the long carriage ride home beside Lord
Dunstan. At the door she did all she could to remain
patient as Dunstan lingered over her hand.

"Good night, Lord Dunstan."

"Good night, my lady. Thank you for a lovely afternoon. May I call on you again tomorrow?"

"I'm sorry. I shall be away most of the day."

"I see." Undeterred, he gave her a knowing smile.
"You realize, each time you refuse, you only whet my
appetite for more. Perhaps the day after?"

Before she could reply he shook his head. "Not now,
my lady. I'll send my driver by on the morrow for your
answer. Good night."

She watched until his carriage faded into the dusk.

Then she closed the door and hurried up the stairs to her room.

Finding Glinna there, she had no choice but to make ready for bed.

"Bridget said she would send up a tray if you wished it, my lady."

"Thank you, Glinna. That would be lovely. Just some tea and biscuits."

"Aye, my lady."

Bridget herself arrived with the tray. When the door was closed, she said softly, "In your absence I saw to our houseguest."

"Thank you, Bridget. How was he?"

"Like all men when they're beginning to heal. Short of temper. Impatient. And prone to self-pity."

AnnaClaire had to laugh. "All those things describe Rory O'Neil. Did he eat?"

"Hardly a bite. As soon as he heard that you would be gone for the day, he pushed aside his tray and sulked."

For some strange reason, that made AnnaClaire want to laugh aloud. Instead she turned away to hide her smile. "I'm sure he'll make up for it. You'd best prepare a little extra porridge on the morrow."

"Aye, my lady." Bridget nodded toward the tray. "I added enough food to see him through the night." She glanced at AnnaClaire. "Just in case you wanted to see him before you retire."

"Thank you, Bridget." She realized that she did want to see him. Very much. "I suppose I could drop by for a moment or two."

"Good night, my lady."

As soon as the housekeeper was gone and the door

secured, AnnaClaire picked up the tray and made her way up the little staircase.

Rory heard the light footfall that signalled Anna-Claire's arrival. He lay watching the door, feeling a strange dryness in his throat. Anticipation had his heartbeat accelerating. He'd missed her. Without her presence the day had been long and dreary, with no end to the pain.

He realized he'd begun to look forward to her visits, even though the vigorous workouts often made him grit his teeth in frustration. The effort was worth the rewards. Not only was he growing stronger, but he was privileged to spend more and more time in her company.

She wasn't even aware of how much she had changed over the past few days. At first, she had reacted with cool disdain, touching him only when necessary, and then with an almost clinical aloofness. But he had discovered inside himself a patience he'd never known he possessed. He had been thoughtful, considerate and as cool as she. Now they seemed to have settled into a cautious truce. But there were times when he could see beneath her calm surface to the turmoil within.

AnnaClaire entered with a swish of skirts and gave him a welcoming smile as she placed the tray on the bedside table.

"Good evening to you, Rory O'Neil. How did you fare in my absence?"

"I spent most of the day sleeping like a babe."

She laughed at his little frown. "Now why does that make you unhappy?"

"Because it's fine for infants to sleep like this. A man of my years should be ashamed of such a thing."

"Shame or no, it's a necessary part of healing." She lifted the lid from a tureen and the fragrance of broth and freshly-baked biscuits filled the air. "Bridget's outdone herself, I'm afraid." She lay a clean cloth on top of the blankets, then handed him a steaming bowl. "She's determined that her cooking alone will work miracles and speed the healing of your wounds."

He sipped. At once his smile returned. "Tell Bridget I consider her a saint, and her cooking indeed a miracle."

"She'll blush like a maid when I tell her." AnnaClaire opened the narrow casement, allowing a fresh evening breeze to sweep the room. Then, while he ate, she laid out clean breeches and a crisp white shirt.

"What need have I of those?"

"They'll replace the ones you were wearing when you came here." She bundled up his torn shirt, and glanced pointedly at him. "When you've time, I'd like you to remove those breeches."

"With pleasure, my lady." He made a move to his waistband, but she held up a hand to stop him.

"I'd prefer that you wait until I've gone."

"And spoil all my fun? Come, lovely AnnaClaire, give me a hand."

"You're a born tease, Rory O'Neil. Just see that you remove them after I've gone."

"Why should I waste good fabric? You said yourself that Bridget managed to boil away the worst of the stains."

"Aye. But she couldn't repair all the holes caused by knife and sword. I've decided that I'd best burn them."

"Burn them?" His eyes narrowed with sudden interest. "Why all this concern?"

"If your clothes were to be found, they could be traced back to you. Everyone who saw you on the docks that day will remember what you were wearing. I'd wager there aren't too many men lying abed in torn breeches and shirt."

His tone went icy cold. "I'll ask you again, AnnaClaire. Why this sudden concern about my clothes?"

Her voice lowered to a conspiratorial tone. "The truth of it is, I learned today that another ship has docked. English soldiers are sweeping the city. Lord Dunstan has put a price on your head, in the hopes of coaxing your countrymen to betray you. He is determined to be the one to capture the elusive Blackhearted O'Neil."

He shoved aside the food. It wasn't the first time he'd given thought to her precarious position. But it was the opening he'd needed to ask the question aloud. "Considering the danger, why did you take me in, AnnaClaire?"

She removed the empty bowl and handed him a plate of beef and cheese and crusty bread warm from the oven, hoping to entice him to eat. "If you'll recall, the choice wasn't mine to make. It was thrust upon me."

"But you could have had me arrested."

"Aye." She poured water into a basin and folded several towels beside it.

When she offered nothing more, he picked at his food. "At least you could have ordered me away."

"I could have." She closed the window, shook back the curtains and lifted a blanket that had fallen to the floor, carefully folding it over her arm.

"But you didn't, AnnaClaire." He caught her hand to still her busy work. "You let me stay, knowing you were placing your entire household in danger. Why?"

She avoided his eyes. "You were in need of my help. I'd no more turn you away than I'd turn away any creature in need."

"For God's sake, AnnaClaire. There's a price on my head. Do you think I don't know what the English will do to you if they find me here?"

"They won't find you." She did look at him then. And felt the heat rise to her cheeks. She lifted her head in what she hoped was a haughty look. "You said yourself. I'm one of them."

"I've said a lot of things. Some of which make me ashamed." His tone lowered. "You're not one of them, AnnaClaire. Nor could you ever be."

"And how would you know that? My father is one of the queen's most trusted counselors. At this very moment he is probably meeting with her, advising her on the best way to handle the 'Irish problem,' as she likes to call us."

"You see?" He shot her a smile. "You just said 'us.' You consider yourself one of us."

"A slip of the tongue. Nothing more."

"Nay. It was no slip. Your mother's people were Irish. And your heart is here. With us." He touched a hand to her cheek. "With me."

She struggled to show no emotion. But each time he touched her she felt the slow curl of heat deep inside, and the quick, sudden tug on her heart.

"You make my words something more than I intended, Rory O'Neil. You were wounded. You needed a place to heal. I'd have done the same for any wounded creature, whether it be a dog or a man."

"Aye. You've a tender heart. It's one more thing I've begun to love about you, AnnaClaire."

"Don't." She brushed aside his hand. "Don't use those pretty words to break down my resistance to you."

"Is that what I was doing?"

"I've the feeling that you always know exactly what you're doing, Rory O'Neil. Now." She sharpened her tone, determined to remain brisk and businesslike. "If you'll sit in that chair, we'll work on your arm before we take our sleep."

"Together?" The teasing light was back in his eyes.

"The only thing we'll do together is move that arm."

He sat and stripped off his shirt, tensing as he waited for the moment when she would first touch him. When she stood behind him and her strong fingers began massaging his shoulder, he closed his eyes and released a long slow breath.

The touch of her was like a drug. The moment her hands skimmed his flesh he could feel the changes. His heartbeat became erratic. His breathing quickened. His mind was swept clean of all thought save one. He wanted more. He was desperate to feel her hands touching him everywhere. And to taste her. To take her. Here. Now.

He clenched his teeth to keep from crying out. Clenched his hands into fists to keep from dragging her into his arms and taking what he wanted.

"You haven't been moving your arm as you should."

"And how would you know that?"

"Because I can feel a knot of tension here." She kneaded his flesh, and he bent his head forward slightly to give her easier access. "And here." She pressed her thumbs over his stiff shoulder, working the flesh in firm but gentle strokes.

"Perhaps the tension is from something other than pain."

"And what would that be?"

He sighed, as much in pleasure as frustration. "I'll leave you to figure that one for yourself, my lady."

She cursed the evening shadows that lent an air of romance to the little attic room. Surely that was the reason why his teasing seemed to have taken on added meaning tonight. As her fingers skimmed his flesh and she patiently worked his arm upward and back, she found herself wishing she could just relax and enjoy what he offered. For if truth be told, she was more and more tempted.

"That will have to do for tonight." With a trace of impatience, she emptied the opiate into a tumbler of water and picked up the tray.

"You're leaving so soon?"

"Aye." She walked purposefully to the door without allowing herself to look at him. One glance at that handsome face, those smiling lips, and that teasing laughter in his eyes, and she would be lost.

"Will I see you on the morrow? Or are you spending another day in the company of your Englishman?"

She did turn then, giving him a haughty look. "You shall just have to wait and see, Rory O'Neil."

When she reached the safety of her room, she set down the tray and slumped against the edge of her bed. It was getting harder and harder to remember why she must keep her wits about her, instead of simply surrendering and enjoying what her houseguest was offering.

* * *

"What was it like growing up in England, Anna-Claire?"

It had become a familiar ritual. AnnaClaire would fetch Rory's meal, and then, while his strength was at its peak, she would help him to the chair and work with him on the difficult task of restoring the use of his arm. While they went through the routine, she would tell him of her childhood, or get him to talk about his, in order to keep his mind off the pain. His parents, Gavin and Moira, his brother, and little sister, Briana, had become as familiar to her as her own family.

"My childhood in England was lonely, I suppose. Because of my mother's delicate health, I was her only child. I remember wishing I had brothers or sisters to talk to. But, since my father wanted me to be educated, I was surrounded by an array of tutors. I was expected to learn comportment, music, and French and Spanish, as well as English." She laughed. "My English tutor constantly berated me for my brogue, which I'd picked up from my mother."

At last he understood why her voice was a strange mixture of English and Irish. And though the brogue had been softened, it was still there. Like a hint of soft, soothing music to his ears. "A pity you weren't educated here. Your Irish tutors would have encouraged your brogue."

"Mistress Morgan would strike me with a rod each time she caught me speaking so."

"She struck you?" The thought of it had him gritting his teeth. "What did your parents say about that?"

"I dared not tell them. My mother had always been in uncertain health. I knew it would upset her to learn that I was being obstinate. So I...took my beatings, and tried to do as my tutors expected."

He felt an unreasonable wave of protectiveness toward this tough little woman. "What about your friends?"

"I had a few. But many of them considered me too Irish. And when I would accompany my mother to Clay Court in the summers, the young people here considered me too English. I suppose that explains why I've learned to keep my own counsel." She was eager to change the subject. "Now, tell me more about Conor. Why did your parents choose to send him abroad rather than you? After all, as firstborn, that should have been your right."

He chuckled. "I wouldn't go. I'd had enough of books and tutors. The monks at St. Brendan's had been cramming their knowledge into my head since I was no bigger than a whelp. But it wasn't books that held my interest. It was my father's land and holdings. For me it's always been the land. Our beautiful Ballinarin."

She heard the softness that came into his tone whenever he mentioned his home. And a yearning that no amount of toughness could hide.

"Why don't you go back then, Rory?"

He shook his head and grunted as she stood behind him, positioning his arm above his head. The pain had greatly diminished this day. "I can't. I'll not go back until this thing is ended."

"This thing." AnnaClaire shivered at the term he used to describe his vendetta with the soldier named Tilden. As she lowered his arm and began to massage the rope of muscle at the shoulder she said, "What good will you be to your family if you're killed?"

"No good at all." He turned his head slightly to

glance at her. "That's why I intend to stay alive. For I truly regret leaving them alone for so long. My father must assume the burden of the work at an age when he ought to be relaxing by the fire, surrounded by grandchildren. And my mother, God love her, is now left with the task of raising young Innis, the only survivor of Tilden's massacre. I resent not being there to see my sister, Briana, grow into womanhood. And Conor." His voice roughened with feeling. "We're closer than mere brothers. One of us used to be able to finish a sentence before the other had spoken the words. Though we're very different in looks and temperament, our souls are one. I miss him every day of my life."

Her hands stilled. She could actually feel the pain vibrating through him. Without realizing it, her fingers closed around his upper arms and she brought her lips close to his ear. "I'm sorry. I know this is so difficult for you. You mustn't torment yourself, Rory."

God in heaven. Did she know what it did to him when she touched him like that? He felt a rush of heat and then a slow, steading throbbing in his loins. The blood roared in his temples.

Too late, she became aware of his tension. And her own. But as she started to pull away he closed his hands over hers, holding her still.

"That isn't all that's tormenting me, AnnaClaire."

She tried to tug free but he held her fast. Her throat went dry. Her words were strained. "It's time I took my leave, Rory O'Neil." The room seemed suddenly far too small and suffocating.

"Nay, my lady." In one smooth motion he stood and hauled her into his arms. "Don't go just yet."

Awed and a little frightened, she tried to make light

of the situation. "It would seem our time together has been well spent. Your strength is indeed restored."

"As is my appetite."

"I'll be sure to tell Bridget."

"I wasn't speaking of food, AnnaClaire. It's you I want."

"Let go of me, Rory O'Neil."

"Why? I'm not alone in this wanting. You want me too."

She felt a wave of panic. "Take your hands off me. I want nothing of the kind."

"Liar." When she started to push away, he muttered, "Do you think I can't see it in your eyes, AnnaClaire? Feel it in the way you touch me? You want. Aye, you want the same thing I want. And the wanting frightens you, doesn't it?"

Her head came up. "I'm not afraid. Not of the likes of you."

"Prove it. Kiss me. Right here. Right now."

She froze at the challenge. Her words were pure ice. "I need to prove nothing to you."

"Aye. But how about to yourself, AnnaClaire? Or are you afraid of what you'll find?" He lowered his hands to his sides, leaving the choice up to her. He wouldn't hold her against her will. Still, he'd come to know her so well. He was counting on the fact that she couldn't resist a challenge.

Very deliberately she lifted herself on tiptoe to meet his mouth, all the while staring into his eyes. Just as her lips brushed his she saw his eyes narrow slightly. Then her mouth was fully upon his and her lashes fluttered, then closed as her lips moved over his. She felt the quick jolt, the sudden heating of her blood even as icy ribbons of nerves coursed along her spine. It all happened in the space of seconds, and yet the feelings rocked her.

When she opened her eyes, she realized that he hadn't moved. His hands were firmly at his sides, his body as still as though nothing had happened. It was an odd stillness that masked the tension humming through him. His lips curved into a hint of a smile. A smile that issued its own challenge.

"So, AnnaClaire, what did you find?"

"Nothing." She felt her cheeks flame for the lie, but refused to back down. "I found nothing. I felt nothing at all. Does that answer your question?"

"Aye. And I say it again, my lady. You're nothing more than a beautiful, beguiling liar."

"I answered your challenge. And that's all I intend…"

Her words ended in a gasp as he swept her into his arms, crushing her against his chest. His mouth covered hers in a kiss so hot, so hungry, she had no choice but to answer with a hunger of her own.

His mouth was so incredibly agile. Tasting. Feeding. Devouring. With teeth and lips and tongue he took her on a wild ride that had her head spinning, her heart racing. The heat instantly became an inferno. Her blood flowed like lava until she felt herself erupting with a passion that threatened to overwhelm her. And all the while his hands, those big, work-worn hands moved along her back, burning a trail of fire.

"Rory. Give me a moment." She pulled back, dragging air into her lungs. "I can't think."

"Don't think, AnnaClaire. Just feel." He ran soft nibbling kisses across her temple, down her cheek, over her upturned nose. The sweetness of it, the gentleness, made her sigh.

He caught her hand and pressed it to his naked chest. "Feel what you do to my heart."

It was pounding, wildly out of control, just as her own heart was.

She lifted her hand and he raised it to his lips, pressing a kiss to the palm. Their eyes met. Each could read the desire in the other.

Without a word they came together, lips mating, bodies straining to get closer.

Rory's hands were in her hair, his fingers kneading her scalp as he took the kiss deeper, then deeper still.

Her arms twined around his neck, needing to hold him, frantic to feel him with every part of her body.

This was madness. He knew it. And yet he could no more stop it than he could stop the sun from shining, or the breeze from blowing across the land. This woman had become a fever in his blood. A hunger that gnawed at him. He had to have her. Or die trying.

"Lie with me, AnnaClaire. Let me love you. Here. Now."

His words, whispered so fiercely against her lips, inside her mouth, had the blood singing in her brain. It would be so easy to take what he offered. And yet she held back, afraid of the feelings that misted her mind, clouded her reason.

"I...can't."

"Can't? Or won't?"

"I don't know. I can't think when you're holding me like this, kissing me like this."

She pushed a little away, struggling for control.

"I understand. A woman like you wouldn't give your love lightly. And there is the matter of the price on my head."

Her eyes flashed. "You think that would hold me back? If you believe that, then you don't know me."

"Oh, I think I know you well enough." He touched a finger to her lips, moist and swollen from his kisses. "You answered my question."

"What question?"

"I've no doubt you want me as much as I want you. You may deny it, but your kisses say otherwise."

"How dare..."

He shot her his dangerous smile. "Are you back to denying? Then deny that you needed no coaxing to kiss me just as passionately as I kissed you."

He saw the protest that sprang to her lips and hurried on before she could speak. "Aye, there's fire in you, AnnaClaire. And a deep dark well of passion just waiting to be set free."

She pushed away. "Damn you, Rory O'Neil."

"Aye. I'm damned, all right. Damned to want a woman who doesn't know her own mind. One minute you're returning my kisses like a woman, the next you're poised to run like a child. You can lie to me. Just remember not to lie to yourself, AnnaClaire. When you're all alone in the dark in that big soft bed, think about the man who lies just one floor above you. Any time you want me, I'll be here. And more than willing to unlock that secret door you keep so tightly closed."

She flounced away rather than stay and fight his words. Especially since they hit so close to the truth. As she made her way down the narrow staircase, she cursed the fact that the taste of him was still on her lips. And the need for him still burned.

Chapter Seven

AnnaClaire awoke to the soft tapping on her door. She'd put in a miserable night, taunted by Rory's words, haunted by the image of him holding her, kissing her.

She slipped out of bed and padded across the room. When she tore open the door, Glinna swept past her and set the tray on a table.

"Why have you begun bolting your door, my lady?"

Caught by surprise, AnnaClaire could offer no logical explanation.

"If you're afraid of the rogues who are said to be hiding out in Dublin, my lady, you need have no fear. Despite what's been said about them, they don't harm women. Even English women. 'Tis said their fight is with the queen's soldiers."

"Thank you, Glinna. That's a comfort."

"Shall I stay and help you dress, my lady?"

"Perhaps later. Lord Davis and Lord Dunstan will be coming by to take me on a picnic."

The little maid was suitably impressed. "Lord Dunstan? The handsome one?"

AnnaClaire nodded. "I'll need a cloak and bonnet.

And you might ask Bridget to prepare some of her tarts. I know Lord Davis has a fondness for them."

"Aye, my lady. Will you ring for me when you wish me to help you dress?"

"I shall indeed. Until then I believe I'll relax here in my room."

As Glinna made her way to the door, she glanced at the heavy tray. "I hope you take time to eat at least some of the food Bridget has sent." She lowered her voice. "If you ask me, I think she's getting a bit daft. Why, until I called her attention to it, she was sending you two cups for your tea, and two bowls of porridge this morrow."

AnnaClaire coughed behind her hand, to cover the laughter that threatened. "Perhaps she's been working too hard lately. I'll have a word with her."

"Aye, my lady." The little maid pulled the door closed behind her. Before she could walk away, she heard the sound of the door being bolted from within.

Alone in her room AnnaClaire slipped on a wrap of cut velvet, tying it modestly at her waist and throat. She was determined that there would be no repeat of last night's temptation. While seeing to Rory's food and comfort, she was determined to maintain her modesty.

With a sigh of determination she picked up the tray and started up the steps to the attic. At the top of the stairs, she nudged open the door with her hip.

"Good morrow, Rory O'Neil." She kept her tone impersonal.

"The same to you." He yawned, stretched, pretending to be drowsy. In truth, he'd been awake for what seemed hours, awaiting his first morning glimpse of her.

He sat up and watched as she bent to place the tray on the table. Despite the proper robe, he could imagine every line and curve of that lithe body.

She handed him a bowl of porridge.

Before she could turn away he caught her hand, drawing her to the edge of the mattress. "You're not joining me?"

She laughed, to cover the little jolt she experienced at his touch. "Not this time. My little maid, Glinna, noticed the two bowls and cups on the tray and accused poor Bridget of being daft. So I'm afraid there's only one bowl and cup today."

"Then we'll share." He lifted the spoon to her mouth. It was an oddly intimate gesture that had her nerves quivering.

He watched her swallow and had to fight the urge to kiss away the moisture that clung to her lips.

"That's not enough to feed a bird." He dipped the spoon and fed her more.

She was achingly aware of him. Of the muscles that rippled each time he moved his arm. Of his eyes watching her so keenly. Of his hair, dark and mussed from sleep, falling slightly over his forehead in a most appealing way.

"You eat the rest. You need nourishment to build your strength." In order to put some distance between them, she crossed to the narrow window and opened it.

"What sort of day is it?"

She kept her back to him, grateful for the chance to escape those eyes. "A bit of fine mist falling. But there's sunshine just to the east. I believe it will be a grand day."

"What will you do today?"

"I'm going on a picnic." She paused a beat before adding, "With Lord Davis, an old friend of my father."

He'd noted her hesitation. "Just the two of you?"

She shook her head. Stared off into the distance. "There will be others. Lady Thornly. Lord Dunstan."

His tone hardened. "How convenient."

"I could think of no way to politely refuse."

"Did you try saying no?"

She shot him a look. "It isn't that simple. Lord Davis is a sweet old dear who is enjoying the role of matchmaker. I simply will not hurt his feelings." Seeing that the bowl was empty, she crossed to Rory, took the bowl and handed him a cup of tea. "I'm sorry that you'll have to be alone all day."

"It's quite all right. Enjoy your day, my lady." His voice was controlled, with no hint of the emotions that simmered below the surface. "I expect I can manage to lift my sword a time or two without your help."

"Well then." She ran her hands along her skirt, wishing she could think of some reason to prolong their visit. "Do you need anything?"

"Not a thing. You've been more than kind."

"Good day to you then, Rory O'Neil."

He inclined his head. "My lady."

She turned away and descended the stairs, feeling strangely deflated. Damn Lord Dunstan, for taking her away from home when she had no wish to be with him. And damn the warrior who lay abed upstairs, as well. Both men had conspired to spoil her day.

"You see, Lynley?" Lord Davis leaned back against the trunk of a gnarled tree and sipped his ale. "I told you there were some splendid places here in Ireland."

"Aye." Dunstan flicked a glance over the table set

up in the shade of a nearby tree where four gentlemen were engaged in a game of cards. There was a time when he would have dominated the game and happily relieved them of their gold. At the moment, however, he had found a more appealing treasure. He turned to AnnaClaire, who was kneeling on a coverlet spread in the grass. In her one hand was a goblet of ale, in the other, a delicately pleated fan. "I am beginning to understand why you wish to remain here, my lady."

She smiled at his unexpected compliment. "Be careful, Lord Dunstan. You might fall under Ireland's spell."

"I believe I already have. But it isn't this land that has a hold on me."

Lady Thornly, caught up in the excitement of budding romance, couldn't help sighing. "Oh, Lord Dunstan. My dear departed husband used to look at me in the same way that you're looking at our sweet AnnaClaire. Isn't that so, Lord Davis?"

"Indeed it is, my dear." The old man shuffled to his feet and offered his arm. "Perhaps we'll take a walk and leave these young people alone."

"If you don't mind, I'd like to go with you." AnnaClaire stood and shook down her skirts, determined not to be left behind. "After that fine lunch your cook prepared, Lady Thornly, a walk is just what I need."

The old woman turned to Dunstan. "Then you must join us as well. I insist."

Pleased, he moved along beside AnnaClaire, offering the support of his arm as she picked her way over the rough ground.

"Have you made any progress in your search for the Blackhearted O'Neil, my lord?"

"Nay. But my soldiers tell me that the offer of gold has caused a stir among the people. It is, after all, more than most of them will see in a lifetime. I have no doubt that someone will come forward."

"It was a brilliant move, Lynley. Brilliant." Lord Davis mopped his brow with a fine linen square, then indicated a fallen log. "If you don't mind, I believe I'll just sit here a moment and catch my breath."

"Then I'll join you." Lady Thornly fanned herself and settled carefully on the edge of the log.

When AnnaClaire paused beside them, Lord Davis signalled her to move ahead. "No need for you wait for us. Go ahead, my dear."

Dunstan pointed to a clearing through the trees. "Come, my lady. We'll walk to the banks of the river."

It was on the tip of her tongue to refuse, but he was already guiding her along a grassy trail. Up ahead she could hear the voices of several of their friends, who had wandered off after eating.

When they reached the river they came upon a cluster of men and women who stood facing a young mother, clad in only a damp chemise and petticoat, standing knee-deep in the water. In her arms was a naked, wriggling infant. Hiding behind her were a frightened boy and girl. It was obvious that they had been interrupted while washing in the river.

"Remove yourselves at once," one of the men shouted. "You're sullying our fine river with your filth."

The others laughed and pointed, while the mother and her children cringed in shame.

"Lord Ramsey." AnnaClaire hurried forward and

said in a soft tone, "You're causing the young woman embarrassment."

"I want her out of there at once. The sight of her offends me. Besides, my wife desires a drink of water."

His wife held a handkerchief to her mouth and nose. "How could I possibly drink the water now, Thomas, after seeing that peasant and her brats? And look." She pointed to the basket of wet clothes lying on the shore. "They actually washed their filthy rags in the river as well."

A second woman pointed to a tiny thatched hut in the distance. "No wonder these people bare their bodies for all to see. Look how they live. Like animals in hovels. Have they no shame?"

Temper made AnnaClaire careless. "Perhaps it is you who have no shame. And no decency. This poor woman had no way of knowing you'd come upon her like this. The least you could do is give her a moment to cover herself and her wee ones and allow her to take her leave with dignity."

"Dignity?" Lord Ramsey's wife was outraged. "How can you suggest that these barbarians have any concept of dignity? Look at them. Filthy beggars."

The laughter of the others caused an ache around AnnaClaire's heart. Striding across the space that separated them, she whisked off her cloak and held it out to the frightened young woman. "Here. Cover yourself with this."

The woman waded toward her through the water, clutching the infant to her heart. The boy and girl clung to her wet petticoat, their eyes wide and terrified.

When she reached the shallows, the young mother shook her head. "I couldn't possibly accept your kind offer, my lady. Your cloak is far too fine. I'd only soil it.''

"I insist." AnnaClaire took a step into the water and draped it around the woman's trembling shoulders.

"I'm grateful, my lady. If you'll wait here, I'll return with it as quickly as I can."

"There's no need. I have another. This one is yours to keep." AnnaClaire glanced at the shivering children. "See that you get them home to a fire quickly."

"Aye, my lady. God bless you."

The young woman wrapped the infant in a ragged shawl and lay him atop the basket, then hurried away without a backward glance, struggling under the heavy load. Beside her the two children had to run to keep up.

When AnnaClaire turned, the others, including Lord Davis and Lady Thornly, were watching her in silence.

"Well." It was Dunstan who finally spoke. "You realize, my dear AnnaClaire, that your fine cloak will fetch a pretty price at market. That little strumpet will no doubt sell it to buy whiskey for her man."

"Perhaps. Or perhaps she'll use it to keep her wee ones warm in their beds."

Dunstan threw back his head and laughed. "I can see that you need someone to save you from your romantic notions, my lady. These people don't give a care about their spawn. From what I can see, they procreate like animals."

"Is that what you intend to tell the queen?" Temper caused AnnaClaire to throw all caution to the wind. "Perhaps you would like England to issue a decree prohibiting them from having children, Lord Dunstan."

"It isn't such a bad idea. And I do think Elizabeth should see that these people can no longer inherit, since they have neither the means nor the will to improve upon their inheritance. Look around you, AnnaClaire. Left in the hands of such as these, this country will soon be fit for nothing more than savages and pigs.''

AnnaClaire's voice rang with righteous indignation. ''You would know something about that, wouldn't you, my lord?''

Before she could say more, Lord Davis draped his own cloak around her shoulders and forcibly turned her away. ''Enough, my dear. There is a chill breeze off the water. I think it's time we got you home.''

''I haven't finished.''

''Oh, but you have.''

Before she could protest further, he hauled her along beside him, leaving the others to follow.

As they made their way back to the waiting carriages, Lord Davis muttered, ''You would be well advised not to anger Lord Dunstan, my dear. He can be a powerful friend, or a dangerous enemy.''

''I care not about Lord Dunstan. Or the others.''

''AnnaClaire. AnnaClaire.'' He gave a sigh of disapproval as he watched his friends approach. ''If you do not care about the others, give a care for me.''

She touched a hand to his cheek. ''You know I love you, Lord Davis.''

He caught her hand and said sternly, ''Then hold your tongue. We will speak no more of this. And if Lord Dunstan is willing to forget, you will do the same. Agreed?''

She took a deep breath, then nodded. ''Very well.''

''Good. Good.'' He patted her hand before helping her into the carriage. And when, a moment later, Lord Dunstan climbed up beside her, the old man breathed a sigh of relief.

Still, as their parade of carriages made its way back to Dublin, Lord Davis couldn't seem to shake off the unsettling feeling that AnnaClaire might have gone too far. He had heard rumors of Lord Dunstan's vicious temper. Those who dared to cross him often found themselves not only out of favor with the queen, but also found their fortunes dwindling and their estates confiscated.

Lord Davis could only hope that AnnaClaire's beauty held enough allure for the powerful Dunstan to keep her in the queen's good graces.

When the carriage came to a halt at the door of Clay Court, Dunstan graciously stepped down and offered his hand.

"Thank you, my lord."

"You are most welcome, my lady." He walked with AnnaClaire to the door. "I would like to call on you tonight."

She forced a smile to her lips. "I'm afraid all this fresh air has conspired to make me weary." She glanced to where old Lord Davis was watching them intently, and carefully added, "Perhaps another time."

"Of course. I'll pay a call on the morrow if I may."

"Thank you, Lord Dunstan. Until the morrow then."

He brushed his lips over her hand. "Good night, my lady."

AnnaClaire stepped inside and leaned wearily against the closed door. The effort to be polite and charming in Dunstan's company had left her exhausted. The feel of his lips on her hand made her skin crawl. Still, she couldn't ignore her old friend's warning. Dunstan was dangerous. She would do well to keep that in mind and behave accordingly.

Moments later as she hurried up the stairs, she felt

the weariness lifting from her shoulders. Could it be because she was about to see Rory O'Neil?

With a smile of anticipation she flung open the door to her room.

"Oh, my lady." Glinna spun around and clapped her hand to her mouth. "You startled me."

"What are you doing here, Glinna?"

"I was hanging your clean gowns, my lady." The little maid darted a look around the room, then started backing toward the door. "Shall I stay and help you undress?"

"That won't be necessary, Glinna. Good night."

"Aye. Good night, my lady." Relieved, the little maid fairly danced out of the room.

From the hurried footsteps on the stairs, AnnaClaire guessed that Glinna must be eagerly on her way to meet one of the stable lads. She couldn't blame her in the least. Wasn't she just as eager to make her way to the one who awaited her in the little attic room above?

She studied her reflection in the looking glass, taking a moment to tuck up a stray strand of hair. A day in the fresh air had put a bloom on her cheeks and a sparkle in her eyes. Smoothing down her skirts, she crossed the room, then came to a sudden halt in mid-stride.

The door leading to the attic staircase was ajar.

She distinctly remembered closing it that morning.

She lifted both hands to her cheeks at the sudden realization. If Glinna had stumbled upon their secret, all their lives were in danger. Everyone knew the maid could never be trusted to keep such a thing to herself. If even one of her friends found out, it would soon be known all over Dublin.

And then AnnaClaire thought about Dunstan's boast.

Though these people were patriots, many of them were also desperately poor. The promise of gold could be too great a temptation for even the most loyal of citizens.

AnnaClaire ran down the stairs in search of her maid.

"Glinna. Glinna." Her voice grew more frantic as she raced from room to room.

In the kitchen she came upon Bridget and Tavis enjoying tea and biscuits.

"Have you seen Glinna?" she asked.

"Aye, my lady. Just moments ago she ran out of here as though the devil himself were after her."

"Sweet Savior." AnnaClaire whirled and left the old couple staring after her as she made a mad dash up the stairs.

Rory O'Neil must leave at once. Else, if what she suspected were true, he would surely face certain death.

Chapter Eight

"Rory. Rory O'Neil."

AnnaClaire was breathless by the time she entered the little attic room. Her gaze swept the empty bed. Rory was standing in the shadows. He was barefoot and shirtless, clad only in the black pants she had provided.

He turned and she was jolted by the force of his presence. It wasn't only the width of his shoulders, or the ripple of muscle, or the carelessly handsome pose. It was an aura of strength, of purpose, that held her transfixed.

"You must take your leave at once."

He strode toward her, catching her roughly by the shoulders. "What's wrong, AnnaClaire? What has happened?"

"My maid, Glinna." She paused a moment to catch her breath. "She was in my room when I arrived home. The door to this room was ajar. Did anyone come up the stairs while I was gone?"

His eyes narrowed. "I slept on and off most of the day. But I thought..."

"You thought what?"

"That I'd heard a footfall. When I investigated, there was no one there. But I was agitated enough that I couldn't get back to sleep."

"I knew it." She turned away and began to pace. "Our secret is no longer safe, Rory. If she knows about you, others soon will. You must leave now. I'll have Tavis prepare a horse and cart."

"Nay." He caught her arm to still her movements. "When I leave here, I mustn't do anything that would lead the English back to you." His tone lowered. "I've tarried here long enough. It's time to resume my search for Tilden."

"You aren't strong enough yet to engage in battle."

"That's what I've told myself for days." He stared down into her eyes. "But we both know I've been lying to myself. My wounds are healed. The truth is, I didn't want to leave here. To leave you." He touched a hand to her cheek. "But I must. Every day that I allowed myself to stay here has put you and everyone in this house in danger."

"I've told you before. My father is a trusted friend to the queen. English soldiers wouldn't harm me."

He touched a finger to her lips to silence her. "This isn't a game, AnnaClaire. It's war. Even your father's friendship with the queen wouldn't save you if they found out you'd been harboring their enemy. Do you understand?"

She studied him a moment, warmed by his touch. Then, as another thought struck, she was suddenly chilled. She would never be able to feel his touch again. Hear his voice. See his face.

She took a deep breath and slowly nodded. "What do you want me to do?"

"Have Tavis send word to my men that the time has

come. They'll know the plan.'' With his knife he forced the small window open. Then, slicing his hand, he very deliberately stained the sill with his blood.

''What are you doing?'' She was horrified at the sight of fresh blood.

''Making it look as though I forced my way into your home. Go now, AnnaClaire.''

She started to turn away. ''I'll have Bridget prepare some food.''

''No food, AnnaClaire.''

''But—''

He held up a hand to silence her protest. ''When I leave here, I will be the most hunted man in Ireland. There will be many, including my own countrymen, who would capture me for the reward. Remember what I said earlier. There must be nothing that would lead my captors back to you.''

She could see the wisdom of his words, even though her heart cried out at the cruel thought of his capture.

''I'll be back, Rory.''

''Nay, my lady. When Tavis is gone, join Bridget in the kitchen.''

''I want to say a proper goodbye.''

He crossed the room and crushed her against him while his mouth moved over hers. ''This is all the goodbye we can manage, AnnaClaire.'' He kissed her one last time, lingering over her lips, wishing he could do more, say more. ''It will have to do. Now go. Hurry.''

She felt a sob catch in her throat as she turned away. She swallowed it down. Not here. Not now. There would be time later for tears. For now, there was so much to be done.

In the attic room Rory hurriedly dressed, tucking a

knife at his waist and another in his boot. Then he prowled the room, overturning a small table, snagging the curtains on the edge of a basin, to make it look as though an intruder had come through in a hurry.

With sword in hand he made his way down the stairs. Seeing no one about, he descended to the main floor. Before he could seek out the others in the kitchen, he heard the thundering hoofbeats of approaching horses.

He cursed the timing. He'd known the English would move quickly once they'd heard of his whereabouts. There was nothing to be done now but to bluff his way through, and hope he could at least save the reputations of those to whom he owed his life.

He stepped into a darkened parlor and listened to shouted commands moments before the tramp of feet sounded on the walkway. From his place of concealment, he watched as Bridget hurried to fling open the door.

Lord Dunstan's imperious voice broke the silence. ''Where is your mistress?''

''In the kitchen, my lord.''

''Out of the way, old fool.'' Dunstan brushed past the housekeeper and strode to the kitchen, followed by at least a dozen armed men.

''Lord Dunstan.'' AnnaClaire set down her cup of tea with a clatter, alarmed at the tremor in her voice. ''What brings you back at such an hour?''

''You employ a maid named Glinna Farley?''

''I do.''

''She has claimed a reward for finding the Black-hearted O'Neil.''

''Our Glinna?'' Bridget paused in the doorway, making a valiant attempt to draw attention from her frightened mistress. She clapped her hands together. "How grand. Where did she find him?"

Ignoring her, Dunstan continued to study AnnaClaire as he said, "She claims he is secreted in a room below the eaves."

AnnaClaire's hand flew to her throat. "Here? In my father's house?"

"That is what she says. Are you saying you know nothing about this?"

"My lord." AnnaClaire got to her feet and grasped the back of her chair for support. "I couldn't say for certain, since I haven't been in that room for many months. But I find it hard to believe such a thing could happen in my own home without my knowledge."

"Then you don't mind if my men search the room in question?"

AnnaClaire glanced at the soldiers, then returned her gaze to Dunstan. "Not only do I not mind, my lord, I insist." She lifted her skirts and swept past him. "Come. I'll lead the way."

"Nay, my lady." Dunstan caught her arm and held her back, saying to the soldiers, "Let the old woman show you the way."

As she listened to the sound of their footsteps, AnnaClaire prayed that her trembling legs wouldn't fail her. She was no good at this playacting. Could Dunstan sense her terror?

Had there been time for Rory to escape? Sweet heaven, what would she do if he was still there? She would be forced to stand here and do nothing as he was taken away in chains.

Several soldiers stood at attention near the door while she and Dunstan listened to the sounds of muted voices and footsteps above. Soon the voices drew nearer and one of the soldiers held up a hand bearing unmistakable stains. "There's fresh blood on the sill, my lord. And more on the door. The O'Neil has been here."

Dunstan's eyes narrowed. "Search the house. Room by room. The lady and I will wait here."

AnnaClaire turned to Bridget. "I am feeling faint. Bring me some ale." As though suddenly remembering her manners she turned to Dunstan. "Will you join me, my lord?"

"Aye." He was studying her carefully, noting the trembling of her limbs, the unmistakable pallor.

As the housekeeper moved around the kitchen, AnnaClaire crossed to the fire and stood warming her hands. She felt chilled to the marrow. Where was Rory now? How could he possibly escape with so many soldiers guarding the house?

"Ale, my lady." Bridget handed her a goblet, then offered a second to Lord Dunstan.

Just as he was about to accept it, the back door was thrust open and Tavis stumbled in. Blood streamed from his head.

Bridget let out a bloodcurdling scream and hurled herself against the old man, cradling his head in her hands. "Tavis. Oh, Tavis love. What has happened to you?"

The old man stumbled a few more steps, then sank down on the floor. Several soldiers came running to investigate the commotion.

"Thieves," he managed as he accepted several linen squares from his wife and pressed them to his head. "Came into the stables, they did. Stole our horses."

"It's the O'Neil," Dunstan shouted to his soldiers.

"Trying to escape. Hurry. One hundred pieces of gold to the man who stops him."

At that the soldiers streamed out of the house and went racing off in the direction of the stables.

"I care not whether he is brought back alive or dead," Dunstan called after them.

He stood watching for several moments as his men struggled to outrace each other for the prize. Agitated, he turned.

The elderly housekeeper and her husband were staring across the room, eyes huge, mouths agape.

"What is it, you old fools?"

Without a word Bridget pointed.

Rory stepped from his place of concealment directly behind AnnaClaire. One hand was clamped over her mouth, to keep her from crying out. The other was holding a knife pressed against her throat.

"Unhand that woman at once," Dunstan ordered.

Rory merely gave him an icy smile. "The woman will die unless you do exactly as I say."

"Do you know the name of the woman you have dared to sully?" Dunstan demanded.

"I neither know nor care. For now, all that matters is that she is going to assure my escape. If your men should attempt to capture me, I shall have to slice her lovely throat."

"Fool. You have made a poor choice of captive. This woman is the daughter of Lord James Thompson, Chief Counsel to your queen, Elizabeth of England. Should you harm her, that same queen will move heaven and earth to exact retribution."

"Elizabeth is not my queen. As for the lady's name and rank, all the better. I will remind you that my sword cares not whether the English blood it spills belongs to a man or a woman.'' He motioned to Bridget. ''Old woman, tie the hands and feet of these two men.''

Bridget was openly sobbing. ''Please, sir, my husband is gravely wounded.''

Rory bit off each word. ''I said bind their hands and feet. If you don't do it quickly, I'll be forced to harm your mistress.''

With great weeping and wailing, Bridget did as she was told.

''Now.'' Rory motioned with his knife. ''Fetch your mistress a warm cloak.''

Within minutes Bridget had returned with a hooded, sable-lined cloak, which Rory draped over his arm. Keeping the knife at AnnaClaire's throat, he began backing her toward the door.

''Where are you taking her?'' With rising fury Dunstan struggled against his bonds.

''Away from every comfort she has ever known. Far across the heathen land you and your queen disdain.'' Rory shoved open the door and dragged AnnaClaire along with him.

Dunstan swore viciously. ''You have just signed your own death decree, Rory O'Neil.''

''Have I now? It's little enough to pay, so long as I'm given the chance to take the life of your queen's soldier, Tilden, in return.'' As he stepped out into the darkness, his muffled laughter was carried back to those inside.

It was followed a moment later by the sound of AnnaClaire's soft cry.

And then there was only silence.

''Rory. Over here.'' At the whispered voice Rory changed directions and veered off toward a stand of trees.

Half a dozen men were already mounted, holding the reins of a seventh horse. As the darkened shadow approached, one of the men called, "What in God's name are you carrying, Rory?"

"This lovely lady saved my life, lads. Her name is Lady AnnaClaire Thompson." Rory pulled himself into the saddle and settled AnnaClaire in front of him, then draped her cloak around her.

"Thompson?" One of the men sneered. "Is she the spawn of Lord James Thompson?"

"The same." Rory arranged the hood of her cloak in such a way that it managed to hide her pale hair. It occurred to AnnaClaire that he had thought of everything. The dark cloak would make her invisible in the night.

None of this was happening by accident. The horses. The men. The meeting place. He had arranged it all. And apparently it had been arranged long before he had come into her home. She had been part of a terrible, intricate plot.

"And this is how you thank me," she muttered between clenched teeth.

She was trembling violently, whether from cold or fear she couldn't be certain. But one thing was certain. The man who had dragged her away into the night was not the same man she had tended all these long days and nights. That man had been good and kind and noble. This man was nothing more than a barbarian. A brutal, thoughtless, hardened outlaw.

"I'll never forgive you for this, Rory O'Neil. For kidnapping me. For having these barbarians beat an old man senseless, and for frightening an old woman half to death.''

Ignoring her he whispered, ''You know the plan, lads. We'll separate now. From this day forward, we have no knowledge of one another. Return to your homes and families. One day, should the need arise, you may receive a summons to come together once more. If not, know that you have earned the undying gratitude of the Blackhearted O'Neil.''

''Aye, Rory. God speed.'' Without another word the horsemen turned and melted into the darkness.

Rory did the same, urging his mount into a gallop.

It was useless to try to speak. With the wind whistling past their heads, all AnnaClaire could do was cling to him and trust that this angry, desperate man, who was fleeing for his life, was the same sensitive soul she had come to know and love in that cramped little attic room. But the thought of poor old Tavis, all bloody and broken, and his beloved Bridget, trembling with fright, had her fighting back the sting of tears.

What had she done?

Sweet Savior, what terrible affliction had she brought upon herself and those she loved?

Her father's name would be forever sullied. His daughter a terrible pawn in a deadly game. And all those who loved her would be forever caught up in this madman's plot for revenge.

Chapter Nine

They rode for hours without stopping. Without speaking. At times AnnaClaire caught glimpses of firelight from tiny huts and villages. She thought about slipping free of Rory's arms and racing to freedom. But fear and confusion held her in a paralyzing grip. Fear of the people she might encounter. Confusion about where she was. Where they were headed.

At times it felt as if they were the only people left in the universe. A universe filled with nothing but blackness, punctuated by occasional stars.

They kept to the forest where tree branches snagged at their hair and clothing and night creatures scurried out of the way as they passed. One time AnnaClaire saw feral eyes watching them. She let out a cry and Rory's arms tightened around her as he drew her close.

Against her ear he whispered, "Just a wolf. He's more afraid of you than you are of him."

It was obvious that Rory had no idea just how deep, how all-encompassing, her fear was. Fear for her safety. Fear that she would never see her home again. Fear that she had put her trust in a man who had become a stranger to her.

When they had ridden past the watchful eyes of night creatures, there were new things to fear. Voices. Laughter. The smell of a turf fire, signalling that people were nearby. But what sort of people were these, who slept under the stars, without shelter, without roots? Friend or foe?

As though asking himself the same questions, Rory veered away and urged his horse into a stream. They followed the path of water until Rory suddenly turned his mount up the steep bank, taking them even deeper into the forest.

Here there was no trace of sky, no glint of stars. Here the trees grew together to form a dark, soothing canopy. The scents, the sounds, the very soul of the forest were all around them. It was peaceful rather than threatening. Like a warm, snug cocoon.

The ground was more level here, and as the horse continued its slow, plodding pace, AnnaClaire found herself unable to keep her eyes open. After the shock and terror had taken their toll, exhaustion set in. Her taut muscles relaxed. With her head resting against the curve of Rory's shoulder, she drifted into sleep.

It was the sudden absence of movement that jolted AnnaClaire awake. She looked around in confusion. Through the branches of the trees dawn light could be glimpsed, just beginning to paint the sky.

"Where are we? Why have we stopped?"

"It won't be safe to go on now. We'll stop here for the day."

"Here?" She threw back her hood and stared around. "In the forest?"

He slid from the saddle and lifted her down. "Aye. In the forest."

Dizzy from sleep she watched as he led his mount toward a small stream and waited while the animal drank. Then he tethered him in a stand of trees. The foliage concealed the horse from view.

Rory turned. Catching sight of AnnaClaire's pallor, he took her hand and led the way through a maze of trees. In their midst, cleverly concealed, was a sod hut. At first it was too dark inside for AnnaClaire to make out her surroundings. But once Rory had a fire started, she could see that it was a cozy dwelling, with a crude table and chairs as well as a big bed, covered with animal hides.

After rummaging in several pouches, he produced tea and biscuits.

"This will hold us until I can catch some fish for our supper."

"Supper?" Despite her hunger she pushed aside the food. "Are you planning to keep me here?"

He sipped his tea and broke off a piece of biscuit. "What did you expect?"

"That you would have the decency to release me after you'd made good your escape."

"Release you? Where?"

She shrugged, too angry and confused to think. "Anywhere. I'm sure someone in one of the villages we passed could see me safely back to my home."

"They might. Or they might take a look at their women and children, shivering in the night, and then at that fine cloak and fancy gown, and decide you're of more use to them dead than alive."

She gave a gasp of indignation. "Are you suggesting that they would kill me for a cloak?"

"They might. Or for that fancy comb in your hair. Or the fine ring upon your finger. These people are starving, my lady. And if they were to learn that your father is the mighty Lord James Thompson, advisor to the Queen of England, they might slit your throat for that reason alone.''

''How can you say such a thing? My mother was Margaret Doyle of Dublin. She was one of them. She belonged here.''

''I don't think that would matter much to a poor farmer whose crops were destroyed by the queen's soldiers. Or one whose wife and daughter were brutalized by those same soldiers while he was out tending his flock. They would care only that your father was a friend to the monarch who was bleeding them dry.''

Disturbed by the images his words caused, and exhausted beyond endurance, she merely buried her face in her hands and began to weep. ''And so,'' she managed between sobs, ''that is why you have become like the very men you despise?''

''Is that what you think? That I would ever take a woman against her will? You can rest assured, my lady. Your virtue is safe with me. I'm not like those English bastards, who rape and pillage. But if I must kill a few innocent soldiers along with the guilty, so be it. In that case, aye, I am like the very men I despise. For someone must stand up and declare that we've had enough.'' A hardness came into his tone. ''For me, it was the murder of a young woman, on her way to her wedding.'' His voice wavered for just a beat. ''And the murder of all her family. For others, it is a mother, a father, a son or daughter, brutalized, murdered, simply because they're Irish.''

''And that justifies what you did last night?''

''Last night?'' He set down his cup, and studied her in the light of the fire. ''What about last night?''

She wiped at her tears, but they continued to flow. "I don't even care that much for myself. I deserve to be tricked, after what I've done. I knew better than to believe in a common criminal. To take him into my home, my...heart."

Because of the tears blinding her, she failed to see how Rory reacted to her admission. His eyes widened. His mouth softened into the beginnings of a smile.

"But Bridget and Tavis deserved better, Rory O'Neil. You had your men beat that dear old man, and frighten that sweet old woman half to death. Not to mention the horses you stole..."

She looked up. He was smiling. Smiling.

Suddenly, she'd had enough. She uprighted the table, flinging tea and biscuits through the air. "Damn you, Rory O'Neil. Damn you for finding this amusing."

"AnnaClaire. Lovely AnnaClaire." Laughing, he caught her hand and lifted it to his lips before she could yank it away. "It was all a trick. All part of our plan."

"Trick?" She pulled her hand away and narrowed her gaze on him. "What sort of trick?"

"Tavis was in on it. As was Bridget. It was all done with chicken blood."

"Chicken blood!" She eyed him suspiciously, still seeing in her mind the look of Tavis, clothes disheveled, head bleeding profusely. "Are you telling me Tavis wasn't beaten?"

"Why would we beat a loyal son of Ireland? The man risked his life finding us shelter until our wounds could heal. If it weren't for Tavis and his beloved Bridget, my men and I would have all perished after the battle on the docks."

She took a moment to digest this. Then, putting her

hands on her hips, she faced him. "If that's true, why didn't they tell me what they'd planned?"

"They weren't certain their sweet young mistress would be able to lie convincingly. They did think, however, that if you had no knowledge of the plan, you would react exactly as you did. With horror and shock and outrage."

"They knew? And you and your men knew?"

He nodded.

"And you've allowed me to worry and fret and weep all night, without a word?"

"Forgive me, my lady. There was no time to explain. In case you've forgotten, Dunstan's soldiers were there before I could even make my escape. And once we were away, they came very close to discovering us several times while we fled. I simply had other things on my mind."

"Other things..." She turned away, to hide the tears of relief that sprang to her eyes. "Other things. Oh, Rory. If you knew what I've been thinking. How I've hated you. Hated myself for trusting you."

She felt his hands at her shoulders as he pulled her back against him. Burying his face in her hair he murmured, "I hope you can find it in your heart to forgive me, AnnaClaire. It was not enough to merely escape. I had to assure that the reputations of all who had aided me would escape detection, as well. Don't you see? Unless I convinced Dunstan that your household was used without your knowledge or wishes, all would have suffered. Tavis and Bridget would have faced certain death. Your father's good name would have been ruined. And his estates would have been confiscated by England. This was why I had to take you along by force. So that Dunstan would harbor no doubts about you. About us.''

She was weeping again. And this time there was no stopping it.

''Oh, Rory.'' She turned and fell into his arms, her tears soaking the front of his tunic. ''None of this occurred to me. Thank heaven for your quick thinking. I am indebted to you forever.''

''Nay, my lady. It was little enough to pay for all you did for me.'' He wiped her tears with his thumbs. ''Now, dry your pretty eyes and settle yourself in bed while I right that table and see to fresh tea and biscuits.''

AnnaClaire climbed under the soft hides and watched as Rory moved around the tiny hut cleaning the mess she had made. A terrible weight had been lifted from her shoulders. Her cruel, wicked barbarian was once again the noble hero she had thought him to be.

She wiggled her toes, stretching her cramped, aching muscles. He had assured the safety of her dear old servants, and had saved her reputation, and that of her father. He had seen to her safety even when she had cursed him for it. And now, at least for the moment, she was safe and snug and warm.

Sweet heaven, it was all too good to be true.

In a haze of contentment, she drifted once more into sleep.

Rory nudged off his boots and, plumping several hides behind his head for a pillow, eased down on the bed beside the sleeping AnnaClaire. He lifted the glass of ale to his lips and whispered a prayer of thanks for the thoughtful soul who had left such ample provisions

behind in the hut. If only the rest of their odyssey could
be this comfortable. He knew it was an improbable
wish. He didn't mind for himself. Over the past two
years he'd learned to take the hardship in stride. But
there was AnnaClaire to think about now.

He glanced at her and found himself alternately smiling and frowning. She looked so peaceful in sleep. Like
an angel come down from heaven. She truly was an
angel. One who didn't deserve this. He hated the
thought of the danger he'd exposed her to.

He hadn't wanted this life for her. But now that he'd
made the choice, there was no turning back. She would
be forced to spend endless nights in the saddle, fleeing
every ghost and shadow that trailed them. And by day,
she would have to hide like a thief.

He thought about her courage and dignity when
she'd thought she was being kidnapped. It must have
seemed like a nightmare, watching her beloved servants being bullied, her own life being turned upside
down. But she had neither fainted nor despaired. She
had instead kept her composure and had displayed a
spirit, a temper that delighted him. No wonder he loved
her so.

Love. The thought struck like a thunderbolt, leaving
him slightly dazed and breathless. He hadn't meant to
love her. He'd meant only to take the shelter she offered. And, he had to admit, whatever else she might
have offered. But that was before. Before lust had
somehow turned to this other, deeper emotion.

Love. He knew what it was to love. To put another's
comfort before his own. To care so deeply, no sacrifice
was too great, no price too high to pay. To know, in
his heart of hearts, that he would willingly die before
he would see her harmed.

Love.

With love came responsibility. Somehow he must get word to AnnaClaire's father that she was truly safe from harm. For her father would surely be told of her capture by the Blackhearted O'Neil. He would have to act quickly to relieve Lord James Thompson of his fear.

Rory drained the last of the ale and set the empty tumbler aside. Numbly he settled himself under the hides beside AnnaClaire, careful not to touch her. Because if he did, there would be no stopping him. He wanted her so desperately, loved her so completely, an entire regiment of English soldiers wouldn't be able to keep him from her, once the passion was unleashed. But he had no right to declare his love for her. Not so long as this thing between himself and Tilden remained unresolved. As a man of honor, he must return her to her father's home as he had found her. Untouched. Unspoiled. With her virtue intact.

He would have to change his plans because of her. There was no way he could drag her around the countryside while he searched for Tilden. A woman like AnnaClaire needed a safe haven.

The thought came at once. He would take her home. To Ballinarin. Though he had planned never to see it again until his quest had ended, he would have to break his vow. AnnaClaire's safety and comfort had to come first.

He fell asleep wondering how his family would feel about offering sanctuary to the daughter of Lord James Thompson.

The sun was high in the sky before AnnaClaire awoke. When she looked around, Rory was nowhere to be seen. Beside her, the hides still bore the imprint of his body. She lay back a moment, absorbing the knowledge that he'd slept alongside her. It was a strange feeling to think they'd shared a bed. Strange and…intriguing.

The door to the hut opened and the object of her thoughts stepped inside, carrying a string of wriggling fish.

"I see you're awake. Good morrow, my lady. How did you sleep?"

"As comfortably as if I'd been in my own bed. In fact," she shot him a shyly seductive smile, "it was all the more comforting, knowing you were here with me to protect me."

He saw the high color on her cheeks and hated himself for the things he was thinking. "If you care to wash, there's fresh water and linens." He busied himself at the table, preparing the fish for cooking. He was determined to remain as busy as possible, to keep from thinking.

AnnaClaire slipped out of bed and crossed to a basin. In the chipped looking glass she caught sight of herself, hair all mussed and tumbling about her shoulders, face smudged, gown wrinkled and torn from brambles. This wasn't at all the way she wanted to look. Especially now that she was alone with Rory.

With soap and water she repaired the worst of the damage, then ran her fingers through the tangles and, swinging her waist-length hair forward, began to plait it into one thick braid.

Across the room Rory tried not to stare. But there was something so intimate about watching AnnaClaire wash her face and fix her hair. Such ordinary things, yet they stirred a longing in him. A yearning that had him clutching the edge of the table to keep from storming across the room and taking her.

She tossed back her hair and smoothed down her skirts, then turned. Catching sight of him she started toward him. "What is it, Rory? What's wrong?"

"Nothing. I..." He shook his head to clear it. "Nothing."

"You're lying." She laid a hand on his arm. "You've heard something. Seen something. Whatever it is, it has you upset. I can tell."

He shook off her hand as though the touch of her burned. "I need...water from the stream." The fresh air would surely clear his head.

"There's water in the pitcher. I'll get it." She crossed the room and returned with the pitcher. "Where would you like it?"

"In that pot." He refused to look at her. "We'll make tea."

He stood very still until she had moved away. Then, relieved that there was some distance between them, he finished boning the fish and tossed them into a skillet. Before he could set it on the fire, she reached for it. The touch of her hand on his made him burn with need.

"I'll cook them, Rory."

He watched her carefully turn the fish as they began to brown. He would keep the conversation as impersonal as possible. "Are you as good a cook as Bridget?"

She gave a delighted laugh. "Who do you think taught me?"

She looked so sweet and fresh, so comfortable, standing in this simple sod hut cooking his supper. He ached to take her into his arms and kiss her until they were both breathless. "What about your mother?"

"She was always in delicate health. There were many days and weeks that she didn't leave her bed. So Bridget became like a mother to me. It was Bridget who soothed my hurts and tucked me in bed. And Bridget who taught me to cook and sew."

He heard her loneliness and was reminded of his own rowdy, affectionate family. It was all he could do to keep from offering her the comfort of his arms.

"When my mother knew that she was dying, she begged my father to bring her back to Ireland. She wanted to die in her family home, surrounded by those who loved her."

"Aye." Rory allowed himself a single touch of his hand on her hair before pulling back. The thought of running his fingers through the tangles, of burying his face in it, had his breath coming faster, harder. "I know how she felt. I want to be laid to rest at Ballinarin."

AnnaClaire turned from the fire and began to arrange the fish on a platter. Breaking off a tiny portion she held it to his lips. Her smile was radiant. "Now you can judge whether or not Bridget was an apt teacher."

He was so stunned by the touch of her fingers against his lips, he couldn't have said whether it was food in his mouth or ashes. The merest touch of her had his vision misting and the blood roaring in his temples.

He managed to swallow before saying, "I nearly forgot. I have to...chop some wood for the fire."

Puzzled by his reaction, her smile faded. "The fire's fine. And there are several logs beside the hearth."

"Not nearly enough." He caught her roughly by the shoulders and moved her aside before turning away.

"But, Rory, the fish will be cold."

"Sorry. This won't keep." He wouldn't look at her. Couldn't. Instead he stumbled toward the door and, flinging it wide, stormed outside, breathing in great gulps of air.

Sometimes a man had to do whatever it took to keep his common sense from slipping below his waist. Even if it meant looking as though he'd completely lost his mind.

AnnaClaire watched in openmouthed surprise as Rory slammed out of the hut. Dejected, she broke off a piece of fish and tasted, expecting it to be spoiled. To her delight, it was fresh. Delicious. Even Bridget's skill could not have improved upon it.

She sank down onto the edge of the bed, deep in thought. If it wasn't the fish that had sent Rory away, it must have been something she'd said. But try as she might, she couldn't recall a single thing that might have caused him to run from her as though being chased by a crowd of banshees. She had tried in every way she could to let him know how glad she was to be here with him. More than glad. She was elated. At last, there were no servants to hide from. No callers to interrupt them. They were alone. All alone. And free to do as they pleased.

And oh, how she wanted to please him. Hadn't she given him her best and brightest smile? Couldn't he read the invitation in her eyes? He'd have to be blind not to know that she'd been inviting his advances. But instead of accepting her invitation, he'd run from her as though she had the plague. But why, when he had seemed so bold in her home in Dublin? What could have changed?

As she sat there, pondering all she'd said and done,

his words of last night came rushing back. *Your virtue is safe with me, my lady.*

She covered her hand with her mouth. Oh, sweet heaven. He was doing this for her. To save her virtue. Even if it meant going without supper. Even if it meant chopping wood when he would rather be warm and snug inside this hut.

She stood and began to pace. She would have to swallow her pride and find a way to let him know how she really felt.

If only Bridget had been as free with her advice about love as she had been about the womanly arts of cooking and sewing, she thought.

She made her way to the door, praying that Rory O'Neil would not make her task too difficult.

Chapter Ten

Rory brought the axe down with such fury the log split in one clean stroke. He tossed the two pieces aside and angled another log in place, then repeated the process.

In frustration he'd flung his tunic aside. A sheen of sweat beaded his torso. With each movement the wound in his shoulder ached. He was actually glad of the pain. It was something to focus on. Something besides AnnaClaire, with that angelic smile and sinfully tempting body.

He'd been very aware of the effort she was taking to make amends for last night's temper. But she had no need to apologize. Her anger had been justified. And now, of course, she was confusing gratitude with love. That was the reason for the way she was throwing herself at him.

He lifted the axe, swung it with all his might, hoping to banish the image of high firm breasts and softly swaying hips. If he weren't trying to be so damnably noble, all that she offered could be his.

The log split with such force the two pieces danced through the air and landed several feet away. As he positioned another log, he saw a blur of movement out of the corner of his eye.

"AnnaClaire." He spun around to face her. "You should be inside eating."

"I don't want to eat alone." She felt breathless, her heart slamming against her ribs as though she'd been running for miles. "I thought I'd wait for you, Rory."

"There's no need. I have all these logs to split."

"Fine. I'll just carry a few of them inside and stack them beside the fireplace. Then I'll come back for more."

As she bent to one he caught her roughly by the arm. Heat rushed through him at the mere touch of her. It would seem that the chill in the air had done nothing to cool the fire that burned within. "I don't want your help. They're too heavy for you."

"I'm not some fragile doll, Rory." She touched a hand to his cheek and felt him flinch. A little thrill shot through her. So, she had been right. He was trying to be noble. But he wanted her. Wanted her. It gave her an exhilarating sense of power. Her voice softened, warmed. "I'm a woman. Or haven't you noticed?"

"Aye." His throat felt too tight. "I'd have to be a blind man not to notice."

Her smile bloomed. "Good. I wonder if you've noticed, too, that I'm a woman with a mind of her own."

He cleared his throat. "It's come to my attention a time or two."

Her hand moved upward, cupping the back of his head. "Right now, I've a mind to taste your lips and see if I can wipe away that frown." There was just a hint of laughter in her voice.

His hand closed around her wrist, stopping the

movement. His eyes were hard as flint. "I'm not in the mood for games, AnnaClaire."

Her heart stuttered, and for a moment she felt a rush of fear. Then she stiffened her spine. "Nor am I. This isn't a game, Rory O'Neil. It's something far more serious."

"Aye. I'm glad you realize that." He made the mistake of relaxing his hand, intent upon stepping back a pace so he could breathe. He realized too late that she had no intention of allowing him his space.

She leaned into him, her breasts brushing his naked chest. Did she know what she was doing to him? All the air seemed to leave his lungs. "What do you think you're doing now, AnnaClaire?"

"I want you to make love with me, Rory."

Her bold words had his jaw dropping. "You want me to take your virtue? So that I'll be no better than one of those English bastards?"

She placed a finger to his lips to silence his words. "You could never be like them. There's a difference. You won't be taking. I'll be giving."

"You'd be wasting the gift. I'm a wanted man. A man with no future. I've nothing to offer in return."

"I'll ask for nothing more than this."

When he opened his mouth to issue a protest, she dipped her finger inside. He muttered an oath. And felt his world begin to tilt dangerously.

He closed a hand over her shoulder to steady himself. "You don't know what you're doing, Anna-Claire."

"I know exactly what I'm doing. I've never been so sure of anything in my life."

He stared down into her eyes and could read all the love, all the longing, that matched his own. The axe dropped from his hand and landed beside their feet with a thud. They took no notice.

His tone hardened. "Once we cross this line there will be no going back, AnnaClaire. Do you understand?"

She nodded.

He dragged her roughly toward him and lowered his head. Against her mouth he murmured, "I thought I could resist. I was determined to return you to your father as I'd found you. But heaven help me, I'm only a man."

"Aye. And the only man I want, Rory O'Neil," she managed, before his mouth crushed hers.

There was such need in him. Such passion as he feasted on her lips. He plundered her mouth, tasting, devouring, like a man who'd been starved. His tongue tangled with hers, teasing, tempting. The hands at her shoulders were almost bruising as he dragged her fully against him. While his mouth learned the taste of her, his hands began a frantic exploration, moving along her back, sliding up her sides until they encountered the swell of her breasts. His clever, work-roughened thumbs found her nipples already hard, and began stroking until she thought she'd go mad.

She pushed against him and lifted her head, taking in a deep draught of air.

He pulled her close, nibbled her throat. "Having second thoughts?"

"Nay." The word came out in a sigh as she arched her neck to give him easier access. "I just need a moment to catch my breath."

Instead of giving her what she sought, he dipped his head lower until his mouth found her breast, further robbing her of breath.

Ignoring the barrier of clothes he began to nibble and suckle until she moaned and caught his face between her hands. ''Do you know what you're doing to me?''

He grinned, sending her heart spiraling out of control. ''I hope it's the same thing you've been doing to me since the day we met, lovely AnnaClaire.'' He kissed her again with such passion he drove her backward until she was pressed roughly against the trunk of a tree.

His hands were tangled in her hair. Almost savagely he pulled her head back while he rained kisses along her cheek, to her lobe, which he took between his teeth, nipping lightly.

She gave a yelp of pleasure and surprise. ''Rory. Wait. There's a big soft bed just inside.''

He growled against her cheek, ''I hope you didn't think loving me would be all neat and tidy.'' His hot breath tickled her ear. But it was his words that had her shivering. ''I'm not interested in a big soft bed, AnnaClaire. With rose petals scattered among the linens. I'll take your love wherever you offer it. Whenever you offer it. But I'll demand the same of you. Love me as I am. Where I am.''

''Oh, Rory. I will.'' She sighed. Swallowed. ''I do.''

His lips covered hers in a kiss so hot, so hungry, she had no choice but to answer in kind. But even as they struggled to fill each other, the hunger between them grew.

The bark of the tree trunk dug into her back, but she was too drunk with his kisses to notice. He brought his mouth to her throat, then swore in frustration. She heard the ripping of fabric, felt the coolness of air against her skin, and was stunned to see her torn gown drifting to the ground, where it pooled at her feet. Then his big hands reached for the ribbons of her chemise, freeing her breasts.

She had always thought she would be shocked, embarrassed, to display herself to a man. Instead, the look in this man's eyes had her throat going dry.

"God in heaven, AnnaClaire. You're even lovelier than I'd dreamed."

And then there was no need for words. His hands, his mouth, told her all that she needed to know. He was a thirsty man, drinking his fill. A desperate man, clinging to her as though to life itself.

She wanted to see him, feel him, in the same way. Nerves made her fumble as she reached for the fasteners at his waist.

He closed his hands over hers to steady them as his clothes joined hers at their feet. When he drew her close and began to press kisses along her shoulder, across her breasts, her legs were trembling so violently she feared they would fail her.

Sensing her weakness, he caught her hand and drew her down. They were kneeling face to face, cushioned by the moss and jumble of clothes.

The last rays of sunlight filtered through the dense foliage, adding to the heat that rose up between them. The air was perfumed with the fragrance of evergreen. High above them a bird called and its mate gave an answering warble. A family of ducks scrambled into the rush of water in the nearby stream. But the two people locked in an embrace were aware of none of this. All they heard was their own shallow breathing and the wild beating of their two hearts. And the roar of blood pounding in their temples.

Rory fought to bank his needs. He had wanted her

for so long. The need to take was almost overpowering. But for AnnaClaire's sake, he would force himself to move slowly. This was, after all, the only thing he could give her. In this act of loving he would take her away from all this. From the harsh life of an outlaw that he had chosen. From the dangers that threatened them. From the differences that separated them. For a little while they could lose themselves in each other and forget.

His touch gentled, as did his kisses. With lips and fingertips he explored her face, her throat, the sensitive hollow between her neck and shoulder. With each touch, each taste, he felt her body grow more tense, her breathing grow more shallow.

As her blood heated and her body pulsed, Anna-Claire felt her inhibitions begin to slip away. She had feared that she would feel shy and uncomfortable with a man. But with Rory she felt no shyness. With him she felt bold and free. Free to be herself. Free to touch him as he was touching her. Free to love him in every way.

She savored this gentler side of his lovemaking. Steeped in pleasure, she sighed with contentment as he kissed and carressed. The pleasant sensations curling deep inside her lulled her into believing that passion, at least her own passion, was a quiet whisper.

His lips trailed her throat, then dipped lower to her breast. Without warning, a demon seemed to spring to life within her. The pleasant sensations were suddenly writhing and twisting, demanding to be set free. The quiet whisper became a roaring of blood throbbing inside her temples.

Rory sensed the change in her and thrilled to it. Here was more than mere pleasure. More even than passion.

This was need, raw, demanding. Need that had long slumbered within her, awaiting the right touch to awaken it. He could read it in her eyes, taste it on her lips. Hot. Wild. Pulsing.

His fingers tangled in her hair as he drew her head back and covered her mouth in a savage kiss.

"Now," he whispered against her mouth, "I'll show you all the things I've dreamed of doing."

He lowered her to the ground. With teeth and tongue and fingers he moved over her body, touching, tasting, until she was unbearably aroused. Following his lead she brought her arms around his waist and buried her lips in his throat. She felt his muscles contract violently. With a new sense of power, she explored him as he had explored her, daring to touch, to taste, to entice.

His body was alive with need. He had planned to go slowly, to make this first time as easy, as gentle as possible. But now, with their passion fully unleashed, he had to call on every ounce of self-control to keep from losing himself in her.

With exquisite tenderness he kissed her until they were both breathless. At her whispered sighs he lowered his head to her breast, nibbling, suckling, until she moaned and writhed and begged for release. Instead of giving her release, he moved to the other breast, feasting until she clutched at the moss beneath her.

She made a sound that could have been a plea or a protest, and still he held back as he drove her higher, then higher still. He was relentless as he drew out every pleasure until it bordered on pain.

The cool air whispered over them, but nothing could ease the heat that clogged their throats or the sheen that pearled their flesh.

AnnaClaire strained against him, her body screaming for release, as he moved over her. Her whole world was now centered on this man. His clever hands. His enticing lips. His demanding tongue.

He felt her stiffen as she reached the first crest. He gave her no time to recover as he moved over her, tracing his lips upward until they found her mouth.

Dizzy with feeling, her eyes darkened with passion. She didn't think it was possible to want more. But she did. She wanted all.

"Rory. Sweet heaven, Rory. Now. Please. Now."

As he entered her she felt an even deeper arousal. It startled both of them when she wound herself around him, needing to hold on to him as the storm began anew.

He filled himself with her, and knew, even as they began to climb together, that he had lost himself completely. Lost himself in the wonder of her. In the beauty of her. In the love of her.

"AnnaClaire. God in heaven, AnnaClaire." Her name was torn from his lips as he closed his mouth over hers and raced toward the very edge of madness.

And then she was moving with him, racing, climbing. And as they reached the final shuddering release, she felt them soar through space and shatter high among the stars.

They lay, still joined, unable, unwilling to move. Little by little they seemed to drift back, to settle, to find a calm after the storm.

It occurred to Rory that this was the first time in two years that he wasn't concerned about his sword and daggers. His weapons lay somewhere in the tangle of their clothes. If the English should come upon them at this moment, he would be helpless to defend himself against them. But at least he'd die happy. Deliriously happy.

"I'm crushing you."

"Nay." She lifted a hand to his cheek, then let it fall away. "Stay."

"You look…" He lifted his head to stare down at her. "…as stunned as I feel."

She managed a laugh. "Aye. Stunned."

Suddenly she was weeping uncontrollably.

Alarmed, he sat up. "I'm sorry, love. I've been such a brute. I didn't mean to…"

Love. The endearment brought fresh tears. She reached a hand to his mouth. "Rory. It isn't you who made me cry. I feel like such a fool for weeping. But it was so…amazing. I never dreamed it would be like this."

He felt his heart begin to beat once more. Pressing his forehead to hers he whispered, "Aye. It was amazing. And wonderful. You're wonderful, AnnaClaire. My sweet AnnaClaire."

"Is it always like that? Like being caught in a riptide?"

He threw back his head and laughed. "An apt description, love. It was like a riptide, wasn't it?"

She nodded.

He nuzzled her mouth. "It isn't always like that. Sometimes loving can be sweet and gentle."

"But not with you."

He laughed again. "I warned you."

"You did indeed." She wrinkled her nose. "And I have nothing against lying here in the moss, mind you. But there is that big warm bed inside."

"Oh, you'd like a bed next time, would you?"

"It might be different."

"Not so different." He found himself fascinated with the delicate curve of her shoulder. The taste of it. The softness of the skin. The way she shivered each time he moved his mouth just so.

"Rory, stop that."

"Why?" He ran wet, nibbling kisses across her throat.

"Because it tickles."

"Sorry. I'll stop. In a few moments." If he could rein in his appetite. But it seemed that the hunger was back. As strong as before.

"By then I'll be covered with gooseflesh."

"Good." He nibbled his way up to her mouth. "That's my intention."

"But can you...? I mean, can we? Again?"

"Aye, love." He wouldn't have thought it possible, but he wanted her. Here. Now. "We can love as often as we please. Again and again and...again."

The words died on his lips as he took her on a slow, leisurely journey. A journey that left them both breathless. And at last sated.

Chapter Eleven

"Are you warm enough, love?"

In answer, AnnaClaire wrapped her arms around Rory's waist and buried her lips against his throat. She would never grow weary of hearing him call her love. Nor would she ever have enough of those strong arms around her, that warm, solid body beside her.

Sometime just before dark he had carried her to bed. They had spent the night alternately loving and sleeping. At times the storm of passion caught them both by surprise. At other times their lovemaking had been slow and languid, as though they had all the time in the world.

Rory knew he was behaving recklessly. Every hour spent here in this simple hut in the forest brought the English closer to them. But he hadn't the heart to leave yet. Not with AnnaClaire finally his. Not when his heart was filled to overflowing with so much love.

Now, with dawn light breaking through the darkness, they would be forced to spend another day here before they could safely take to the trail.

He glanced down at the woman dozing in his arms.

What a delight she was. Who would have believed that she would prove to be such a fierce little temptress?

"You're smiling, Rory O'Neil." She yawned, then lifted a finger to trace his lips.

"Maybe because I'm enjoying such happy thoughts."

"Care to share them?"

"They'd make you blush."

"I think, after last night, nothing could ever make me blush again."

He threw back his head and roared. "Aye. You are a constant source of amazement to me, my lady. Who would have thought the very proper AnnaClaire Thompson could think of so many…inventive ways to please me."

She sat up and surprised him even further by straddling him, leaning forward and pressing her mouth to his. "You promised to teach me even more ways."

"So I did. But you may wish to wait a day or two."

"Why?" Her lips turned into a most enchanting pout.

He traced a finger over them and grinned when she nipped at it. "Because, my girl, you may be a bit sore today."

"Perhaps you're the one who should worry about being sore." Her fingers played with the dark hair on his chest, sending delicious curls of pleasure along his spine. "After all, you're the one who was wounded and required all that time to mend. You may have…strained something."

"True enough." He caught her hand to still her movements. "But if you don't stop doing what you're doing, I'll have to strain even more. And I'll hold you personally responsible for whatever happens."

She shot him a wicked smile. "Promise?"

"Oh, AnnaClaire, what am I to do with you?"

Her eyes danced with mischief. "I suggest you do what you do so well, Rory O'Neil."

He gave a mock sigh. "A warrior's work is never done."

He rolled her over and kissed her long and slow and deep until she was gasping for breath.

She gave a sigh and fluttered her lashes. "Oh, my big, brave, strong warrior..."

He kissed her again, cutting off any further taunts. "Ah," he muttered against her lips. "I see I've found an effective way to silence you, wench."

With soft sighs they drifted once more into that wonderful world of love. A world where there was no longer any need for words.

"Hungry?" Rory lay in a tangle of pelts, one arm above his head, the other wrapped around AnnaClaire's waist.

Late morning sunshine filtered through the cracks in the walls.

"Famished." She rested her head on his shoulder. "We never did eat that fish you caught."

He twirled a lock of her hair around his finger and watched the sunlight turn the ends to gold. "As I recall we had more important things to think about."

"Aye. But now you must feed me, Rory O'Neil."

"And if I don't?"

She smiled. "I suppose I'll just be too weak to do more than kiss you."

He sprang up out of bed and began pulling on his clothes. "Don't move. Just rest here and I'll see you properly fed, my lady. I wouldn't want anything to steal your energy now.''

She knelt up in the middle of the bed, unmindful of the fact that she was naked. "I can't believe how easy that was. Is that all it will ever take to get you to do my bidding?''

He tangled his fingers in her hair and tilted her head back, kissing her with a thoroughness that had her heart racing. "Only for the next hundred years or so. After that we'll probably be eager for a few minutes apart.''

With that he strode out of the cabin.

AnnaClaire stared after him, convinced that even a hundred years wouldn't be enough time with Rory O'Neil. Her heart was so filled with love it was overflowing. Still, she had to nudge aside the little twinge of regret. They had made no promises. No commitments. And they both knew that when they left here, he would once more become the hardened warrior she had first encountered on the docks.

"You weren't exaggerating." Rory polished off his third helping of fish, then leaned back to sip strong hot tea. "Your cooking really is as fine as Bridget's.''

Now that AnnaClaire was the one receiving his compliment, she understood how her old servant had felt. She positively glowed. "It's a good thing she taught me how to ply needle and thread as well. Look at this gown.'' She held it up. "You practically shredded it.''

"I was in a hurry to get you out of it.''

"We were both in a hurry, as I recall.'' She bent to her sewing. "Next time, all you need do is ask.''

She was wearing nothing but her chemise and petticoat as she mended her gown. Her hair spilled forward in a wild tangle of burnished curls. For now, watching her, Rory could almost forget the pain of the past. He could pretend that they were just a man and woman wildly in love, without a care in the world.

She glanced up and caught his little frown of concentration. "What are you thinking, Rory?"

"That I'd never expected to feel such happiness again."

She set aside the gown. Crossing the room she knelt in front of him and caught his hands in hers. "It's the same for me, Rory. I'd despaired of ever meeting a man who touched my soul." She looked up at him, eyes swimming. "Do you understand?"

"I do." He lifted their joined hands and brushed a kiss over her knuckles. "Perfectly."

She began to untie the ribbons of her chemise. "Love me, Rory. Right now."

He closed his hands over hers to still her movements. When she gave him a quick look, he flashed that dangerous smile she'd come to know so well.

"Let me." He untied the ribbons and eased away the bit of cloth. In one quick motion he lifted her onto his lap.

She sighed when his lips made contact with her flesh. And then, while the sun slowly made its arc across the sky, they told each other, without a single word, all the loving things that were locked in their hearts.

"It's time, AnnaClaire." Rory spoke without turning.

Evening shadows were beginning to gather. Twilight was just settling over the land. It had always been his favorite time of day. But now, he dreaded its coming. For it meant an end to their idyll.

"Are you ready?" He tucked a knife at his waist, a second in his boot.

Behind him AnnaClaire pulled on her cloak, and lifted the hood to hide her pale hair. "Aye. I'm ready."

He checked to make certain that there was no smoke from the fireplace. Then he made his way to the stand of trees and led the horse back to the little hut.

AnnaClaire pulled the door shut and latched it, then walked to his side. "I wish we could just stay here forever and hide from the world."

He pulled himself into the saddle and reached down, lifting her easily in his arms. As he settled her in front of him he brushed a kiss over her cheek. "Aye, love. I wish it, too. But we both knew this would only be a moment's respite."

He urged his horse forward, and they started off through the forest. Within minutes the leaden sky opened up, and the rain began. A sprinkle soon turned into a downpour that soaked through their clothes and left them shivering with cold.

As the horse scrambled up a sodden hillside, Rory suddenly jerked the reins, bringing the animal to a halt.

"What is it?" AnnaClaire turned slightly to study his face.

"I thought I heard something."

They listened intently, but could hear only the drumming of raindrops.

Rory lifted her to the ground. "Wait here. I'll go on ahead and check."

Her first instinct was to clutch at his sleeve and beg to go with him. But she merely nodded, knowing that he had to do this his way.

She stood very still, straining to keep him in her line of vision.

As horse and rider moved ahead, she saw him draw his sword. Moments later half a dozen English soldiers on horseback formed a solid wall in front of him. Instinctively he swung his mount, only to find another line of soldiers who had stepped from concealment behind him.

"Lay down your weapon, Rory O'Neil," came a shout from the leader of their regiment.

"And if I choose not to?"

The man snarled. "You are badly outnumbered, Irish scum. You'd best do as you're told."

"Ah. I see." Rory's laughter had them looking at one another in astonishment. "But you are mistaken. You are the ones who are outnumbered."

While the soldiers were looking over their shoulders uneasily, hoping to spot his comrades, Rory took advantage of the situation by riding into their midst, wielding his sword with a skill that left them bloodied and begging for mercy.

"You there," the leader shouted to his regiment. "He's only one man. Take up your arms and defeat this brigand."

Three men on horseback came at him from three different sides, but he managed to evade their blades, driving one of them back while sending the other two sprawling in the dirt. When the foot soldiers formed a protective wall and began an attack, Rory urged his horse to rear up again and again, driving some of them back, crushing others beneath those powerful hooves.

One of the soldiers hurled a lance, sending it through the neck of Rory's mount. The horse reared up, nostrils flaring, eyes wide with pain. Rory leapt free of the saddle just as the animal went down on its side.

From her position on the hillside, AnnaClaire

watched the churning of mud, the flailing of hooves. Wiping rain from her eyes she gasped as Rory's sword flashed, parrying thrusts from the half dozen soldiers who faced him.

He had them almost beaten. Just a few more, he thought. But as he lifted his sword to fight back another soldier, he felt a sharp pain, followed by the warmth of blood. Once again he had taken a blow from a sword to his recently-healed shoulder. Ignoring it, he fought on, driving the remaining soldiers back. But as he attempted to raise his sword yet again, a strange thing happened. His arm refused to obey his command. He stared in mute surprise at the limb which hung at his side. While he watched, his sword slipped from nerveless fingers and landed with a thud. He reached with his other hand for the knife at his waist, but the tip of a sword shot forward, piercing his hand. The knife, too, fell to the ground.

With a smug smile the leader of the regiment strode forward, sword at the ready. But before he could drive his blade through his opponent's heart, he looked up in surprise at the woman running toward him.

"Praise heaven," AnnaClaire shouted, throwing herself into the leader's arms.

He was so startled, he dropped his sword.

"Lady Thompson? Is it you? Are you still alive then?"

"Aye. You've saved me from this madman." She kept her gaze averted, unable to bear the sight of the blood that oozed from Rory's shoulder. Instead, she tossed back the hood of her cloak as she walked from soldier to soldier, giving each man the favor of her smile.

The soldiers were so dazzled, they could only stare

at this lovely woman who was alternately laughing and weeping.

"I thought I would surely die out here in this wilderness, at the hands of this…this animal." She chanced a quick glance at Rory, then away. "But thanks to all of you, I am safe now." She fluttered her lashes. "My father will want to personally thank each one of you. And I think perhaps the queen herself will offer a handsome reward for your courage when you return the O'Neil to her in chains."

"Return the Blackhearted O'Neil?" The leader blanched at the thought of keeping this dangerous enemy alive. It would be so much easier to simply kill him and be done with it.

"But of course. The queen will want to see this man who has caused such chaos in the land. I'm certain there will be many honors for the brave soldiers who brought down the Blackhearted O'Neil."

"Bind him at once," the leader called importantly, as visions of being presented at Court danced through his mind.

While the men hastened to do his bidding, Anna-Claire hugged her arms around herself and gave a violent shiver. "Would you possibly have some ale, captain? I'm so very cold."

"Aye. At once, my lady." He sent another man scurrying toward the horses.

When the soldier returned with a cask of ale, AnnaClaire gave him her brightest smile. "And if I could have a fire? Just until this chill leaves me."

In no time AnnaClaire was seated under a tent of hides, sipping ale and warming herself beside a roaring fire. Some distance away Rory sat slumped against a tree, his wrists and ankles bound securely. One soldier was assigned to guard him, while the leader and his two remaining soldiers huddled around the fire, staring in fascination as Lady AnnaClaire Thompson regaled them with the tale of her kidnapping.

"The barbarian boldly invaded my home, and then even more brazenly took me hostage when it appeared he would be captured. For that I shall never forgive him."

The men nodded in agreement.

She held out her goblet. "I believe I could use a bit more ale."

The leader poured, then topped off his own glass and that of his men.

AnnaClaire lifted her skirts. "My new boots are soaked clear through. Another thing for which I'll hate the O'Neil."

The three men were too busy staring at her shapely ankles. Seeing the direction of their gazes she wriggled her feet. "Do you know what I'd like?"

The men shook their heads.

"I'd like the O'Neil's boots. It would serve him right to have to travel all the way to England in bare feet. Wouldn't you agree it's a fitting punishment for the lout?" As soon as the leader of the regiment nodded in agreement she jumped up and raced from the tent to where the lone soldier stood guard. "Your captain has said I might have the O'Neil's boots."

"His…boots, my lady?"

"Aye. Mine are soaked. I want his." She nodded toward the tent and the warm fire. "Go ask your captain, if you wish."

"I…" He glanced from the prisoner, who appeared to be unconscious, to the woman, who was shivering in the rain, and then to his leader, who nodded in agreement. "If the captain gave the order, my lady, I shall see to it at once."

He bent to Rory's boots and began to pry first one, then the other. As they slid off, AnnaClaire scooped them up. When her hand closed around Rory's knife, she held it hidden in the folds of her skirt. Then, turning, she allowed the knife to drop into his lap before she strode back to the tent.

The soldiers, warmed by the fire and made drowsy by the ale, sat slumped around the fire. They watched in silence as she began removing her dainty kid boots. Seeing that she had their attention, she slowed her movements, deliberately lifting her skirt higher to rub her hand over her ankle.

"Ooh." She closed her eyes a moment. "It will be so good to get into dry clothes and sleep in a warm bed."

One of the soldiers sighed. She gave him a most engaging smile. Her smile froze when a sword was thrust through the hide directly at his back. The soldier went rigid, then slumped forward. Before the other two could react, Rory tore aside the hide tent and stood facing the remaining two soldiers.

"How could you...?" The leader reached for his sword, but he was too late.

Rory's blade pierced his heart. He was dead before he fell. The other soldier backed away, then turned and started to run. Rory tossed his knife, and it found its mark. The soldier let out a cry, then dropped to the ground.

AnnaClaire stared around at the scene of carnage like one awakening from sleep. She had once thought of Rory O'Neil as a barbarian because of this very thing. But this time, she had no one to blame but herself. She had been a party to the deaths of these men. Loyal English soldiers. The thought was staggering.

Before she could stumble, Rory's arms were around her, holding her firmly against him. "Are you all right, love?"

"I…Yes." She took a deep breath. "I'm fine."

He gave her a long look. "Indeed you are. You'd make a fine outlaw, AnnaClaire."

"I think not. Oh, Rory. I was so frightened."

"That's a natural reaction. But what's important is how you dealt with your fear." He touched a hand to her cheek. "You could have remained hidden in the forest, and no one would have blamed you. You are, after all, a gentle noblewoman." He pulled her close and soundly kissed her. "This is the second time I'm indebted to you for my life."

She touched a hand to his cheek. "And I'll be sure to collect that debt, Rory O'Neil."

"Count on it." He led her to a seat beside the fire, then checked each of the bodies before rounding up their horses and gathering up their weapons. It seemed a fine irony that the very men these English soldiers hated would now ride their mounts and use their swords against their countrymen.

He chose the sturdiest of the animals as his own, then tied the others behind and led them to where AnnaClaire was waiting.

"Pull on your boots and cloak, love. We must be far from here before the rest of their regiment comes searching for them."

"Aye." She finished dressing, then walked to where he was extinguishing the fire. "Just think," she mused aloud. "Bridget and Tavis thought I was too innocent to carry out a lie to Lord Dunstan. I guess I showed them. And you, as well.''

Her laughter suddenly died in her throat as she caught sight of the dead soldiers. The realization of all that she had done sank in. Her face lost all its color. Her knees wobbled, and she began to stumble.

Rory scooped her into his arms and hugged her to him in a fierce embrace. Against her cheek he murmured tenderly, ''Aye, my brave, magnificent little firebrand. You showed them. You showed us all.''

She was beyond hearing as she slid into unconsciousness.

Chapter Twelve

The rain continued throughout the day. Though it made their journey uncomfortable, Rory was glad for the protection it offered. The sound of the raindrops masked their horses' hoofbeats. The puddles obliterated their trail. He hoped, too, that the intensity of the storm would force their pursuers to seek cover.

It was a calculated risk to travel during the day, but he felt they had no choice. He was desperate to get AnnaClaire to a place of safety.

AnnaClaire. He glanced down at her as she slept in his arms. What an amazing woman she was. Who would have believed that this gentle, well-bred lady could prove to be so resourceful?

"There's that frown again." Her lashes fluttered open. With a fingertip she smoothed the line between his brows.

"I seem to do that whenever I look at you." He struggled to keep the grin from his lips. "It's probably because you're so hard to look at."

"Am I?" She angled her chin.

"Aye. I've never much cared for hair that gleams like the color of ale when it's held to the firelight."

He allowed a strand to sift through his fingers before tucking it behind her ear. "Or eyes the color of the sea. Especially when you're angry." His voice lowered. "Or lips so perfectly formed, that each time I look at them, all I can think of is—" he brushed his mouth over hers "—kissing them, just so."

"Oh, Rory." She snuggled closer, warmed by his words. "I don't believe I've ever heard a lovelier compliment."

"'Tis a gift of the Irish. We've a way with words. Now it's your turn."

"My turn for what?"

"To pay me a compliment."

"Ah." She pretended to concentrate for several moments. "I suppose I could say I like your eyes. They can cut to the quick when you're angry. And they actually twinkle when you laugh."

"My eyes twinkle." He thought that over while he urged the horse across a narrow stream. "That's a start. What else?"

"And I do so like your chin."

"My chin?"

"Aye. It's very strong."

"I have a strong chin and eyes that twinkle. Is that all you can say about me?"

"Well." She paused a moment before saying, "I guess I could manage one more compliment."

"I should hope so. Go ahead. What else do you have to say about me?"

"For an arrogant man, you can be quite…subdued when you're in pain."

He looked down at her, then threw back his head and roared. "So much for the proper English and their compliments. For an intelligent woman you can be quite—'' he touched a finger to her nose ''—amusing when you want to be.''

''I'm glad I amuse you, Rory O'Neil.''

''Oh, you do, my lady. You do indeed.'' He tilted her face up and gave her a hard, quick kiss before returning his concentration to the trail before them.

When they emerged from the forest, they were buffeted by a bitter wind that added to the discomfort of wet garments.

''I'm truly sorry we can't stop and warm ourselves by a fire, AnnaClaire.''

''Hush, Rory. I'll be fine.'' She drew her cloak around her and clutched at her hood to keep it from blowing loose.

As day slipped into night, and the cold wind and bitter rain continued, he marveled at her strength of will. Another woman might have wept in despair. But AnnaClaire was unlike any woman he'd ever known. She accepted the pain, the discomfort, as she had once accepted the elegance of her surroundings. With grace and quiet dignity.

They could have stopped for the night. As they passed darkened huts, Rory knew that he would find the welcome of food and warmth within. The desire to seek shelter from the elements nearly overpowered him. But he was driven by an urgency to see to AnnaClaire's safety. It was uppermost in his mind as they rode past the tiny villages around Galway, and as they skirted the slopes of the Maamturks.

Dawn was just beginning to light the sky when they passed through a gap in the mountains. The silvery waters of a lake glistened up ahead.

Rory brought his horse to a halt at the top of the rise and drank in the beauty of the scene before him.

AnnaClaire lifted her head from his shoulder and rubbed her eyes. "What is it, Rory? Where are we?"

"We're home, AnnaClaire."

At the reverence with which he spoke the word, she glanced at him. There was a look in his eyes she had never seen before. As though he were in the presence of the Almighty. She met his smile, then turned to take in the view. And caught her breath at the wild, primitive beauty of it.

"That great pinnacle over there is Croagh Patrick. It has stood guard over Ballinarin for thousands of years."

"Look." She pointed. "Waterfalls. They're spectacular."

The water streamed from the highest peaks, cascading all the way to the floor of the valley, where it joined the swiftly running water of the lake.

Looking up she said, "It seems to glitter in the early light."

"Aye. We call that the jewels of Croagh Patrick. 'Tis caused by fragments of quartz and mica."

AnnaClaire studied the narrow floor of the valley, sheltered from the winds and gales, strewn with tall conifers and clumps of rhododendron. "How much of this belongs to your family?"

He nudged his horse into a trot. "All of it."

"All?" She couldn't seem to take it all in. "The lakes? The mountains? All the land?"

"Aye." His voice was little more than a whisper. As though unwilling to break the spell of this, his first glimpse upon returning home. "There are thousands of acres of moorland, mountain, water and woods. Those who have been fortunate enough to visit say it's the grandest place in all of Ireland.''

She could see that he spoke the truth. As they passed through just-waking villages, the houses appeared clean and prosperous. The fields were planted with crops. Flocks of sheep grazed on nearby hillsides. Old men doffed their caps and young lads clapped in delight when they recognized the man in the saddle.

''Ye'r home then, Rory O'Neil?''

''Aye, Paddy.''

''God bless ye, Rory,'' an old woman called from her window as she shook a linen cloth.

''And you, Mistress Fallon.''

A lad on horseback took off at a run to spread the word that Rory O'Neil had returned.

''Oh, Rory.'' As they rounded a bend AnnaClaire had her first glimpse of his home.

The castle had been built of soft gray stone possibly mined from Croagh Patrick, since it shimmered in the morning mist like the mountain. It soared several stories high, with softly rounded turrets on either end. The road leading up to it was planted with tall conifers that stood at attention along the winding, twisting path. At the front was an enormous gated entrance. Even before they passed through to a paved courtyard, they could hear the sounds of shouting as the word of his arrival was received by those within. And then they were nearly overrun by the pack of hounds that circled their mount, yelping and baying a mournful welcome. At a sharp word from Rory, they settled down.

The door was flung open and a lass still clad in her nightshift raced down the steps and burst into tears. At the sight of her, Rory slid from the saddle and gathered her into his arms.

"Oh Rory. Rory. We haven't had a word in so long. We were so afraid you were..." She burst into fresh tears and hugged his neck so fiercely he winced.

"Easy now, Briana. You wouldn't want to choke the life from me now that I'm home, would you?"

But there was no stopping her. She couldn't let go. Nor could she stop the tears that flowed freely down her cheeks.

From the back of the horse AnnaClaire watched the scene in silence. So this was Rory's little sister, Briana. He had described her perfectly. From the flaming hair to the adoration she felt for her big brother. At the moment her emotions had completely taken over. She was alternately laughing and weeping as she clung and hugged and kissed this brother who had been gone for so long.

A handsome young man came rushing out the door, struggling to fasten the tunic he'd hastily thrown on. As tall as Rory, he was slighter of build, and his hair was more brown than black. But the face was every bit as handsome. And the smile was radiant.

"Praise the saints you're back with us, Rory."

"Aye, Conor. I've been gone a bit longer than I'd planned."

The two young men grinned at each other for a full minute before falling into each other's arms.

"Ah, Rory, I've missed you."

"And I've missed you, Conor."

They both looked up at the sound of a cry. In the doorway stood a beautiful woman in a gown of white wool. Auburn hair sprinkled with gray strands was coiled atop her head like a crown. Her face was majestic. High cheekbones. Small, straight nose and full lips. Eyes as blue as a summer day, with fine laugh lines feathering the pale skin.

Standing in front of her was a solemn little boy, with blond hair and blue eyes so wide and unblinking, he looked like a statue.

"Mother." Rory closed the distance between them and caught his mother in a fierce embrace.

"Rory. Oh, my beloved son. It's been so long." Moira's shoulders shook as she silently wept against his chest.

"Hush, Mother. I'm home now." As they stepped apart, he placed his hands on either side of her face and tenderly kissed away her tears.

Then he stared down at the little boy who had taken refuge behind her skirts. He stooped down and studied the somber face. "So, Innis. You've grown."

The boy lowered his head, refusing to look at him.

"How old are you now?"

When the boy held his silence Moira said gently, "Innis…doesn't speak much. He's nine years old now."

Rory shook his head. "Nine years. I've missed so much. Do you know who I am, Innis?"

The fair head bobbed. The words were slow, halting. "You were going to be my uncle. But now…" His lips trembled.

Seeing the pain in her son's eyes, which matched the pain in the lad's, Moira said, "But now you're home."

"And home to stay, I hope," came a voice behind them.

Rory got to his feet and turned to the white-haired man who stood framed in the doorway.

"Welcome home, my son." Despite the bright smile, the older man's voice shook with emotion.

"Father."

The two men embraced. When they stepped apart Gavin O'Neil studied the battle-weary face of his eldest son. "Is it over then? Have you had your revenge against the English bastard?"

He saw the shadow that passed over Rory's features before he composed himself. "Not yet. I've not come home to stay."

"Why then?" The older man's voice lowered with feeling. "It isn't fair to torture us if you must leave us once more."

"I've brought someone who needs the protection Ballinarin can offer."

Gavin turned from Rory to the woman astride the horse.

The others followed suit.

With servants peering from windows and hanging over balconies, calling out greetings, Rory walked to the horse and helped AnnaClaire to the ground. Her hands were as cold as ice. She was trembling. He clasped her hands between his, offering some measure of warmth and comfort.

"This is AnnaClaire Thompson. When I was gravely wounded she offered me shelter and the safety of her own home, at great peril to herself and all those of her household. Had it not been for AnnaClaire's generosity, I would not have survived."

While the others merely stared in mute surprise, Moira hurried forward.

"Then you are welcome at Ballinarin, AnnaClaire Thompson. For as long as you wish, our home is yours."

"Thank you." AnnaClaire struggled to swallow the lump in her throat. Seeing the love and warmth of

Rory's family, and their unquestioning acceptance of a stranger, made her feel like weeping.

A tiny, hunched woman barrelled through the open door, then came to a sudden halt and stood wheezing for breath. White hair had been drawn back into a tight knot at her nape. Her skin was so pale and transluscent, the lines of blue veins could be easily traced. But though her eyes were watery, they danced with delight.

"They told me, in the scullery, that ye were back, Rory."

"Mistress Finn." Rory had to bend nearly double to hug the birdlike creature. "Come, meet our guest. This is AnnaClaire Thompson. AnnaClaire, Mistress Finn has been the housekeeper at Ballinarin since my father was a lad."

"Aye. I watched him grow as I've watched his sons. Warriors all, they are," she said with a trace of pride as she patted Rory's cheek. "Welcome to Ballinarin, my lady." She took AnnaClaire's hands. "You're shivering. Your clothes are soaked. What were ye thinking, Rory, to keep a lady out on such a night?"

Moira motioned to the housekeeper. "Bring our guest inside at once. Briana and I will see to her comfort."

At her mother's words Briana rushed to her brother's side, clinging to his arm. "I want to stay with Rory. I want to hear all about his adventures."

"You'll have plenty of time to see your brother and hear his tales. For now, you'll help me make our guest welcome."

The young girl knew better than to argue with that tone of voice. It was a tone mothers had perfected throughout the ages.

Mistress Finn motioned to a freckle-faced servant.

"Heat some water, Velia. These two must have warm baths and dry clothes." She looked up, where the windows bloomed with onlookers. "The rest of ye get back to work. We've a welcome to prepare for Rory O'Neil."

Under the housekeeper's watchful gaze the servants scurried away. Moira and her daughter led a dazed AnnaClaire through the doorway and up the stairs to the sleeping chambers on the second floor.

Rory started up after them but was stopped by his father and his brother, who draped their arms around his shoulders.

"There'll be no bath for you, boy-o, until you answer a few questions."

Realizing that AnnaClaire was in good hands, Rory relented. "I'll tell you as much as I can over one glass of whiskey. But only because it'll warm me. Then you'll just have to wait for the rest."

The two men glanced at each other and grinned. He could sleep all day or all week. So long as he first told them every detail of the past two years of his exile.

"And have you never again spotted this Tilden bastard?" Conor handed his father and brother glasses of whiskey, then helped himself to the third.

The three men were seated near the fire, with the hounds at their feet. Their plans to keep Rory talking until they'd heard every single detail had been thwarted when Moira had intervened and ordered her son up to bed. Now, hours later, bathed, rested and dressed in a fine tunic bearing the family crest, Rory had found his father and brother eagerly awaiting him in the library.

"Aye. I spotted him. On the docks of Dublin. I

might have killed him, too, had he not hidden behind the swords of a boatload of soldiers fresh from England.''

''That's when you were wounded?'' Gavin asked.

''Aye.'' Rory rubbed at the inflamed shoulder. ''Damned wound was opened up again when we encountered those English soldiers in the forest. Nearly cost me my life.''

From the doorway came his mother's voice. ''You should have said something before you dressed. I'll have Mistress Finn fetch one of her special ointments. Let me have a look at that.''

She hurried across the room to reach out a hand to his sleeve.

Rory brushed a kiss over her cheek, then waved her away. ''We'll deal with it later. For now, the whiskey will numb the pain.''

She was about to argue when she saw his head come up sharply.

Briana paused in the doorway. ''I told you we'd find them here. Come on in, AnnaClaire.''

AnnaClaire stepped inside, then halted when she realized that everyone was watching her. Even the dogs looked up from their stupor caused by the warmth of the fire and began to sniff the stranger.

As soon as he spotted her, Rory set aside his whiskey and crossed the room to take her hand. For the space of a heartbeat he simply looked into her eyes. Then he led her toward the fire.

Briana became aware of the sudden silence in the room. ''Mum said I could choose what dress to give to AnnaClaire, so I thought the green one would be perfect with her hair and eyes. Don't you agree, Rory?''

"Aye." Rory glanced at his family, who were all watching the young woman closely. "It is indeed perfect."

The gown had a rounded neckline that displayed just a hint of high, firm breasts. The sleeves were long, with points of lace at each cuff. Her tiny waist was accentuated by a darker green sash. The flounced skirt was gathered here and there with matching green bows to display a lace underskirt.

"Will you have some ale or whiskey?" Conor asked.

"Thank you. A little ale would be nice." AnnaClaire accepted the goblet from a maid and sipped, all the while aware of the scrutiny of Rory's family. Her cheeks turned a becoming shade of pink.

"Mistress Finn has prepared a feast, Rory my boy." Gavin downed his drink in one long swallow and poured himself another. "The entire household can't wait to greet you after we sup."

Rory grinned. "I'm glad they agreed to wait. AnnaClaire and I haven't had a single morsel since yesterday. I believe I could eat an entire lamb by myself. Raw," he added, "without even skinning it."

The others burst into knowing laughter.

"You always had a healthy appetite," Conor said dryly.

"Aye. It could be the reason this whiskey is going straight to my head. Or it could be the vision before me."

Again, AnnaClaire felt the scrutiny of the others and felt herself blushing.

When a servant announced that the dinner was ready, Rory set aside the tumbler and offered AnnaClaire his arm. "Now," he said laughingly, "you can judge whether Fiola is as good as Bridget."

"Who is Bridget?" Briana asked as she bounded by his side.

"AnnaClaire's housekeeper in Dublin, who managed to make even porridge taste heavenly."

"I believe I'll have to meet this sorceress," Conor said with a laugh as he followed Rory and AnnaClaire from the room.

Behind them, as Gavin started to take his leave, Moira caught hold of his sleeve and held him back.

"What is it, love?"

Moira's fingers closed over his arm, then tightened. "Did you see the look that passed between Rory and this young woman?"

"Aye." He bit back the smile that threatened. "I'd say our firstborn is smitten."

"He's much more than smitten, Gavin. He loves her. I'm sure of it."

Gavin patted her hand. "Moira, my darling. Our son is only home from his war for hours and already you have him lovestruck."

"A woman knows these things. That look was unmistakable. Rory and this woman have grown… intimate."

She saw her husband's expression alter slightly. Even his chest seemed to puff up a bit. Sweet heaven, what was it about men? Her own heart was stuttering with fear over what she'd seen pass between Rory and this stranger. And all Gavin could feel was some sort of masculine pride that his son had won a beautiful trophy. But who was this woman? Where had she come from? And what did she feel for their son? So far they knew nothing more than her name.

Moira carefully composed her features as she entered the dining hall beside her husband.

Gavin took his place at the head of the table, with his wife at his right side, and his eldest son at his left. As everyone was seated the servants entered bearing trays of mussels swimming in butter and platters of brown soda bread.

Each servant paused beside Rory to offer a warm smile and a word of welcome. Even the cook stood in the doorway, beaming with excitement.

Knowing they were waiting for his reaction, Rory took his first bite and closed his eyes in appreciation. ''Ah, how I've missed this. Fiola, I'll bet you caught them fresh this morning.''

''Aye.'' The cook gave a sigh of relief that she had managed to add to the family's celebration. ''Along with the salmon.''

''Wait until you taste the salmon,'' Conor remarked as he helped himself to a second helping. ''And the lamb. No one can cook lamb like our Fiola.''

AnnaClaire watched in astonishment as course after course was brought to the table and devoured by people who were apparently accustomed to working hard and eating well. There was mutton and beef, fish and seafood, and the tastiest breads she'd ever eaten. Even young Innis forgot his shyness long enough to get caught up in the spirit of the occasion. Two of the hounds had positioned themselves on either side of him beneath the table, grateful for the scraps he offered. By the time the servants offered brandied cakes heavy with currants and nuts, the lad could manage but a single slice before he allowed the hounds to lick the crumbs from his fingers.

Rory sipped his ale and sat back with a sigh. "For two long years I've thought of nothing but this."

Briana glanced at him from across the table. "Wherever did you sleep, Rory. And what did you eat?"

"I slept in haylofts. Fields. And sometimes in the cottages of those who've heard of our cause. I ate whatever I could catch. Fish mostly. An occasional stag when I had the luxury of time to hunt." He laid a hand over AnnaClaire's. "Until that fateful day when I was wounded on the docks. Then, for the first time in two years, I slept in a feather bed and was fed the nectar of the gods."

"Tell us about yourself, AnnaClaire." Gavin signalled to a servant, who filled his goblet. "How did you happen to save our Rory?"

"It was…quite by accident, I assure you." She turned to see Rory's knowing smile.

So, he wasn't going to help her. She took a sip of ale and said, "I was at Clay Court, my mother's home in Dublin, when I found Rory, badly wounded, in my kitchen."

"How did he get there?" Conor asked sharply.

"My servants had smuggled him away from the docks in my wagon. Hidden beneath my lap robe."

"How romantic." Briana clapped her hands in delight. "And so you nursed him back to health."

"It wasn't quite that simple," Rory remarked dryly. "My presence in her home gave the lady quite a shock."

"But she did nurse you back to health?"

"Aye. In time. But by doing so, she placed herself and her household in peril, for there was a price on my head."

"Loyal citizens care naught about that." Conor frowned. "Any one of us would have done the same."

Moira picked up on the thing that had caught her attention. "You mentioned your mother's home. What did she think about the danger?"

"My mother is dead."

Hearing the pain in her words, Moira felt a flash of regret. "I'm sorry."

"And your father?" Gavin lifted the goblet to his lips. "Is he dead as well?"

"Nay. My father…" AnnaClaire glanced at Rory, then stared down at her plate. "My father is away."

"Where?" Gavin asked.

"In England."

His hand paused in midair. "What business takes him to England?"

When AnnaClaire didn't immediately respond, Rory said, "AnnaClaire's father is Lord James Thompson."

"The same James Thompson who is Counsel to England's queen?" Gavin's face clouded with shock and disbelief.

"Aye." Rory nodded. "The same."

Gavin's hand tightened on the stem of the goblet until the glass shattered. Ignoring the blood that gushed from his hand, he leapt to his feet and stared at AnnaClaire as if seeing a monster.

The hounds, sensing the sudden tension, slithered away from the table and cowered in a corner.

"Gavin, you've cut yourself." Moira stood and caught his hand but her husband shook off her touch.

He kept his gaze fixed on AnnaClaire, whose face had lost all its color. His tone rang with righteous anger. "I'll not have the spawn of that devil James Thompson beneath my roof for even one night." He pointed a bloody finger at her. "Woman, you will leave Ballinarin at once."

Chapter Thirteen

Startled by the fury in Gavin's tone, the servants stopped in their tracks. For the space of a heartbeat there wasn't a sound in the room. Then, one by one, the rest of the family got to their feet and formed a half circle behind him. Briana scowled at the hated Englishwoman. Innis couldn't bring himself to even look at her, so deep was his hatred of all things English.

Rory shoved back his chair and glared at his father across the table.

"If you order AnnaClaire from Ballinarin, you are ordering me as well."

"Rory…"

He turned at the sound of his mother's voice, cutting her off with a look. "AnnaClaire Thompson risked her life, and that of her entire household, to save me. I'll accept no less from my family."

Gavin's voice rolled like thunder. "Her father is meeting right now with the monarch who is plotting the destruction of our land. I'll not give aid and comfort to our enemy."

"Had it not been for this woman you call our enemy,

I wouldn't be here having this discussion with you, Father.''

"This is not a discussion." Gavin pounded his fist on the table, sending crystal and silver flying. "This is an order. This is my home. I have the right to say who'll reside here and who won't. And I say…''

Conor stepped between his father and brother. He'd learned the art of mediation from his earliest days as middle child in this passionate family. Though he was as shocked as the others by the news of AnnaClaire's parentage, his tone was deliberately conciliatory. "Father, after two long years, Rory has come back to us. You know how you've grieved. How we've all grieved. And now he's back, as though from the dead.''

"Aye. I've grieved. And now, what do I find? My firstborn in the clutches of our enemy.''

Conor's voice lowered, gentled. "You raised us to be honorable. Would you deny Rory's debt of honor?''

"You know I would not." Gavin's anger was still apparent, but he was beginning to see where Conor was leading him. And he bitterly resented it.

"The woman who saved Rory's life is now in danger because of her generosity to him. He's brought her to us for protection. Can we do less than this noblewoman has done?''

Gavin wouldn't give up without a fight. "Her father is bloody English.''

"And her mother was Irish." Rory's voice was as defiant as ever.

"Irish?" Moira glanced at AnnaClaire, relieved for any break in the tension, no matter how trifling. "What was her name?''

AnnaClaire refused to look at her. At any of them. She hated being put in this humiliating position. This tug-of-war between father and son. Hadn't she warned Rory that his family would resent her?

Rory answered for her. "Her mother's name was Margaret Doyle."

There was a new excitement in Moira's tone. "Was her father Hugh Doyle? From Kerry?"

AnnaClaire's eyes narrowed. If these people dared to say a single word against her beloved mother, she would flee this horrible place without a backward glance. "Aye. Her father was Hugh. Her mother was Claire."

"Oh, Gavin." Moira clasped her husband's arm. "I know of her. I knew Margaret when we were girls. I'd heard she'd wed an Englishman and had left to make her home in London. I'd heard, too, that he was good to her. Despite the conflicts, he didn't force her to abandon her faith." She lowered her voice and turned back to their guest. "I'd heard that they were very happy. And you say she is now dead?"

AnnaClaire's chin came up defiantly, to hide the pain. "Aye. Almost two months now."

After a moment's hesitation Moira rounded the table and placed a hand on AnnaClaire's shoulder. "So soon. 'Tis still a raw wound. I'm sorry for your loss, my dear. Margaret was a darling girl. I'm sure she was a loving mother and that you miss her very much."

AnnaClaire nodded, too stunned and moved by this woman's words to speak. She would not embarrass herself by shedding tears in front of these people who considered her their enemy.

"Gavin, we need some time to ponder all these things. It's all so new. So confusing." Behind AnnaClaire's back, Moira stared long and hard at her husband.

It was a look he knew only too well. He glowered at her and cleared his throat. "Very well. We'll talk no more of this tonight. But on the morrow..." At another look from his wife he turned to a servant. "We'll take our whiskey in the library."

Moira exited beside her husband, followed by Innis and Briana.

"That was a close one," Conor muttered.

"You could always charm the birds from the trees." Rory clenched his hands at his sides, still itching for a fight and feeling oddly deflated. "But I didn't need your help."

"Nay. Not much. If I'd left it up to you, by now the shouts would have led to blows. Left on your own, Rory, you and Father would settle everything with your fists or your swords."

"There are times when even your silver tongue won't win the argument. When it happens, Conor, you'll be grateful for my sword." Rory turned his attention to AnnaClaire, whose pallor was a clear indication that she had been badly shaken by this outburst. "Come, my lady. The worst is over."

She shook her head. "I won't be the cause of trouble between you and your father, Rory."

"He's my father, AnnaClaire. I'll handle him."

"I'll not remain where I'm not wanted. I must leave here."

He fought to keep the anger from his voice. "If you leave, I'll leave as well."

He saw her look of surprise. Noting her hesitation he pressed his advantage. "And I was so looking forward to sleeping in my own bed tonight."

She saw the slight curve of his lips and knew she was being manipulated. Still, with a sigh, she relented.

"I suppose I can stay. But only for the night. On the morrow…"

He touched a finger to her lips to silence her. "We'll speak no more of this until the morrow."

She nodded. But as she walked beside him toward the library, she vowed that this would be the last night she would spend under the same roof as these hateful, volatile O'Neils.

"What brought you to the docks in the first place?" Gavin demanded.

After a few failed attempts at polite conversation, father and son had settled on something safe. Something they both shared. The love of battle and the hatred of the enemy.

"I'd heard the rumor that Tilden would be there. For two years I've always seemed to be just one step behind him. I thought this was my chance."

"And it turned out to be a trap," Gavin muttered.

"Nay. Tilden was there. But we hadn't counted on the fact that a boatload of soldiers would be there as well."

"You don't think it was planned?"

Rory shook his head. "I think we caught him by surprise. I believe our little skirmishes are hurting the English. Tilden has lost so many men he had to send for reinforcements. I think, too, his queen will soon demand to know why an entire regiment of trained soldiers can't put a stop to these annoying Irish peasants."

AnnaClaire studied Rory with new admiration. Hadn't Dunstan said nearly that same thing at Lady Thornly's? When she saw Gavin O'Neil studying her, she flushed. Perhaps he thought she was some sort of spy for the enemy. Needing something to do, she began to move around the room, while the conversation droned on in the background.

As soon as she stood, several of the hounds circled her, sniffing her skirts. But when she scratched their ears and ruffled their fur, they lay back down, tongues lolling.

Like all the rooms at Ballinarin, the library was massive in size. One wall housed a collection of books the likes of which AnnaClaire had never seen outside an abbey. It would seem the O'Neils and their ancestors were educated.

A blackened stone fireplace dominated another wall. Above the mantel hung a coat of arms depicting a lion, a stag and an ornate jeweled crown. It was the same coat of arms Rory wore on his tunic. It had been on his cloak as well, before Bridget had cut it away to tend his wounds. The lion, AnnaClaire knew, was the symbol of a warrior. The stag symbolized a hunter. But the crown puzzled her until she remembered that Rory had boasted that his family had descended from the first king of Ireland. No wonder his father was so arrogant, she mused. His temper would be a match for the English queen he so despised.

She turned away. A third wall had three arched windows looking out on a formal garden planted with hedges and conifers, arranged in an intricate pattern along paved walkways. An inviting, restful view.

The scarred wooden desktop was littered with ledgers, a clear sign that a great deal of business was conducted here. But there were several groupings of overstuffed chairs and settles as well, that added a look of comfort to the room.

To one side of the fireplace stood a small table, with a chair on either side. AnnaClaire paused beside it.

Covering the entire tabletop was a hand-carved wooden chess set. She studied the pieces and was jolted when she realized that one set depicted Irish swordsmen, the other English soldiers.

"It's not been used since Rory went away." Conor's voice beside her made her jump. He pointed to the two horsemen standing guard before a queen. "That was the last play our Rory made."

"Does no one else play?" she asked.

"Aye. But Father lost heart when Rory left. He said my brother was the only one who could ever truly offer him a challenge."

"A pity." She studied the players for a moment, then said, "When Rory challenges your father again, Gavin will want to move that rook into position. Else he'll find himself helplessly locked in checkmate."

Hearing her, the O'Neil was across the room in quick strides, studying the pieces. After several minutes he shook his head. "'Twould be a foolish move. My opponent would then be free to move this bishop."

AnnaClaire shrugged and noted that the others had stopped talking to watch and listen. "Suit yourself, Gavin O'Neil. I have no wish to fuel your temper again this night."

Anger sparked. The cheek of the woman! He turned to his firstborn. "Come here, Rory. It's time I taught you a lesson or two in the art of strategy."

"Perhaps it's you who'll need the lesson, Father." Rory's mouth twitched in amusement.

The two men took their seats, while the others stood in a circle watching. Both men studied the pieces.

Rory looked across the table. "I believe the first move is yours, Father."

"Aye." Gavin glanced up at AnnaClaire, thought

about what she'd said, then dismissed it and moved another rook instead.

Rory glanced at his father in astonishment. "Are you certain this is what you want to do?"

"I am."

Rory moved his chess pieces and said, "You should have listened to the lady, Father. I have you in checkmate."

Gavin's eyes grew stormy, and for a moment AnnaClaire thought there would be another outburst. He fixed her with a steely look. "You did that on purpose, didn't you, Englishwoman?"

"Did what?" She could feel her cheeks growing warm as the others turned to stare at her.

"Offered advice, knowing I'd be quick to reject it, since it came from the likes of you."

She shrugged. "I intended nothing of the kind. But if you wish to think so, I have no way of changing your mind."

"There may be a way."

She met his look.

"Do you think you could beat me, AnnaClaire Thompson?"

"I've been playing chess with my father since I was a child. And routinely beating him."

"Ha. But he is a bloody Englishman. I challenge you to a game of chess with a wily Irishman."

AnnaClaire glanced around at the others, who looked as surprised as she felt.

"But, Father." Briana's eyes were wide. "You've always refused to teach me the rudiments of the game, because you said it's a strategy only men can understand."

"Aye. A game of war. A game of wiles and wit. The

female mind simply cannot comprehend such things. Well, my lady? Are you afraid I'll humiliate you?''

As he'd suspected, she couldn't possibly refuse his taunt. ''I accept your challenge, Gavin O'Neil.''

''Let's get started then.''

Moira touched a hand to her husband's shoulder. ''Gavin, the lass must be growing weary. Think of the difficult journey she has undertaken in the last few days.''

''She can sleep as long as she pleases. As soon as the game is over.''

Before Moira could protest further, Conor draped an arm around his mother's shoulder and led her toward the settle. ''Come. We'll warm ourselves with some ale and listen to Rory's tales of adventure.''

For the next hour or more Rory made a half-hearted effort to oblige. But he found himself distracted by the image of AnnaClaire facing his father across the chess board. Did she have any idea what she'd gotten herself into? To his father, this was no game. It was war, about which Gavin O'Neil felt passionately. By the time it was over, lovely AnnaClaire would no doubt be reduced to tears.

''I've backed you into a corner, Englishwoman.'' Gavin's eyes danced with delight. They had begun at a slow, leisurely pace as each player tried to surmise the strategy of the other.

He'd been surprised by the lady's quick mind. She'd very cleverly determined where he was going, and effectively blocked every move. But now she was about to face defeat.

''Aye. That you have.'' She studied the options left

open, then gave him a slow smile. "So I'll just have to say....checkmate, Gavin O'Neil."

"That's impossible. I thought out every move. By all that is holy…" His voice exploded, bringing everyone out of their chairs to hurry over.

Rory and Conor were studying the chess pieces, while Moira was staring at her husband, trying to gauge the depth of his anger. She didn't want another outburst like the one they'd witnessed in the dining hall.

Behind her, young Innis hung back, as he'd done all evening, and kept his gaze fixed on the floor. The arrival of Rory O'Neil and this strange woman had added to his agitation. And the news that she was English had sent him into some dark place in his mind.

Briana clung to Rory, as she had all evening, needing desperately to assure herself that her adored brother was really here with her. But it was AnnaClaire who had captured her attention. All her young life Briana had heard about the cruelty of the English. Yet this female was far from cruel. AnnaClaire Thompson was unlike any young woman she had ever known. She'd actually risked her life to save a stranger. She had traveled clear across Ireland, facing unknown perils. And she sat here calmly playing a confusing game of strategy with a man who considered her his enemy.

Though she knew it was treason to entertain a kind thought about the English, she was almost sorry AnnaClaire would have to take her leave on the morrow. Briana found her fascinating.

"I do believe you've lost, Father." Conor's tone was incredulous.

"The woman is a sorceress." Gavin downed a tumbler of whiskey, then studied the pieces again, looking for a way out.

"Face it, Father. She's bested you."

The older man shook his head. "It isn't possible."

Moira patted his shoulder. "It's time we all took our rest, Gavin. After all, 'tis only a game."

"A game?" His eyes narrowed. "This is no mere game. And I've never met a woman whose mind could grasp the strategy of war."

"You've met one now." Rory set his tumbler down and caught AnnaClaire's hand. "Well done, my lady." With a bow, he brushed his lips over her knuckles. "Now, whether you like it or not, Father, AnnaClaire has earned a well-deserved rest."

"Rest is it?" Gavin stared at the chess pieces, then at the woman who'd beat him. "Aye. We'll all rest. But on the morrow, after we break our fast, we'll match wits again."

Before anyone could stop her, Briana blurted, "But Father, you ordered the Englishwoman to leave on the morrow."

"I did indeed." To hide his discomfort Gavin broke the silence with a roar. "No bloody Englishwoman will leave Ballinarin until I have the chance to redeem myself." He stared hard at AnnaClaire. "Is that clear?"

She gave a slight nod of her head. "Quite clear, Gavin O'Neil. I'll give you that chance on the morrow, before I take my leave of this place. Now I bid you all good night." She walked out of the library beside Rory.

When she was gone, Gavin glanced at his family. "Well? What are you looking at? I think it's high time we all took our rest."

"Aye. Good night, Father." Conor kissed his mother's cheek, then herded Briana and Innis out the door, with the hounds following.

Alone by the fire, Moira studied her husband for long, silent moments. "You like her, don't you?"

"Like her? How can I possibly like her? She's bloody English."

"Aye, though she has some Irish blood in her." She peered at him from beneath her lashes. "And you like her."

"I don't like defeat." He took her hand and led her from the room.

As they climbed the stairs she whispered, "Admit it, Gavin."

He shot her a sideways glance. "I admit nothing."

Moira sighed. Gavin O'Neil had always been an obstinate man. But it was one of those things she'd always managed to overlook. He was, after all, the love of her life.

But in this instance, she had to admit that her husband was right to order the young woman to leave. AnnaClaire Thompson might have won the heart of their son, but she was still the enemy. And they had no way of knowing if this Englishwoman truly returned their son's affection, or if she was using him for some sinister purpose.

Perhaps she was part of a plot to bring the English soldiers into the O'Neil stronghold. If so, she would soon learn that the O'Neils would do whatever it took to keep their loved ones safe from all harm. Especially here in their own home.

Chapter Fourteen

"Oh, my lady." As AnnaClaire stepped into her bedchamber, Velia, the little servant, sprang up from the chaise where she'd fallen asleep. "Forgive me."

"It's quite all right, Velia. I'm sure you've put in a very long day."

"Aye, my lady." The girl shoved stiff, corkscrew curls from her eyes. "I was up before dawn so I could go down to the village and see..." She bit her lip, wondering how much to reveal. Her voice lowered. "There's a farmer, you see. Titus O'Malley. I bake him bread and biscuits and bring them to him before he leaves for the fields."

"A farmer? Is he courting you?"

Velia nodded.

AnnaClaire studied her with surprise. "But you're so young."

"Not so young. I'm ten and three. And long for a family of my own. Sometimes, when my chores are finished, I go into town and help my sister with her young one. She has a wee babe, and needs a bit of help now and then."

"The O'Neils don't mind that you leave?"

"Nay. They encourage it. They know how much my sister means to me, now that she's the only family I have left." She blushed. "Well, my sister and Titus."

"What happened to the rest of your family?"

"My parents and younger brother were killed."

"I'm sorry, Velia. How did it happen?"

"They were taking some sheep to market across the river, and were attacked by English soldiers..." The minute the words tumbled out of her mouth the little servant looked away. By now she had heard, as had all the household, the truth of AnnaClaire's parentage. The O'Neils' furious response to such news had been repeated by all the servants. "Forgive me, my lady. I've been known to trip over my own tongue."

"You have nothing to apologize for, Velia."

"Oh, but I do. No matter what, you are a guest at Ballinarin. Here, let me help you." She hurried forward, eager to make amends. "'Twouldn't do for you to feel neglected. Especially now that himself gave you a wee taste of his temper."

"A wee taste?" AnnaClaire couldn't help laughing. The sound of it eased the tension in the little servant.

"Aye, my lady. You wouldn't wish to feel the full force of the O'Neil's temper." At the thought of it, even Velia's freckles seemed to shiver. "For 'tis fierce indeed. Like a great storm blowing in from the sea. All who know him fear the O'Neil. Now, let's get you out of that dress."

AnnaClaire carefully removed her borrowed gown and slipped on the nightshift Velia offered her. "Have all the O'Neils inherited their father's temper?"

"I'd say Rory and his sister are the most like the O'Neil. Not that Conor doesn't have a temper, but, like his mother, he's learned to subdue it."

"Rory told me that Conor prefers talking to fighting."

"Oh, aye." Velia broke into a sunny smile as she led AnnaClaire across the room to an ornate dressing table. "A silver tongue that one has. I think his mother wishes he would use his gift to spread the faith."

"A man of the church? Do you think he will consider it?"

"So far Conor's been busy using his gift to charm the maidens."

In the mirror AnnaClaire could see the little spots of color on the girl's cheeks. It would seem that despite her courtship by a young farmer, she was not immune to Conor O'Neil's charms.

Velia removed the combs from her hair and ran a brush through the tangles. "Not that Rory O'Neil hasn't always made the maidens' hearts flutter as well. But everyone knew he had eyes only for his Caitlin."

AnnaClaire felt a quick jolt around her heart. "Did you know her, Velia?"

"Oh, aye. And all her family. It doesn't seem possible even now that all are gone. Except Innis, poor lad."

"Tell me about Innis."

She lowered her voice. "He's very bitter. He never smiles. Hardly even speaks. And never about...that day."

The two young women fell silent, each lost in thought.

Finally, to banish the sadness, AnnaClaire glanced down at the filmy nightshift, edged with lace at the hem and sleeves. "It was so kind of Briana to offer me the use of these beautiful clothes."

"She's a lovely, generous girl." Velia set aside the brush. "Besides, she cares nothing for such things."

"What does she care about?"

"Swords. Horses. Anything that Rory likes. He's always been the one she looked up to. It near broke her heart when he left. She was like a bird without wings. And now, oh, the look on her face when she realized her hero was truly home."

AnnaClaire nodded, remembering. Briana's tears of happiness had stained her cheeks all the day long.

The little maid turned down the bed and drew the heavy draperies at the windows. Then, adding a log to the fire, she said, "I'll bid you good night now, my lady, and leave you with my family's blessing. May the angels bless your dreams until the morrow."

"Thank you, Velia." AnnaClaire was touched by her gentle words. "Where will you sleep?"

"I've a room here at Ballinarin. I've been assured it is my home, for as long as I choose. And for that I'll be forever indebted to the O'Neils."

AnnaClaire settled herself on the edge of the bed and watched as the maid took her leave. For a moment she stared at the flickering flames of the fire and thought about all Velia had told her. No wonder Gavin O'Neil had reacted so violently at the mention of her father's name. She regretted the fact that English soldiers were the cause of so much pain and suffering for these good people. Still, it was unfair to blame one man. If only they knew her father as she knew him.

She thought again about Gavin O'Neil's outburst. It was difficult to reconcile that man with the one who had opened his home to the orphans, Velia and Innis. It would seem that despite his famous temper he was a kind and generous man as well.

It seemed a shame that men of different nations, different loyalties, could not know each other as their families and friends knew them.

She shook her head, weary at being torn apart by all this.

With a sigh she sank into the softness of down. But just as her eyes closed, she heard the opening of a door. She looked up, and saw Rory, barefoot and shirtless, striding across the room.

"I thought she'd never leave."

"Who?" She sat up, unmindful of the blankets that slipped away, revealing the sheer garment.

But Rory took notice and felt his throat go dry at the sight of her. "Your long-suffering maid."

She was shocked. "You were listening at my door?"

"Aye." He gave that dangerous smile she'd come to know so well. "How else would I know when you were alone?"

As he began stripping away the last of his clothes she whispered fiercely, "Rory, you musn't be here."

"And why not?" He lifted the blanket and slipped into bed beside her.

"Because this is your parents' home. It isn't right."

"Tell me this isn't right." He cupped the back of her head and kissed her, long and slow and deep.

It was impossible to think, or to resist. She clung to him, returning the kiss.

Then, coming up for air, she pushed him away a little. "You know what I mean. The servants will talk. Your parents will know. The entire household will know by morning that you shared my bed."

"Aye. If they don't already know, they must be blind." He combed his fingers through her hair and began nibbling her chin, the corner of her mouth.

She could feel the heat, the need, beginning to build deep inside.

"I've missed you, AnnaClaire. All day, all evening, all I thought about was you. About this." He drew her down into his arms and kissed her again until they were both breathless. "Tell the truth. Haven't you thought about me, as well?"

"Umm." She nodded, too overcome for words.

"Just think." He ran soft kisses over her nose, her cheek, her eyelid. "No matter how long the day seemed, we have the whole night now to ourselves."

"Oh, if only it could always be so."

"It will be, love. I promise."

With exquisite tenderness he took her on a long slow journey of love.

"Good morrow, my lady." Using her hip to open the door Velia backed into the room carrying a pitcher of water and an armload of fresh linens. Several of the hounds bounded into the room behind her.

When she turned, she realized her mistake. "Oh, forgive me, I thought surely you were awake by now."

At her words AnnaClaire forced herself upward from sleep like one who'd been drugged. For a moment she couldn't recall where she was. Then, suddenly wide awake, she looked around in dismay, afraid that Rory was still asleep beside her. Seeing the bed empty, she gave a sigh of relief. She could vaguely recall his whispered words in the early hours of morning. She touched a finger to her cheek where he placed a gentle kiss as he'd left her. But somehow she had drifted back to sleep, with a promise to write her father that she was safe and well.

As the little maid began to edge from the room,

shooing the dogs as she went, AnnaClaire called out,
"No, Velia. Please stay."

"You're certain, my lady?"

"Aye. I can't recall when I've ever slept so
soundly."

"And so you should. From what I've heard, you
endured a long and perilous journey, my lady. All the
household is abuzz about your courage."

As the little maid opened the draperies, AnnaClaire
could see that the sun was already high in the sky.

"I was given orders that you were not to be disturbed." Velia moved around the room, filling a basin
with water, laying out an assortment of fresh clothes.

"That was kind of your mistress." AnnaClaire
climbed from bed and scratched each hound's ears before crossing to the basin.

"'Twas not the mistress of the house who gave the
order. 'Twas Rory O'Neil himself. He forbade anyone
from coming near you."

AnnaClaire busied herself at the basin to hide the
color she knew was on her cheeks. She would speak
to her bold lover about this later. For now she must
prepare herself to leave. "Is everyone below stairs?"

"Aye, my lady." When AnnaClaire finished washing, the servant helped her into a chemise and petticoat,
then held up a gown the color of the sky. "Does this
meet with your approval?"

"It's lovely. But I had hoped to wear my own gown
and cloak, especially since I'll be leaving today."

"As you wish, my lady." The little maid appeared
distressed. "Your garments were badly soiled. But I'll
have them brought to your room as soon as I have them
in good repair."

AnnaClaire slipped on her kid boots and studied her

reflection in the looking glass as the little maid dressed her hair. Then she hurried down the stairs, in search of Rory.

The sound of voices led her to the dining hall. When she entered, those around the table looked up in sudden silence. It seemed clear that they had been discussing her. And, she thought, probably wondering how soon they would be rid of her.

"Ah, AnnaClaire. Good morrow." It was Conor, ever the gallant one, who crossed the room and took her hand to lead her smoothly toward his family.

"Good morrow, Conor." She bowed a greeting to the others, who responded with cool nods.

"Rory had thought you'd stay abed for hours." He held a chair, and she had no choice but to take her place to one side of a scowling Gavin.

She accepted a goblet of hot mulled wine and sipped before asking, "Where is Rory?"

Gavin and Moira exchanged glances. It was Moira who said, "Rory needed to ride. There are...places he wanted to visit. He's been away a long time."

A servant paused beside AnnaClaire, offering a tray of steamed fish and mutton. She refused, accepting instead a slice of bread, still warm from the oven.

When the servant walked away she said, "I've instructed Velia to have my gown and traveling cloak ready. I can leave as soon as Rory returns."

"You can't leave yet, Englishwoman." The temper was still in Gavin's tone. "You owe me a chance to redeem myself at the chess table."

She kept her tone deliberately cool, refusing to give an inch. "That shouldn't take long, Gavin O'Neil. I can beat you at chess and still be on my way in an hour or less."

The nerve of the woman. He pushed away from the table and shot her a steely look. "Unfortunately I must ride to the village first. Then we shall see who wins and who loses."

AnnaClaire nodded. "Very well." What little appetite she'd had was now gone. Where was Rory? Why had he left her alone at such a time? He had to know how awkward this was. All his lovely promises made under the cover of darkness had been snatched away by the light of day.

Seeing her restlessness Moira said, "Perhaps you would be more comfortable in the gardens."

"Aye. Thank you." AnnaClaire got to her feet, grateful for the chance to escape.

"Come, Briana," her mother called. "You will accompany us."

As AnnaClaire followed them outside, the ever present hounds trailed, circling her legs.

"Oh." AnnaClaire's earlier frustration was forgotten as she stepped through the doorway. "This is lovely."

The gardens were in the manner of the formal English gardens, with carefully planted hedges, curving stone walkways, and comfortable stone benches set here and there among the plantings.

"It will be glorious when the summer sun has had a chance to work its magic on the blooms."

"Even without the flowers, there's a feeling of peace and beauty here," said AnnaClaire.

Moira's quick smile was so much like Rory's, AnnaClaire felt a little jolt around her heart. "Aye. The first time I came here, as a young bride, I felt it."

"How old were you?" AnnaClaire asked as she lifted her face to the thin sunshine.

"Ten and five."

AnnaClaire turned to study her. "So young."

"Aye." Moira shook her head. "No older than Briana is now. It's hard to believe I could know my own mind at such a tender age. But the moment I saw Gavin O'Neil I knew he was the man I wanted."

Despite his stern countenance, AnnaClaire could see why a young woman would lose her heart to such a bold, proud warrior. Hadn't his son touched her own heart in much the same way? "Did your father have nothing to say about it?"

"Oh, indeed he did. And none of it good."

"Why?"

Moira indicated a bench in the sunlight, and the three women sat.

"Gavin O'Neil had a reputation as a fierce warrior. Such men often leave young widows behind. My father was determined that his only child would wed a man who would give her both a peaceful life and a comfortable one. He refused to accept Gavin's request for my hand. When Gavin pressed, my father said there would be no dowry, and thus, no wedding."

AnnaClaire arched a brow. "It's obvious that your father gave in. How did Gavin convince him?"

"Gavin didn't convince him. I did." Moira held her hands to her cheeks, surprised that even after all these years, the telling of the tale could make her blush. "I tried begging, pleading. Then I did the only thing I could. I sent a message to Gavin asking him to come for me, and signed my father's name to the missive. When Gavin showed up to claim his bride and her dowry, I was waiting by the river's edge, with nothing but the clothes on my back. I told him that the only way he could have me was to take me as I was." She gave an embarrassed laugh. "As you can see, he did."

"Were you forced to sever all ties with your father?"

Moira smiled. "I'd expected to. But blood is deep. When he learned that I had given birth to his first grandson, he sent word that he wished to visit. He made his peace with my choice, and in time, he and Gavin became fast friends. Until his death there were many joyful visits between us."

The older woman looked up when she saw the cook heading toward them. "I must speak with Fiola. Briana will keep you company in the garden, since you seem more comfortable here than in the keep."

"Thank you." When she was gone, AnnaClaire glanced at the scowling young woman beside her and realized that Briana was here against her wishes. Hoping to put her at ease she said, "Your home is as lovely as Rory had said."

"He told you about Ballinarin?"

"Aye. And always there was such love in his voice when he spoke of it. It was the same when he spoke of all of you."

"Then you have us at a disadvantage, Englishwoman. For we knew nothing about you. Oh, why did you have to come here and turn our world upside down?"

AnnaClaire touched a hand to the young woman's sleeve. "I know you're distressed, Briana. But it's just as distressing for me. This was not my choice. Nor, I think, was it Rory's. Circumstances forced him to bring me here."

The young woman pulled away as though the mere touch of her burned. "I wish my brother had never met you. I wish things could be as they were, before the slaughter began, before Rory had to go away. I don't want you here. You're a millstone around Rory's neck."

With that she lifted her skirts in a most unladylike fashion and ran back to the keep.

With a sigh AnnaClaire stood and shook down her skirts, wishing she could escape as easily as Briana had. Feeling restless and edgy, she began to follow the winding walkway which was bordered on either side with thick hedges. Beyond the hedges she could hear the sound of a voice, speaking in low tones. Puzzled, she continued on until she came to a break in the hedge. The voice was louder here. She peered around and saw Innis. But this was unlike the shy lad she had seen yesterday. He was speaking as fiercely as the O'Neil, gesturing wildly.

Hoping to find Rory with him, AnnaClaire stepped through the opening and found herself in a circular courtyard, with benches all around, and a fountain in the middle. The carved figures at the base of the fountain depicted a mother holding a child. In the child's hands was a bouquet of flowers, which he was offering to his mother. There were identical looks of love on the faces of both mother and son.

When AnnaClaire looked more closely, she realized that Innis was alone. And speaking to the statue.

"She's English," he was saying. "Bloody, hateful English. I must never forget that, though she looks just like you. When I first saw her I thought it was my mother come back from the grave. But now I know she can never be…"

At a slight sound behind him he whirled and caught sight of AnnaClaire. His words died. His eyes flashed with a fire that reminded her of a soldier in the heat of battle.

"I'm sorry I startled you." AnnaClaire stood very still. Aware of the boy's tension, she looked over his head and pretended to study the fountain, to give him time to compose himself. "She's very beautiful."

He held his silence.

"If I lived here, I would want to visit this place often. It's soothing to the spirit." She glanced at the statue, then at Innis. "Does it remind you of your mother?"

He looked away, refusing to meet her eyes.

Her voice lowered with feeling. "I lost my mother two months ago. I don't know if the ache will ever leave my heart. Sometimes I find myself weeping for no reason at all."

His voice was tight, angry. "The O'Neil says it isn't right to cry."

It was the first time he'd spoken to her. Though she could hear the anger in his tone, she felt a quickening of her heartbeat. It was a crack in the wall of hatred he'd built.

She chose her words carefully. "The O'Neil isn't God almighty. I'll wager he's been wrong a time or two."

For a moment he merely stared at her, too stunned to respond. Then, with a look that might have carried just a hint of a smile, he turned away. In almost a whisper he asked, "Are you looking for Rory?"

"Aye. Do you know where he went?"

Instead of responding, he merely turned away. With a glance over his shoulder to see that she was following, he led her through the garden, across the sloping lawns, past the small chapel, and out onto the old bog road.

As they walked AnnaClaire drank in the beauty of

this wild, primitive place. The sides of hills were dotted with stunted, twisted shrubs and trees. The sky above was a harsh gray-green, the swirl of clouds threatening rain. The wind blew, sharp and chill, whipping the ends of her skirt, flattening it against her legs.

They continued walking, following the bend in the road, until Innis came to a sudden halt.

The land looked no different from the surrounding countryside. Yet AnnaClaire felt a shiver course along her spine. No sheep grazed here. No crops had been planted. A single bird circled overhead, calling to its mate. Its lonely cry seemed to echo in the stillness.

Up ahead she could see a horse standing very still, bridle dangling. At first she thought its rider may have fallen. But when she looked more closely she could see Rory kneeling on the ground, his face buried in his hands.

AnnaClaire pressed a hand to her mouth as the realization dawned. Dear heaven. This was the place where his Caitlin and her family had been slaughtered. She felt a thrust of pain, sharp and deep, around her heart. Jealousy? For a dead woman? She struggled to deny it. But the truth was, it hurt to realize that Rory was grieving for a lost love. Still, she consoled herself, had it not been for the massacre that had occurred here, she would never have met him. Would never have lost her heart to this wild Irish warrior.

"Have you come here since…?" She couldn't bring herself to speak of the slaughter of this lad's entire family.

Innis ran a hand over a rough stone, standing like a lone sentinel in the field. "I come here every day."

"Every day? But why?"

"To remember." His big eyes looked sad. And old. And haunted.

AnnaClaire shivered. "I should think you'd rather forget."

"Forget?" He whirled on her, anger blazing in his eyes. "I'll never forget." His brow drew together in a small frown. "I must remember. So that I can see it never happens again."

"And how can one small boy accomplish that?"

"Do you see this?" He revealed a small dagger hidden at his waist. "Each day since Rory left, I've come here to learn, to practice until it's now second nature. With this, I could cut the heart from a bird in flight."

As he took aim at the lone bird overhead, Anna-Claire closed a hand over his wrist. "Nay, Innis. I couldn't bear to see a bird killed."

"Liar." He jerked free of her touch. "Unhand me, Englishwoman. If I had to, I could even cut out your heart." With fierce concentration he tossed the knife. He turned at the last second so that instead of the bird, he tossed the knife at a leaf, trembling on a high, barren branch. The dagger pierced the leaf and brought it tumbling to the ground.

AnnaClaire was shocked at the violence in the lad. Though he had grudgingly avoided killing the bird, she had the distinct impression that he would have preferred to aim his weapon at her heart.

As he retrieved his dagger and returned it to his hiding place beneath his waist he muttered, "When I'm big enough, I shall join Rory O'Neil on his quest for vengeance. And together we'll rid this land of all English."

"Oh, Innis." She felt her heart contract at the venom in his tone. "I pray that day never comes." With tears stinging her eyes she turned away. "Now I must leave this place at once." She began stumbling over the rough terrain.

He moved easily by her side. "Why do you flee, Englishwoman? Are you afraid to see what your countrymen have done?"

"I have no right to be here. I'm..." *The enemy.* The words were burned into her mind. She clamped her mouth tightly shut and began to run.

They both looked up at the pounding of hoofbeats.

"AnnaClaire." Rory brought his horse to a halt. His eyes were raw and gritty. The heaviness in his heart made his voice rougher than he intended. "What are you doing out here?"

"I asked Innis to show me..." She groped for words. "...this place. He comes here every day."

Rory swiveled his head. "Do you, lad?"

Innis stared boldly at the warrior whose name was spoken with such reverence, he was almost a god. The boy could still see, in his mind's eye, the savage look on Rory's face when he'd first come upon the scene of the massacre. At night the lad was often awakened by the sound of his own cry, echoing the heart-wrenching sound that had broken from Rory's lips when he'd found his beloved Caitlin. But if Innis wept in sleep, by day he could only mimic the man whose eyes had been dry and dead and lifeless by the time he'd stood over the graves and vowed revenge.

"Can you speak, lad?" Rory slid from the saddle and knelt beside him. "Are you afraid of me, Innis?"

The boy met his look. "Nay. I do not fear you. Though some call you the Blackhearted O'Neil. They say you're the most feared man in all of Ireland."

"The only ones who need fear me are English soldiers, Innis."

"They'd best fear me as well. For if I come up against them again, they'll not find a wee lad hiding behind his da's back."

Rory studied this boy, so like himself. Then his look darted to AnnaClaire.

She looked away quickly, avoiding his eyes. She'd seen the pain. Had heard it in his voice. "I'd like to go back to Ballinarin now."

"Aye. There's a storm brewing, from the looks of that sky. Here, we can all ride."

Rory bent and lifted AnnaClaire to the saddle, then handed the boy up to her. As Rory was pulling himself up behind them, AnnaClaire felt the lad shrink from her touch.

As the horse carried them back to Ballinarin, AnnaClaire held herself stiffly, pondering all that she'd seen and heard. Perhaps, if she could win over one sad little boy whose soul had been so scarred, there would be hope for the others at Ballinarin as well.

But perhaps, her heart taunted her, it was too late. The evil deeds of others had surely turned the hearts of all at Ballinarin against her. And had sealed forever the fate of two star-crossed lovers.

Chapter Fifteen

The storm broke before they could reach the shelter of the stables. With the wind whipping fiercely, and rain pelting them, Rory turned his mount toward the small chapel just ahead.

"We can take refuge in here." He slid from the saddle and lifted AnnaClaire and Innis down. Leading them through the downpour he leaned into the heavy door and forced it open.

Inside, the air was perfumed with the fragrance of oil and beeswax and incense.

"Here, love." Rory shook the rain from his cloak and wrapped it around AnnaClaire's shoulders. "I'll build a fire." He crossed to the fireplace and piled several logs on the grate, where a thin flame flickered. Then he positioned a plain wooden bench nearby and urged AnnaClaire and Innis to sit. Soon the little chapel was snug and warm while the storm raged beyond its walls.

Rory rubbed his hands together. "All we need is some bread and cheese, a little church wine, and we'd be as comfortable as if we were home."

"Did someone say wine?" A man's deep melodious voice sounded from behind the altar.

"Friar Malone." Rory hurried forward to embrace a hunched old monk in a coarse robe. Though his face was as wrinkled as old leather, and his hair was a wild thatch of white, his eyes were as dark and piercing as a blackbird's. And as alert and intense as a child's.

"Ah, Rory, lad. I'd heard you were home." The old priest held him a little away, noting the lean hardness of his body, the layer of warrior's muscles. "I offered my mass this morning in thanksgiving for your safe return."

"Thank you, Friar. I'm grateful."

The priest turned his look on Innis. "I missed you at mass this morning, lad."

The boy stared down at the floor.

Rory took the old man's arm and led him closer. "Friar Malone, may I present Lady AnnaClaire Thompson."

"My lady." The old priest took both her hands in his. "I offered my mass for you, as well, when I'd heard that it was your goodness and courage that saved our Rory."

"Thank you, Father," she answered.

"And how would you have known about Anna-Claire?" Rory demanded.

"How else?" Friar Malone had a twinkle in his eyes. "Your mother was here at dawn, requesting a mass of thanksgiving. After we prayed together, Moira was most eager to tell me all she knew." He turned to study AnnaClaire. "She told me that your father is Lord James Thompson."

Though she wasn't aware of it, AnnaClaire's spine stiffened. "Aye. She told you true."

"The same Lord James Thompson who advises Elizabeth of England?"

AnnaClaire nodded.

"As I recall he married an Irish lass. Were you allowed to keep your mother's faith, or were you required to accept the faith of England?"

It was on the tip of her tongue to refuse to answer. Instead, AnnaClaire said, "My father left the choice to me."

"I'd wager my boots that you chose to follow the faith of your mother. For in your heart you're Irish, AnnaClaire Thompson."

Her tone sharpened. "I'm both Irish and English. And proud of it."

At her quavering tone, Innis lifted his head to study her.

The old priest turned away to hide his smile. "I believe you were wishing for bread and cheese, Rory. Why don't I fetch some from my room?"

"That would be grand. And don't forget the wine, Friar Malone."

The old man was already shuffling away. Over his shoulder he called, "One thing I'd never forget is the wine, for it warms not only the blood but the soul."

Moments later he returned. Setting a coarse blanket on the floor in front of the fire, he invited them to sit with him while he broke off hunks of bread and cheese, and filled goblets with wine.

"Do you live here in the chapel?" AnnaClaire asked.

"Aye. Gavin and Moira graciously offered me a chamber in their home, but I prefer the simplicity of my life here in the chapel. 'Twould be too easy to forget my vows of poverty and humility if I were to indulge myself in the good life.''

AnnaClaire nodded as she sipped the wine which he'd poured from an earthen jug. ''I've met the men of the church who surround the queen at Court. It's as you say. They have forgotten the people who live outside the walls of the castle. Most of them are arrayed in such splendor, they begin to think of themselves as royalty.''

''It shames me that men of the church can so easily forget their vows.'' He shook his head before refilling her goblet. ''What do you think of the queen?''

''She is fascinating. Strong. Fiery. When she enters a room, all others fade from view. I believe Elizabeth was truly born to rule. Even the men who advise her are cowed by her will.''

Friar Malone was watching AnnaClaire's face as she spoke. ''There are those who denounce the monarch as a bully and a tyrant. Yet you admire her.''

''Aye. She is a woman in a man's domain. And yet she is fearless. How could I not admire that?''

The old priest broke off another piece of cheese. ''Moira told me that you placed yourself and your household in grave peril by helping our Rory.''

AnnaClaire flushed. ''I didn't think of that. At least not often.''

''How can you say that?'' Rory's voice was dangerously soft as he turned to Friar Malone. ''There was a price on my head. And English noblemen paying visits at her door. Though the lady may say that she gave it no thought, she is merely being humble. She knew exactly what she was doing. And was well aware of the price she might have to pay for her kindness.''

Innis was staring at AnnaClaire with a look of wonder. "Could you have been killed for helping Rory?"

"Perhaps. But don't look so worried, Innis. I'm here now. The danger is over."

"And you weren't afraid?"

"I was often afraid. But I couldn't let the fear keep me from doing what I knew was right."

"It must have seemed strange for a highborn woman to have a rough swordsman under her roof," Friar Malone said.

"Not so strange. For I've always admired warriors…" She glanced over until she met Rory's look. "…both the brave and the foolish."

The priest chuckled as he poured more wine. But Innis, somber and silent, continued to watch and listen. There was much about this Englishwoman that was unexpected.

They lingered over their lunch, enjoying the rich voice of Friar Malone as he related the history of Ballinarin to AnnaClaire.

"Rory told me that St. Patrick himself baptized his ancestors here. Can it be true?" she asked.

"Oh, indeed. The family can trace its origins to Irish kings." He winked. "And a few scoundrels."

"Ah." She smiled. "So, Rory O'Neil, the blood of scoundrels flows through your veins as well as the royalty of which you boast."

Beside her the boy almost giggled before he caught himself.

"Aye. And I'll warn you that not all of my forebears were gentlemen. So you'd best watch your tongue, woman."

"And you'd best watch your back." She drained her goblet, feeling warm and content. "Else the same woman who saved your life may see that you forfeit it." She heard a snort from the lad beside her, who was clearly enjoying this teasing banter.

Still laughing Rory looked up. "I think the storm has blown over." He crossed to the door and looked out, then returned to help the old priest to his feet.

"I'll help you clean up, Father," AnnaClaire offered.

"Nay, my dear. You go along with Rory." He caught her hands and gave her another long look before his face creased into a warm smile. "I've enjoyed this time together."

"As have I."

"And Innis," he called as the three began to take their leave, "I hope I'll see you at morning mass."

The boy ducked his head.

The old priest watched as Rory lifted AnnaClaire and Innis to the saddle, then pulled himself up behind them.

When they waved, he lifted a hand and called, "Go with God's blessings, my children."

He continued standing until they were out of sight, then turned with a sigh. Moira had been right. The two were clearly in love. But unlike Rory's worried mother, he felt a sense of peace at the knowledge. Rory O'Neil had been a man shattered by brutality, and driven by a hunger for vengeance. Perhaps now, with a gentlewoman like AnnaClaire, the healing could begin.

As he began clearing up the remains of their picnic, he remained deep in thought. What was more fascinating was the reaction of young Innis to this stranger. The lad wanted to hate her for being English. But somehow she had touched a chord in him. It would be interesting to see how their relationship progressed.

* * *

Rory helped AnnaClaire and Innis from the back of the horse, then turned the animal over to a stable lad. As they crossed the courtyard and entered the house they were greeted by Velia.

"Your da and mum are waiting for you in the library with Conor," she said.

"Thank you, Velia."

As they climbed the stairs AnnaClaire clapped a hand to her mouth. "Oh dear. The chess game. I'd forgotten all about it."

When they entered the library, Briana and Conor and their parents were seated before the fire, their heads bent in earnest conversation. As soon as they spotted Rory their heads came up sharply.

"Forgive me." AnnaClaire hurried across the room. "I truly forgot about the chess game. We were caught in a storm and..." Seeing the look on their faces she stopped, swallowed. "You're angry, Gavin O'Neil."

"Aye. Nay." He stood and caught her hand before she could swing away. "Not with you, lass. 'Tis something else. Rory." He glanced at his son, then at the little boy who stood just behind him. "We must talk. Alone."

AnnaClaire looked from one to the other. "If this is about me, I have the right to hear."

Gavin looked to his son, who nodded. He sighed in defeat. "Conor and I rode to the village this morrow. And we heard some unsettling news."

Rory's eyes narrowed. "Is this about English soldiers?"

Gavin nodded. "They're combing the countryside, searching for you and the lass."

Rory made a sound of disgust. "And I've brought them to our doorstep."

Gavin touched his arm. "You had no choice, my son. There was nowhere left to go."

Rory shook off his touch and began to pace. "There were plenty of other places. But I had this foolish notion about coming home."

His mother got to her feet. "Foolish? Is that what you think? I'll remind you that this is where you belong, Rory."

"Aye." His father nodded agreement. "Besides, you're safe here. Ballinarin is a natural fortress. They'd dare not storm it."

Rory ran a hand through his hair. "Father, I have James Thompson's daughter. Do you really believe they'll leave without her?"

"If they try to take her," Conor joined in, "they're fools, for many will forfeit their lives."

Rory nodded. "Some. But not all. They'll send for more soldiers, and more, until they get what they want."

AnnaClaire studied the worried faces of Rory and his family. "Then why not give them what they want?"

Her words had them all staring at her in disbelief.

Moira started toward her. "Do you know what you're saying, lass?"

"Aye." AnnaClaire held up a hand to stop her. "I'll…" She thought a moment, her mind racing. "I'll tell them I escaped from your son's clutches. That I slipped away without anyone knowing. They'll be so relieved to have me safe, they'll forget about Rory."

Moira saw the look in AnnaClaire's eyes and felt her heart sink. It was as she'd suspected. This woman would do it. Because she was a woman in love. But there was more than one involved in this love match.

Rory's voice, low and deep with feeling, cut through his mother's thoughts. "Even if they should have you safe and sound, they'll never forget about the Blackhearted O'Neil. One Irish peasant has managed to beat them at their own game. I've humiliated them. Made them look like fools before their own countrymen. Before their queen. They'll hunt me until they run me to ground. And even then they won't be satisfied until my head is on a stake outside the Tower of London."

AnnaClaire clutched her arms about herself, her eyes filled with anguish. "Don't say that, Rory."

"Why not? 'Tis the truth." He crossed the room and gave her shoulders a hard shake. "So think about this, AnnaClaire. If you should offer to give yourself up to save me, it will be a noble gesture, but all for naught. For it isn't only you they want. It's me. Do you understand?"

Seeing the way her eyes filled, the others looked away in uncomfortable silence. It was as they had all feared. These two had forged a bond which, when broken, would shatter them both.

When a servant announced that their meal was ready to serve, Moira looked from Rory to AnnaClaire. "We'll speak no more of this tonight. For at least one more night we will gather as a family, to eat, to talk, to laugh." To pray, she thought fiercely, as she placed her hand on her husband's arm and followed the others to the dining hall.

"Your nightshift, my lady." Velia, sensing the family's tension throughout the evening, hovered over AnnaClaire as she prepared for bed.

"Thank you." She slipped the sheer garment over her head, smoothed the skirt. "You may go now, Velia."

"But your hair, my lady. I'll brush it loose before you retire."

With a sigh AnnaClaire relented, sitting before the looking glass, watching as the little maid painstakingly smoothed every tangle.

"There now, my lady." Velia set aside the brush and crossed the room to turn down the covers. "I hope your dreams will all be as sweet as those of the angels."

"Thank you, Velia." AnnaClaire kept her smile in place. "Good night."

As soon as the door closed behind her, AnnaClaire stripped off the nightgown and slipped into her own gown, which had been carefully cleaned and mended.

She'd had plenty of time to think about what she planned. This night, while the household slept, she would slip away and ride to the village. She was certain she could persuade the soldiers that she had escaped from Rory, and that they had a duty to take her home immediately. After all, she was the daughter of Lord James Thompson. They would dare not defy her. Especially if she invoked the queen's name.

She would have to be a good enough liar to persuade the soldiers to be satisfied with her safe return, and to give up their search for Rory. If, however, they were determined to return for him, at least she would have bought enough time for the people of Ballinarin and the surrounding villages to prepare a defense.

Just as she picked up her cloak, she heard footsteps outside her door. With a little cry she flew across the room and jumped into bed, tugging the covers to her chin.

Rory opened the door, then closed it quickly and leaned against it. The way he stood looking at her made her throat go dry. Could he see through her little charade?

"What is it, Rory? What's wrong?"

He seemed to pull himself from dark thoughts. "I just wanted to look at you. You're so lovely, Anna-Claire." He crossed to the bed and stood over her.

Fear assaulted her. Would he know that something was amiss? Could he hear the sound of her labored breathing? Or perhaps the thundering of her heart? Sweet heaven. What if he wanted to sleep with her this night? She had to send him away, and quickly.

With her mind racing she pretended to yawn, then lifted a hand to stifle it. "Forgive me, Rory. I fear the excitement of the day has caught up with me. I can scarcely keep my eyes open."

"Aye. I know the feeling, love. My bed beckons as well."

She felt a moment of triumph. Her tension began to ease. "Good night then, Rory. Until the morrow."

He leaned down, brushing his lips over hers. "Good night, my love." Against her mouth he whispered, "It gladdens my heart that my family has begun to soften toward you. It will ease my burden to know that you and they have each other."

"What are you saying?" She clutched at his shoulders as he started to straighten. "What burden? Rory, what are you planning?"

As he caught her wrists, the covers slipped away, revealing the fact that she was fully dressed. His eyes narrowed. "I might ask you the same thing."

Mortified, she simply stared at him, refusing to speak.

"You were planning to sneak away, weren't you, AnnaClaire? To draw the soldiers away from me."

She folded her arms over her chest and regarded him in stony silence.

"Little fool. Do you know what kind of men they are?" When she said nothing, he snarled, "They're hardened by years of being far from home. The killing, the brutality, have robbed them of their humanity."

"Need I remind you that I am the daughter of Lord James Thompson?"

"To them you are a helpless female. No more. No less. They'll do to you what they've been doing to women old and young all across Ireland."

She sat up straighter. "They wouldn't dare. I would tell my father. And he would tell the queen herself."

Her outrage might have amused him at some other time. Now, he realized he had to convince her of the seriousness of what she was planning. "Dead women don't talk, AnnaClaire. And when they bring your body, battered and broken, back home, they will claim it is another horror committed by the Blackhearted O'Neil. Now who do you think your father and the queen will believe? Their own loyal English soldiers? Or the word of an Irish outlaw?"

She could see the truth of what he was saying. Still, she had to try to make him see her point. "It's my fault the soldiers are here. I believe if they're appeased, they'll leave your family alone."

"Aye. And that's the truth of it." He saw her brows lift in surprise. He lowered his voice. "That's why I must go now, AnnaClaire. I can lead them a merry chase. I'll be halfway to Dublin before I let them catch me.''

"Let them…?'' She started to get out of bed but he put a hand on her shoulder to stop her. Now she realized for the first time what she had been too blind to notice before. He was dressed for riding, in boots, tunic and heavy cloak. Her heart leapt to her throat. He had come here to say goodbye. "What are you saying, Rory?''

"Listen to me, AnnaClaire. I've watched you with my family. Though there's been little time, they've accepted the fact that you are precious to me. Soon enough they'll see the goodness in you, and they'll love you for it. For yourself. What's more, Innis has even begun to look at you in a new way. My mother has told me how deeply he has grieved. For two years he has been sullen and silent. In just two days he has begun to speak to you. Soon, when he knows you as I do, he'll open to you like a flower to the sun. The boy needs you. Once I'm gone, the others will need you as well. Your strength. Your sweetness. Your courage.''

"And what about what I need?''

He heard the quaver in her voice and firmly shook his head. "I made you no promises, AnnaClaire. I knew I had no right. My duty now lies with leading the soldiers away from here. And when they finally catch me, I'll tell them you're dead.''

"You'd let them hang you for my murder?''

He touched a hand to her mouth, and felt the jolt, sharp and swift. He would have given anything for one more night in her arms. But it was not to be.

"A man can only hang once, AnnaClaire. I've always known 'twould be my fate.''

"I won't let you.'' She pushed against him and

scrambled out of bed. "I'll shout down the household. Your father will stop you. Your brother..."

He clapped a hand over her mouth to stifle her cries until he could gag her with a linen square from her night table. "I'm sorry, love. Truly I am."

While she kicked and struggled, he clasped her two hands in front of her and tied them tightly with the sash of her gown. Carrying her to the bed he laid her down, and tied her ankles as well. Then he pulled the covers up to her chin.

"I hope in time you will find it in your heart to forgive me, AnnaClaire. If you think but one thing of me in years to come, let it be this. I love you. More than I ever believed I could love anyone again." He pressed a kiss to the cloth covering her mouth. Against her temple he murmured, "How can I fear death, when I love you more than life itself?"

He crossed the room and let himself out without a backward glance. For to do so would have torn his heart from his chest and robbed him of all resolve.

As the door closed, hot tears scalded AnnaClaire's lids and spilled over to run in rivers down her cheeks.

Though she struggled and twisted and tugged, she was forced to admit that she was as helpless as a lamb being led to slaughter.

Her tears fell harder, faster. But it wasn't she being led to slaughter. It was Rory. And oh, the thought of it was more than she could bear.

Chapter Sixteen

Innis was having another nightmare. It was always the same. He was crossing the field with his family, dressed in his finest clothes. Up ahead was the tip of Croagh Patrick, gleaming gold in the sunlight. After an early morning rain it had turned into a sunny day, with only a sprinkle of clouds in the sky. A fine day for a wedding, his father was saying.

His Aunt Caitlin, his father's youngest sister, was surrounded by her smiling family as she made her way to Ballinarin and her soon-to-be-husband. Some were on horseback, some in wagons and carts. The rest were walking. Someone was singing. A high, lyrical voice that carried on the slight breeze. Because of the murmur of happy voices, and the occasional shout of a child, they didn't immediately hear the approaching horsemen. Then someone let out a cry. The crowd stopped, turned, and found themselves already under seige.

The soldiers had fanned out so that none of their victims could run to safety in the nearby forest. They targeted the men and boys first, so that the women and children would be unprotected.

Innis watched his father unsheath his sword as the first horseman attacked. His da was able to unseat the soldier, but before he could run him through, a second horseman approached from the other side and struck out, knocking the sword from his hand. A second blow sent the soldier's sword to his da's heart.

As the young father fell, he landed on top of his son, pinning him to the earth.

"Don't move, Innis," he managed to whisper. "If they think you're dead, lad, you'll survive."

They were the last words Innis ever heard his father speak. And every night since, he heard them as the nightmare unfolded in his mind. He'd been forced to lie there beneath his father's body, listening to the screams, watching as women and young girls were brutalized, then murdered. The soldiers had saved the worst for his own beautiful mother, and the young bride-to-be, Caitlin. And through it all he'd been forced to remain helpless.

The sound of his own cries awakened him.

He sat up, clenching his fists. He hated the night. Hated the dreams that tormented him. Hated these feelings of helplessness.

Hearing a loud thump from somewhere nearby, he climbed from bed to investigate. He wasn't afraid. After what he'd been through, nothing else would ever frighten him again. Except the night and its terrors.

Taking up a candle he let himself out of his room and began to move slowly along the hallway. Outside AnnaClaire's door, he paused to listen. There it was again, only louder. He knocked, then put his ear to the door. The pounding increased.

He pushed open and door and stared at the strange sight.

AnnaClaire was lying on the floor, caught up in a tangle of bed linens, kicking her feet against the wall.

"Englishwoman." He rushed to her and held the candle aloft. Seeing her bound and gagged, he hurriedly set aside the candle and began to pry loose her bonds.

"Who has done this terrible thing to you?" he demanded.

She was as angry as a spitting cat tossed in the river. For a moment she didn't make any sense.

"Rory O'Neil, damn his imperious hide. And when I catch him, I'll make him pay for this. But first, Innis, you must fetch me a horse and a weapon."

"A...weapon?"

"Aye. For before I make him pay for this I must first save his wretched, miserable life."

AnnaClaire moved quickly. There was no time to waste. Rory was rushing headlong toward disaster.

She pulled on her traveling cloak, then hurried down the stairs and out into the night.

At the stables Innis was waiting as he'd promised. When she drew near she saw him holding the reins of two horses.

"What do you think you're doing?" she demanded.

"I'm going with you." He boosted her to the saddle, then pulled himself up to the other horse.

"You'll do nothing of the sort." She caught his reins. "Get down at once. I'll not have you riding into danger."

"And how do you propose to stop me? I'll merely follow you when you've gone."

"Oh, Innis." She tugged fiercely on the reins, hoping to make him understand the seriousness of what she was about to do. "Give me your knife and go back to bed."

"And what would you do with the knife?"

"I can...brandish it. No one need know that I've never actually used it before."

"Aye. Well, I can take out a man's eye at twenty paces." He caught her arm, forcing her to look at him. "You need me, Englishwoman. I'll not let you go alone."

She glanced at the darkened keep and knew that she would never be forgiven for this, should the lad be harmed. But there was no time. She had to stop Rory before he made a terrible mistake.

She nodded. "All right, Innis. We go together. May God go with us."

She turned her mount and he did the same, racing across the sloping lawns of the estate, until they reached the silvery ribbon of road that led to the village.

Rory stood in the shadows and watched as the two soldiers passed a jug between them. From inside he could hear the sounds of rough voices and raucous laughter.

It was a simple matter to slip past the guards and climb through an upper window. From there he made his way along a balcony and down the stairs until he came to the public room of the inn.

With his face hidden beneath the hood of Friar Malone's coarse brown habit, he counted no more than a dozen soldiers. Puzzling. There had been twice as many horses at the stable. That meant that there were an equal number of soldiers somewhere in the village. Perhaps they were wenching and sleeping, he reasoned.

"Will ye' have an ale, Friar?"

Rory nodded and accepted the tankard from the young tavern wench. As he lifted it to his lips he studied the faces of each soldier. His hand froze in midair when he caught sight of the yellow hair.

All his carefully laid plans were forgotten. The disguise. The need for secrecy. The ruse he'd planned to get them to follow him out of the village and into the forest beyond. Suddenly, all he could see was a red blaze of fury as the image of Caitlin's bloody, battered body swam through his mind.

He hadn't expected this. After all these long months, the brawls, the battles, the physical hardship, the emotional toll, his goal was within reach. This changed everything. If it was indeed Tilden, there was no way he could simply leave and lead him on a merry chase. Still, though he was caught off guard, he managed a sip of ale, all the while waiting for the man to turn, so that he could be certain. He didn't want to make the same mistake he'd once made, killing an innocent soldier instead of the brute, Tilden.

A cluster of soldiers burst into laughter. The yellow-haired man turned. And Rory could see the puckered scar that ran from his chin to his eyebrow.

His blood pounded hot in his temples. Two years. Two years of pain and misery and unbelievable suffering. And it had all come down to this village, this pub, this man, who didn't deserve to live another minute.

AnnaClaire and Innis left their horses at the edge of the village, then made their way stealthily toward the lights of the tavern.

They darted behind a wall when they heard the sound of laughter.

"English soldiers," the lad said.

"How can you tell?"

"At this hour the villagers are abed. They'll be up tending their fields and flocks by dawn." He glanced around. "Odd."

"What is?"

"There are no guards out here."

"Why is that odd?"

"These soldiers are on foreign soil, Englishwoman. They've no reason to trust the people of the village. Unless…"

"Unless what?" she whispered fiercely.

His puzzled frown turned into a scowl. "Stay here," he said suddenly.

Before she could ask what he intended, he seized the low-hanging branch of a tree and began to climb. With all the grace and speed of a squirrel he climbed until he reached the upper window of the tavern, where a curtain fluttered in the night breeze.

For the space of several moments AnnaClaire watched. Then, cursing the clumsy skirts and petticoats that hampered her movements, she followed.

Innis was just about to ease open the door when he turned and caught sight of her.

"You should have stayed below, Englishwoman. Now wait here out of sight."

"I will not. Tell me what you suspect, Innis."

He took a deep breath. "All right. I think the English bastards are expecting a visit from the Blackhearted O'Neil this night. Why else would there be no guards outside?"

"A trap? Oh, sweet heaven." Her hand flew to her mouth. "Come, then, Innis. Open the door."

With a sigh he did as she ordered. The two stepped

into the hallway and made their way silently down the stairs toward the public room.

Rory felt as if time had stopped. At last his goal was within his reach. All the pain. All the misery. All the hatred. And the object of that hatred stood just a sword's length away.

His hand went to the weapon at his waist. As he unsheathed it, every man in the room turned to stare at him. The crowd had gone so silent he could hear his own heart beating in his chest.

The hair at the back of his neck prickled, and he realized too late that he had walked into a trap. He had seen it. Smelled it. And had chosen to ignore it. All because he'd let his emotions blind him.

A voice directly behind him said, "Lower your weapon, O'Neil. Or this will be the last breath you ever draw."

Rory swiveled his head to find a dozen sword tips pointed at his heart. "Aye, it may be my last breath," he said softly, "but at least I'll have the satisfaction of taking this bastard to hell with me."

Anticipating Rory's fury, Tilden caught the young serving wench and held her in front of him like a shield, pressing the blade of his knife to her throat with such force he drew blood. "Drop your weapon, O'Neil, or the wench dies."

The girl let out a shriek, and her father, the tavern owner, dropped to his knees and began to weep and plead for his daughter's life.

So near, Rory thought. So tantalizingly near, and yet, no matter how desperately he wanted Tilden, he couldn't let it cloud his sense of right and wrong. He mustn't be the cause of an innocent girl's death.

He let the sword drop from his hands. In the silence, it clattered to the floor. One of the soldiers kicked it away, to insure that Rory couldn't retrieve it.

''Now kill the Blackhearted O'Neil,'' someone shouted, and the blades of a dozen swords began slicing his flesh. A sword tip pierced his shoulder, branding him with searing fire. Another sword thrust through his arm, rendering the limb useless.

With blood streaming from a dozen wounds, Rory staggered, then dropped to his knees. But before the fatal plunge could be made, Tilden's voice broke through the shouting.

''Nay. Hold. I want this man kept alive.''

''Why?'' one of the soldiers demanded.

''Just do as I say. Bind him and put him on a horse.'' Tilden shoved the wench ahead of him toward a small back room. ''I have some unfinished business here.'' At the shouts and laughter that followed, he favored the others with an evil grin. ''But it shouldn't take long. These peasant lasses are little better than bloodless corpses. When I've finished with her, we ride to Dublin. There is a ship leaving for London on the morrow. And I intend to be on it. With the Blackhearted O'Neil in chains.'' He swaggered from the room, already savoring his homecoming.

With the Blackhearted O'Neil as his trophy, the queen would surely hail him a hero. As would all of England.

''Let go of me. Let go.'' AnnaClaire pushed furiously against the hand that had covered her mouth, stifling her cries. ''Don't you see? I must go to him. I must.''

She shoved at the lad who barred her way. But despite his slight size, Innis was amazingly strong.

"Nay, Englishwoman. Listen to me." He caught her arm and shoved her roughly against the wall, then suddenly shielded her body with his own as a line of soldiers trouped out, dragging Rory with them. "To show yourself now is to die."

"I don't care." The tears were dangerously close to the surface, and she wiped at them with the back of her hand. "Did you see him, all bloody and wounded? Innis, I must go to him."

"What you must do is save his life," he said on a hiss of fury. "And you'll not do that by revealing yourself to these bastards. If you do, they'll do worse than kill Rory O'Neil. They'll torment him by torturing and killing you before his eyes. Now what do you think that would do to him, my lady?"

"How would you know about such things?" The lad sounded so much like Rory, she could scarcely believe her ears.

"I saw what they did to my mum. And the others." His voice was tight, to keep the fear at bay. "It'll take more than the two of us to save Rory. But at least for now he's still alive."

When the room emptied he caught her hand, dragging her out into the darkness.

"Where are we going?"

"We must ride to Ballinarin. Our only hope now is to get the O'Neil to amass an army."

AnnaClaire was grateful for the boy's cool head. For, though she knew that he spoke the truth, her heart broke at the thought of riding away and leaving Rory in the hands of his cruel captors.

While she went through the motions, pulling herself into the saddle, taking the reins of her horse and following behind Innis, she couldn't get the image of Rory, all bloody and wounded, out of her mind.

Chapter Seventeen

As they raced along the road leading to Ballinarin, AnnaClaire wasn't certain which was pounding harder—the horses' hooves or her heart. The image of Rory, bloody and broken, was indelibly imprinted on her mind. It tore at her heart. Twisted inside her with a pain far worse than any knife. She had to save him. Had to. She wouldn't let herself think about the horrors he would have to endure. For to do so would leave her shattered.

She glanced at the darkened cottages of the villagers as she rode past. These simple men were farmers. Crofters. Shopkeepers. For so long, they had been downtrodden by the whims of imperious men from across the sea. Even if they were to rise up to defend one of their own, what chance would they have against seasoned soldiers?

Oh Rory, she thought. *Hold on. Please hold on. We'll find a way.*

Following Innis' lead, she leaned low over the horse's head and urged him into a run until they raced across the lawns and came to a stop in the courtyard.

"Wake the household," she shouted to the startled housekeeper as she and Innis burst through the door.

"But, my lady, they are still abed."

"I said wake them, Mistress Finn. Tell them to come at once to the library." To avoid further protest AnnaClaire hurried away, with Innis running alongside her to keep up with her frantic pace.

Gavin and Moira were the first to arrive. Though they were dressed, it was obvious that they had done so hastily, and weren't at all happy with being summoned like servants in their own home.

"You'd better have good reason for this, Englishwoman," Gavin muttered as he drew a cloak around his shoulders and ushered his wife closer to the fire.

Conor, his clothes disheveled, his hair flying, entered the room directly behind Briana.

He glanced around. "Where's Rory?"

"He's the reason I woke you." AnnaClaire stopped her pacing and glanced toward the doorway, where Friar Malone was just rushing in. He was the only one who looked as though he'd been up for hours. No doubt in prayer.

"Rory's been captured by English soldiers."

"And how would you know that?" Gavin demanded.

"Because I witnessed it."

The older man's eyes narrowed. "What are you saying, woman? Explain yourself."

"Rory planned to lead the soldiers away from Ballinarin, in order to save those he loved. But he fell into a trap. When he arrived at the village tavern, the soldiers were expecting him."

Briana's eyes rounded. "Is he dead then?"

"Nay." AnnaClaire heard the collective sigh of relief from his family. "But he was wounded. There were dozens of soldiers surrounding him as they led him away."

"Where will they take him?" Gavin asked.

"Tilden said he would take him to England."

Conor caught her arm in a rough grasp. "Tilden? That bastard's here?"

"Aye. He was the bait they used to trap Rory."

His eyes were hot and fierce. "And how is it that you were able to witness all this? How did you know what Rory was planning?"

"He came upon me as I was preparing to leave."

"Leave?" Gavin's tone was clipped. He took a step toward her.

"I was…planning to ride to the village and give myself up to the soldiers."

The older man's eyes narrowed in suspicion. "So that you could lead them to Rory?"

"Nay. So that I could lead them away. But when Rory heard my plan, he insisted that his was better. And safer. When I tried to stop him, he bound my hands and feet so I couldn't follow."

"Bound hand and foot and still you managed to escape?" It was clear that Gavin O'Neil didn't believe her.

"'Tis true," Innis said softly. "I heard her struggling. When I freed the lady and heard that she planned to go to the village alone, I insisted on going with her."

"Two fools. Two bloody fools." Gavin began to pace furiously before the fire. "I'll summon the chieftains of every village. Within days I'll have an army assembled. We'll stop the bastards."

AnnaClaire shook her head. "Even a day or two will

be too late. By then Rory will be on his way to Fleet Prison.''

"Damn them. Damn them all.'' Though Gavin was itching for a fight, he could see the wisdom of her words. "Aye. The bastards will want to parade their prize before the queen.'' He turned to his middle son. "Conor, you'll go to England at once. Use whatever contacts you have to prepare a defense of Rory at the Court of Elizabeth while I prepare an army.''

"Aye.'' Conor was relieved to have something tangible to do. It would replace this terrible, wrenching fear that his brother was doomed.

As he started toward the door AnnaClaire followed. "I can be ready to travel within the hour.''

"And where do you think you're going?'' Gavin's booming voice had everyone turning.

"Why, to England. With Conor.''

"Nay, lass. You'll stay here and honor Rory's wishes. This was what he wanted. That you stay here at Ballinarin where you'd be safe. And we'll damned well abide by his wishes.''

"That may be what he wanted. But it isn't what he needs.''

"And I suppose you claim to know what he needs?'' Gavin's tone was contemptuous.

"Aye. What he needs is someone who is comfortable at Court. Someone familiar with the people who surround the queen. I can introduce Conor to the men who have the queen's ear. Lest you forget, one of them is my father. I intend to plead for his help.''

Gavin pounded a fist on the mantel. "Your father is a bloody Englishman. Do you really think he'll care about the plight of an Irish outlaw?''

Her voice lowered with feeling. "He'll do it because

I'll ask him. And whatever else you think of him, he is a father who loves his only child.''

When the older man opened his mouth to protest, Moira touched a hand to his arm. "She's right, Gavin. Rory needs all the help we can give him. If AnnaClaire can help, we must accept it.''

Feeling betrayed, he fixed his wife with a look of fury. But the anger died when he saw the pain in her eyes. He closed a hand over hers, then gave a grudging nod of his head. "All right, lass. You'll go with Conor.''

They were all surprised when Innis said, "I want to be allowed to go, too.''

"To England?" Briana placed her hands on her hips. "You'd leave Ballinarin?''

"Rory needs me. More, Lady AnnaClaire needs me.''

"The Englishwoman?" Briana's eyes widened. "And why would she need the likes of you?''

"If I hadn't gone with her tonight, she'd have charged into the tavern and flung herself into the thick of the battle.''

Gavin studied the young woman with new respect. "A scrapper, is she, lad?''

"Aye. When she saw Rory's blood, I thought she'd scratch out the eyes of every soldier in the place.'' Innis turned away when he saw the look AnnaClaire sent him. "I have to go with her, or she's bound to do something foolish and dangerous.''

Moira's voice was choked with tears. "Nay, Gavin. You mustn't let him go. I couldn't bear it if I were to lose all my men this day.''

The older man's shoulders sagged. The thought had occurred to him, as well. Their family reunion had been so brief. And now they would once again scatter far across the sea. If this was all he could do, at least he would keep the youngest safe at home.

"You'll stay at Ballinarin, lad."

"It isn't fair. It's my fight as much as yours. I've lost my family. All of them. I don't want to lose Rory and…the Englishwoman as well."

Gavin's voice grew stern, to cover his churning emotions. "You heard me, boy. You'll stay here. We're your family now. And we'll keep you safe."

At that Innis pushed his way past AnnaClaire and Conor and raced up the stairs.

"Mistress Finn." Moira turned to the housekeeper, who stood just beyond the doorway, holding the hem of her apron to her eyes. Throughout their entire exchange she had taken in everything with sighs and moans, endlessly crossing herself. "Take the lad some broth later to cheer him. Now you'd best order a hearty meal before AnnaClaire and Conor depart."

The housekeeper nodded before turning away.

Friar Malone watched and listened in silence. Hadn't he just been wondering what sort of relationship would develop between the lad and the Englishwoman? And now, in the space of mere hours, so much had changed between them.

Perhaps it was the fact that AnnaClaire, like Innis, was an outsider, brought to Ballinarin for protection. But the old priest thought it was something much deeper. In his lifetime he'd seen every facet of human nature. If he had to hazard a guess, he'd say the lad had long harbored guilt that he hadn't been strong enough to save his mother from a horrible death. A death he'd been forced to witness, and relive in his mind over and over. Perhaps the lad was reasoning that with AnnaClaire he was being given another chance to protect a gentlewoman from all manner of frightful things.

Or perhaps, with the Englishwoman's coloring, the lad was beginning to see her as the mother he had lost.

Friar Malone shook his head. He hoped Innis would never be called upon to prove his courage. For if he were, the lad had the singlemindedness of one who would lay down his life before he would admit defeat again.

"Safe journey," Moira whispered as she kissed AnnaClaire's cheek.

"God go with you both," Friar Malone intoned as he lifted his hand in a blessing.

AnnaClaire and Conor pulled themselves onto their mounts and prepared for the long ride to Dublin. The wagon bearing their trunks and young Velia, who would serve as lady's maid to AnnaClaire, had already gone ahead.

AnnaClaire looked around the courtyard. All the servants had assembled, as well as many of the villagers, who had been summoned from the fields.

"I don't see Innis," she said.

Briana let go of her brother's hand and dabbed at her eyes. "The last I saw him, he was lying across his bed sulking."

"I wanted to tell him goodbye. And to thank him again for his help. He was so brave. He truly did save me from leaping into the fray."

"I'll tell him." Briana's voice was little more than a whisper. "He isn't the only one who is brave. I think what you're doing for my brother is the bravest thing I've ever known. You love him, don't you?"

AnnaClaire nodded.

Weeping, the girl turned away.

Moira stepped closer to press AnnaClaire's hand to her cheek. She looked up, meeting the younger woman's eyes. "I'm grateful for what you are doing."

"I have no choice. I have to be there, to do what I can."

"I know. I know now that you love Rory every bit as much as his father and I love him." Her lips trembled, but to her credit she kept her voice controlled. "You'll see that my son comes home to me?"

AnnaClaire nodded, suddenly too overcome with emotion to speak.

"And AnnaClaire," Moira said as she released her hand and took a step back. "I want you to come back to us as well." She nudged her husband. "Tell her."

The O'Neil cleared his throat. "Englishwoman..." He swallowed and tried again, his voice softening. "AnnaClaire Thompson, our home is yours. If you should..." He stopped, corrected himself. "*When* you manage to free our son, we pray you will return with him to Ballinarin."

"Thank you." It was all AnnaClaire could manage to whisper over the lump in her throat.

"Come," Conor said as he turned his horse. "We've a long journey ahead of us."

"Goodbye. God speed," came a chorus of voices as the horses' hooves clattered across the courtyard.

AnnaClaire looked over her shoulder, hoping to see Innis waving at one of the windows. But he was nowhere to be seen.

It was her last glimpse of Ballinarin. The sun was just burning off the mist that shrouded the towers. She felt a sharp tug and knew that this raw, savage land, like the man who loved it, had captured her heart.

AnnaClaire leaned on the rail of the ship and watched as the land seemed to slip away. So green. With that strange light casting a soft halo all about it. There was a softness, a gentleness, about the land that defied description. Rolling meadows dotted with sheep. Ancient stones keeping their silent sentinel on distant hillsides. The turrets of castles and graceful manor houses rising up beside thatched-roof cottages that looked as though they sprang up from the very earth. And in the bay, fishermen in their rough boats, casting their nets, as their fathers and grandfathers had before them.

Conor joined her at the rail. "Regretting your decision to leave?"

She shook her head. "I couldn't stay. Not knowing Rory is bound for Fleet." She drew her cloak firmly around her shoulders as the wind whipped up, filling the sails, sending the boat flying over the waves. "I can't bear to think of him in that filthy place."

"We'll free him, AnnaClaire." Conor looked down at her, saw the pain and the fear she couldn't hide.

She swallowed. Lifted her chin in that manner he'd come to recognize. "Aye. We will. Or die trying."

He touched a hand to her cold cheek. "I see why my brother loves you."

She turned away to hide the ache around her heart. "It isn't love, Conor. It's gratitude he feels for me. For taking him in. For hiding him."

"If you think that, my lady, you're sadly mistaken. I've seen the way Rory looks at you. What I see in his eyes isn't gratitude. It's love." He tipped up her chin and smiled. "I see the same look in your eyes, and it gladdens my heart."

"Truly?"

"Aye. I'd hate to think Rory had lost his heart to one who didn't share his feelings." His voice lowered. "'Tis a miracle that his broken heart could mend so thoroughly. But now that I've come to know you, I can understand it. You're good for him, AnnaClaire Thompson. Maybe the best thing that's happened to my brother in a very long time."

She felt tears burn her eyes and blinked furiously. Her emotions were entirely too close to the surface. She lifted herself on tiptoe and brushed a kiss over Conor's cheek. "Thank you, Conor. This wind is…stinging my eyes."

She hurried below deck to seek shelter from the wind, and from the storm that was whirling around her heart. Once inside her cabin, she closed the door and leaned wearily against it. Though she had put on a very brave face for the O'Neil family, the truth was, she had no idea how her father would react to her sudden appearance at Court. Especially when he learned that she had aligned herself with an Irish outlaw.

She slumped down on the edge of the cot. "There's no turning back now, my girl. You're bound for England."

"Are we truly?"

At the sound of the muffled voice, she jumped up and stared around the cramped cabin, then crossed to the tiny wardrobe. When she tore open the door she stared in shock and disbelief at the figure huddled beneath her clothes.

"Innis. How did you get here?"

"I hid myself in your trunk. Then, once it was carried aboard ship, I slipped out and mingled with the workers until Velia left your cabin. Then I sneaked in here to wait until we were underway.''

She shot him a look of indignation. ''Do you know what you've done?''

''Aye. I've disobeyed the O'Neil. He'll be furious.''

''Of that I have no doubt. And since I've tasted his temper, I don't envy you. But what about Moira? She'll be desperately afraid when she finds you missing, Innis.''

''I left her a missive, tucked under my bedcovers, explaining where I've gone and why. By the time she finds it, 'twill be too late to catch me. Just as it's now too late for you to send me back.''

''Is that so? What makes you think I won't?''

''Because you'd dare not waste the time it would take, Englishwoman.'' He stepped jauntily from the wardrobe and rubbed his damp hands along his sides. ''Twas a bit warm in there. But not nearly as uncomfortable as the trunk.''

''Oh, Innis,'' she said on a sigh. ''What am I to do with you?''

''You might try feeding me. I've had not a bite all day.''

She shook her head in exasperation. Then, at the realization of what he'd done, she wrapped her arms around him and drew him close. ''We may, none of us, come out of this alive, Innis. Have you thought of that?''

Feeling shy and awkward, he took a step back. ''Aye, Englishwoman. But if I must die, at least I'll die nobly, as my father and grandfather did. And I'll be in good company, with Rory and Conor.''

"Conor. Oh, sweet heaven. What will he say when he learns what you've done?"

"No more than you, I expect." He climbed up on her bunk and stared out the tiny porthole. "I've never been to England. Will it be so much different than Ballinarin?"

She stared at the little boy, who was so determined to be a man. With a sigh she muttered, "You'll see soon enough for yourself. Now I think it's time for us to go to Conor. You might prepare yourself for his temper."

He followed her from the cabin, completely unconcerned about what was to come. With the innocence of youth, he gave not a thought to those he'd left behind to fret and pace. Or to the dangers that awaited him at journey's end. For now, all that mattered was that he was here, aboard ship with the lady who, though one of the hated English, reminded him of his beautiful mother. And together they were about to embark on the adventure of a lifetime.

Chapter Eighteen

"Oh, my lady." Velia, trailing behind AnnaClaire and Conor, couldn't stop staring at the sights and sounds of the London docks. "I'm dizzy just seeing all this."

Innis, walking beside her, kept swiveling his head so he wouldn't miss anything. There were crates of animals. Monkeys, chattering to each other, to the delight of the crowd. A sleek tiger pacing back and forth, issuing fierce growls, while his handlers watched from a safe distance. There were baskets of fruit and sacks of teas and pungent spices. But it was the people who were the most fascinating. There were tall dark men with turbans, and exotic ladies with almond eyes and body-skimming gowns. Beggars, calling for alms from those who passed by. Elegant carriages bearing the wealthy, titled ladies, who shielded their faces from the sun with wide-brimmed bonnets and parasols. Gentlemen in fine coats, returning from voyages to India and France and Spain. And dandies in satin breeches and plumed hats, haggling with merchants and vendors.

In the midst of such chaos, AnnaClaire was grateful for Conor's quiet competence. It was clear that he had often traveled abroad and was comfortable dealing with their trunks and arranging carriages.

As their driver began lashing the trunks to the back of the carriage, Conor helped the others inside, then took his place across from AnnaClaire. "Are you certain your father will have no objection to sharing his London townhouse with members of the O'Neil household?"

"I have no way of knowing his reaction." She couldn't suppress a smile. "But I think it's safe to say he'll greet you at least as warmly as your father greeted me when he learned he had an Englishwoman at his table."

Conor winced. "My father's famous temper was a part of our daily lives. We were as accustomed to it as the winds that blow across Croagh Patrick. It must have been a shock to your delicate sensibilities, my lady."

"It was…interesting." She glanced at Innis, who was staring wide-eyed at the passing parade. "Just as London is proving to be interesting to our young lad. What think you, Innis?"

"So much to see. So many strange people. And all of them hurrying somewhere."

"Aye." She leaned back, feeling drained from their journey. "After my months in Dublin, I'd forgotten how frantic the pace of London can be."

The driver climbed to his seat and cracked the whip and the horse moved ahead with a slow, steady gait. Leaving the teeming masses of the docks behind, they rolled through the broad streets of London.

"The tailors work here." On Bond Street, AnnaClaire pointed to the cramped narrow shops. "And up here the butchers and bakers." They inhaled the fragrance of freshly baked bread that wafted from the shops.

In a pretty green park, children played under the watchful eye of their mothers or nurses, who sat gossiping on stone benches. Warm spring sunshine added to the gaiety of the scene.

The carriage slowed, then veered along a winding drive planted with hedges. "This is where my father lives when he is in London," AnnaClaire said simply.

It was an elegant home of three stories, with a caretaker's cottage in front and a splendid carriage house off to one side.

When the driver reined in his horse, the front door opened and a servant, spying AnnaClaire, came forward with a bright smile.

"Oh, my lady. We received no notice that you were coming home."

"I know, Wilona. There was no time to notify my father. Is he home?"

"Nay, my lady. He is with the queen at Greenwich Palace."

"Then the queen is in residence here in London?"

"Aye, my lady. We've scarcely seen your father since the queen returned. He spends all his time at Court."

AnnaClaire gave a sigh of resignation. She had hoped for some time alone with her father, to explain all that had happened to her, and to seek his counsel on the wisest course of action regarding Rory. Now, she and Conor, it would seem, would have to make their choices blindly.

"Wilona, this is Velia. If you'll show her to my rooms, I'll be along shortly. My friends and I would like to refresh ourselves in the parlor."

The little maid nodded. "Aye, my lady. I'll ask Cook to see to it at once."

AnnaClaire led Innis and Conor through the familiar rooms of her family home until they reached the parlor. Unlike the keep at Ballinarin, this room was light and airy, with peach-colored walls and soft draperies at the windows that fluttered in the afternoon breeze. Despite the warmth of the day, a fire burned on the hearth, adding to the coziness of the room.

Innis moved around the room, pausing to study a miniature portrait on a highly-polished table before snuggling into the comfort of a chaise. "Is this where you live?"

AnnaClaire nodded. "Sometimes." She glanced around at the familiar things she'd known since her childhood. "We have a lovely estate in Berkshire, and another in Surrey."

Conor, feeling restless, paced to the window. "With so many homes here, why did you go to Dublin?"

"It's where my mother wanted to be." AnnaClaire's tone softened, as it always did when she spoke of her mother. "She knew she was dying and wanted to die on Irish soil. At the time, I didn't understand. But now I do. Ireland held her heart. Just as it now holds mine."

Both Conor and Innis were watching her with identical looks of surprise and pleasure at her admission. She looked up as the maid entered carrying a silver tray.

"Cook asks if you and your guests will be staying for supper, my lady."

AnnaClaire looked to Conor for confirmation. At a shake of his head she said, "Not tonight, Wilona." She glanced at the boy, who was struggling to keep his eyes open. "But you can take young Innis above stairs to my chambers. After he rests, he'll take a meal with Velia.''

"Aye, my lady." The maid poured tea and uncovered a plate of thinly-sliced beef and an assortment of fruits and cheeses. Then, with Innis in tow, she started to leave the room.

At the door the lad turned and walked back to AnnaClaire. Catching her hand he said, "When this is over, will you return to Ballinarin with Rory?"

She squeezed his hand. "It is my fondest wish, Innis."

"And mine." He chose his words carefully. "I've long wished that Rory would be my father. I'd like you to be my mother. Would you mind, Englishwoman?"

"Mind?" She dropped to her knees and gathered him close. "Oh, Innis. More than anything, I would have you for my son."

He drew back and stared into her eyes. Then, with that solemn look she had come to recognize, he turned and followed the maid from the room.

For long minutes after the door closed behind them, she was unable to speak over the lump in her throat.

At last she turned to Conor who was watching her carefully. "Have you a plan?"

"Of sorts." He, too, was moved by what he'd just seen and heard. And more determined than ever to succeed. "We must request an audience with the queen. I was hoping your father might arrange that. But first, I must find a way to see Rory. I need to see for myself that he is…" His voice trailed off. He couldn't stop thinking about the gruesome tales he'd heard of the treatment of Irish prisoners on the journey to Fleet Prison, and in the prison itself.

AnnaClaire had no need to hear. Just seeing the look

on his face had her heart nearly stopping. She set down her cup with a clatter and started toward the door. ''We'll find a way to see him. Perhaps we could bribe a jailer?''

Conor closed a hand over her arm, stopping her in mid-stride. ''Hold, my lady. Fleet is no place for you. You'll stay here with Innis.''

''I'll do no such thing. I've come this far, Conor. I'll see it through. Besides, I know the streets of London. I can lead you to Fleet and back. You see, Conor, you need me, if you hope to get through the next few days.''

He took one look at the lift of her chin, the set of her jaw, and burst into laughter. ''By the heavens, I'm beginning to see what my brother had to put up with. All right. We'll go together. But I warn you, my lady, you'll be shocked by what you'll see in that filthy place.''

AnnaClaire was more than shocked. She was stunned. Horrified. Her stomach rolled and she gagged with every step, as she and Conor descended rough stone steps that led into the very bowels of the cavernous prison.

It was dark as a tomb. Except for tiny slits cut in the rough stone walls, allowing for a little light, there was no way of knowing if it was day or night. The fetid air reeked of human waste and decay. Some cells held more than a dozen prisoners, some chained, others lying about, too weak to stand. All around them were the sounds of sobbing, wailing, moaning. It was a scene out of a nightmare.

It had taken a purse of gold to persuade the jailer to lead them to the Irish prisoner. Even then he probably would have left them lost and confused had Conor not had the foresight to withhold half the purse until they were standing outside Rory's cell.

"Here." Conor thrust the rest of the gold into the man's outstretched hand. "See we're not accosted. If you do so, and warn us of anyone approaching, there will be more when we leave."

"Aye." The burly guard shoved the coins inside his tunic and handed Conor a torch before striding away.

Conor held the torch aloft and strained to see beyond the bars of the rusted door. This was a single cell, far from the others. Inside, a lone prisoner was sprawled on the cold stone floor.

"Dear God." For a moment Conor thought he might be dead. "Rory. Rory, speak to me."

The figure lifted his head and moaned. Conor and AnnaClaire turned to each other with identical sighs of relief.

"You're alive then, Rory," Conor called.

For a moment the figure blinked against the light of the torch. Then, holding an arm to his face to sheild his eyes, he muttered, "Barely. Is it you, Conor?"

"Aye."

"I'm here too, Rory love."

At the sound of AnnaClaire's voice he struggled to his knees and turned away from the light. "For God's sake, Conor, get her out of here."

"Oh Rory." She tried to keep the jumble of emotions from her voice, but it was impossible. "We've come to plead for your life. We'll go to the queen. We'll…"

"You're wasting your time." He cut her off abruptly. "My life is over. Tilden has said he'll see me dead before he'll ever release me from this hell. He's a hero now. His queen is about to welcome him in a lavish ceremony. When it's over, he'll announce that I attempted to flee and my jailers had to kill me." With his back to them he said, "Now take her out of here, Conor. And see that she doesn't come back."

AnnaClaire's voice trembled with emotion. "I never thought you a coward, Rory O'Neil."

"A coward?"

"Aye. A coward who would give up without a fight."

He did turn then and struggled to his feet. In that moment both AnnaClaire and Conor had a chance to see just how devastating his wounds were. His clothes were torn and bloody, his hair matted with dried blood. His face had been battered viciously. One eye was closed. The other bore a gash from brow to temple. He had tied a dirty rag around his thigh to stem the flow of blood from a gaping wound, and his left arm hung uselessly at his side.

"Oh, my beloved." Though AnnaClaire couldn't stop the tears that streamed down her face, she forced herself to go on. "If you must give up, then so be it. But I will not. I'll never give up." She opened her cloak and slipped a bundle through the narrow bars of his cell. "We've brought you warm blankets, and food, and ointment for your wounds. And tomorrow we'll go to the queen. We'll beg, we'll plead, we'll do whatever we must. But we won't stop until you're free of this place and safely home in Ballinarin." She wiped at the tears with the back of her hand. "I love you, Rory O'Neil. And even if you've stopped believing, I never will. Nor will I stop fighting for you. With my last breath I'll fight for you."

At her impassioned words he staggered across the

cell and touched a finger to her face. "Oh my darling AnnaClaire. My fierce little angel. Of course I'll fight. Until there's no life left in me, I'll fight to be free. But I can't bear that you see me like this, in this place."

She lifted a hand to his bruised, bloody face. "Conor tried to keep me away. But I had to come, Rory."

They stared hungrily at each other for long silent moments.

At last Rory turned to Conor, and the two brothers clasped hands through the bars.

"Ye' must leave," came the whispered warning of the jailer. "Soldiers are coming. If ye're found here, we'll all lose our lives."

"Come. Quickly." Conor placed an arm beneath AnnaClaire's elbow, forcing her away from Rory's cell.

Without another word, they followed the jailer through the maze of darkened hallways until they were once more breathing the air of freedom.

As their carriage bore them back to the townhouse, neither of them spoke a word. But their thoughts were as dark, as bleak as the cell in which Rory lay bleeding.

"Your father is home from Court, my lady. He anxiously awaits you in the library."

"Thank you, Wilona." AnnaClaire had washed and changed her clothes since her return from prison, and had eaten a cold supper with Conor.

She turned to him with a weary sigh. "It's best if I see him alone."

He nodded and followed the maid up the stairs to the guest chambers. AnnaClaire made her way to the library, where she found her father standing at the window, staring into the darkness.

"Father. Oh, I've missed you so."

At the sound of her voice Lord James Thompson turned. "Can it be? Oh, my dear AnnaClaire. How I've worried about you."

She rushed to his arms and was caught in a warm embrace.

For the longest time, he couldn't seem to let go of her as he kissed her hair, her cheeks, her temple, all the while murmuring words of love. At last he held her a little away.

He narrowed his eyes and took the time to study her. "You look...different. I believe you've lost weight." His brows drew together. "Have you been ill? Have the O'Neils treated you unkindly?"

"Oh, nay." Her brows shot up. "You received my missive then?"

"Aye, AnnaClaire. And another, earlier one from the one they call the Blackhearted O'Neil. He wanted to assure me on his honor as a gentleman that you were safe and well. But, knowing his reputation as a rogue and outlaw, and hearing the way Dunstan and Lord Davis have spoken of him, I couldn't stop fearing the worst. Now, you will tell me everything, AnnaClaire."

He led her toward a chaise. As he sat, he clasped her hands. "Wilona has said you did not come alone."

"I've brought...friends with me."

"Are these friends from Dublin?"

"Nay. Their home is far from Dublin. But..." She released his hands and began to pace in front of the fireplace. "Oh, how can I tell you all that has happened since you left Dublin?"

Seeing her agitation, he folded his hands and regarded her carefully. "Perhaps you should begin at the beginning."

* * *

AnnaClaire made her way to her chambers. The house at this hour was silent. Outside, the midnight sky was ablaze with starlight. But her thoughts weren't on the stars, or sleep, though she'd put in an exhausting day.

Her father had been so silent, so thoughtful throughout her narrative. So unlike the O'Neil. She had anticipated his calm, cool reaction. He was, after all, a man who had long ago accepted the fact that his daughter had a mind of her own. But she could see also that his feelings were raw and wounded. And all because of her carelessness.

"Did you not stop and think about the consequences of your actions?" he had asked.

"Nay, Father."

"And even now, you continue to rush to judgment. You bring the O'Neil's family into my very home. And you dare to ask for an audience with the queen." He had looked at her with sad, tired eyes.

She paused outside Conor's door and was still twisting her hands together when the door suddenly opened.

"Conor. I didn't even knock yet."

"I know, my lady. I've been pacing, and waiting, and listening." He ushered her inside and quickly closed the door.

Across the room Innis slept so soundly, he didn't even stir.

"You told your father?"

She nodded. "Everything."

"How did he react?"

She shrugged. "As I'd expected. My actions have caused him much pain. He fears he has raised a fool for a daughter."

Conor winced, recalling his own father's fury. "That's it, then. I'll find lodging in London on the morrow. And then I'll begin calling in favors from everyone my family has ever known. Sooner or later someone will show me the way to petition the queen for an audience."

"Someone already has." She caught his hands, squeezed. And, despite her exhaustion, her smile was radiant. "Though my father is hurt and angry, he is still my father. It took a great deal of convincing, but he has agreed to take us with him on the morrow."

"Take us with him?"

"To Court, Conor." She kissed his cheek. "To see the queen."

"Oh, my lady." As soon as AnnaClaire entered her sleeping chamber, the little maid rushed to her side to assist her. "I was afraid you wouldn't get to sleep at all this night."

"Sleep doesn't matter, Velia. Nothing matters now except getting Rory out of that filthy prison."

"You saw him then?"

"Aye." AnnaClaire struggled to put aside the memory. "I must be up at dawn, Velia."

"At dawn? But why so early, my lady?"

"Conor and I must go over our plans once more, before we leave for Greenwich Castle."

"Greenwich?" The little maid clapped a hand to her mouth. "You will see the queen?"

"Aye." AnnaClaire climbed beneath the covers and watched as Velia blew out the candle.

In the darkness Velia whispered, "How does one prepare for such a momentous event, my lady?"

AnnaClaire felt the knot of fear that no amount of

false bravado could hide. "All one can do now is pray."

"Then I shall pray, my lady. For you. For the O'Neil family. And for the queen, that she will regard your petition with kindness. Good night, my lady."

When she was alone, AnnaClaire felt hot tears well up and spill down her cheeks. After what she had been through, she had thought she was beyond crying. But the truth was, she was terrified of what was to come on the morrow. Elizabeth, the willful fierce young monarch said to be as unyielding as her father, held the fate of Rory, his family, and his beloved country in her hands.

Chapter Nineteen

"There is Greenwich Castle." AnnaClaire watched the reaction of Conor and Innis as their carriage started up the long curving drive.

The queen's standard flew from the turret, announcing that the monarch was in residence. If that were not enough, the long columns of soldiers standing guard along the perimeter made their own statement.

"Why does the queen require so many soldiers?" Innis asked. His voice, AnnaClaire noted, was not quite steady. But to his credit, he had insisted upon coming with them. AnnaClaire realized that he had appointed himself her protector.

"They are members of the queen's own guard. It is their job to defend her at all times, against all danger."

Lord Thompson glanced at the handsome young man seated next to his daughter. Though they had exchanged less than a dozen words, he had already discovered, much to his surprise, that Conor O'Neil was educated and well-spoken. "Have you thought of what you will say to the queen?"

"Aye."

When he offered nothing more, James changed the

subject. In an aside he whispered to his daughter, "Do you think it wise to bring the lad?"

"Conor and I could see no way of refusing. If we'd ordered him to remain behind, he'd have simply found a way to defy us and would have turned up at Court anyway. At least this way, we'll know what he's up to. Otherwise, we feared we might find him joining Rory in Fleet."

"Is that how the Irish are raising their young?"

"It isn't just an Irish flaw." She looked at her father. "Last night you called me defiant. And foolish."

He smiled and caught her hand. "Aye. You are both, I fear. Traits you inherited from your defiant, foolish parents."

She flushed with pleasure, and was even more surprised when he lifted her hand to his lips. "Have I told you that I'm proud of you, my dear?"

She felt both surprise and happiness at his words. Before she could respond, the carriage came to a halt and a footman hurried to assist them.

Once inside the splendid castle, Lord Thompson led them past the throngs of titled people who milled about and ushered them into the Throne Room, where Elizabeth held Court.

He turned to Conor and Innis. "I must ask that you relinquish any weapons you may possess."

Conor touched a hand to the sword at his waist. "Why must I give this up?"

"Because you will be in the presence of the queen. The soldiers who guard her person will arrest anyone found concealing a weapon."

Conor grudgingly removed his sword from its sheath and handed it over.

When Innis made no move to follow his lead

AnnaClaire nudged him. "I know you carry a knife. You must give it up."

"Never, Englishwoman."

She glanced at Conor for support. At a nod of his head, the lad bent and removed the sharp dagger from his boot, placing it in Lord Thompson's hand.

As her father walked away, Innis turned to her with a scowl. "You've left me defenseless, Englishwoman."

"I think it is a better choice than being jailed."

They turned their attention to the colorful pageantry around them. Most of the nobility came to watch the proceedings, which offered them a constant source of entertainment. Elizabeth, enjoying her power, presided over everything from petty crimes to squabbles between vendors and their patrons. Her wit was said to be quick and cutting. Her wisdom was admirable. And her patience was always on a short tether.

Lord Thompson spoke with a man in gold and scarlet robes, who listened, nodded, then walked from the room. When her father returned to her side he said to AnnaClaire, "You and your friends will wait here until you are summoned before the queen."

Conor watched him walk away. "Your father won't be waiting with us?"

AnnaClaire shook her head. "My father is one of the queen's counsellors. He must stand by her side to assist if she should have any questions regarding the law of the land. But he cautioned me that there is little he can do or say that will help our cause."

Just then AnnaClaire looked up and gave a little groan of dismay. Walking toward her was Lord Dunstan.

"My dear lady. I just heard the good news from your

father.'' He caught her hand and lifted it to his lips, then stepped back to give her a long, appraising look. ''You seem none the worse for your ordeal.''

''I'm fine, my lord. Truly,'' she added when he gave her a look of skepticism.

''You'll be much better when you've had time to wash the taste of that filthy island from your lips.'' He placed her hand on his sleeve. ''Come. We'll sit with Lord Davis and Lady Thornly.''

''They're here?'' She glanced around and, seeing her old friends, waved to them across the room.

''Aye. They returned aboard ship with me, to lend whatever solace they could to your father during these trying times. Praise heaven you've been rescued from that madman.'' He turned to glance at the young man and boy who flanked her. ''And who might this be?''

''The madman's brother.'' Conor's tone was carefully controlled.

''Conor O'Neil, this is Lynley Lord Dunstan.'' As the two men nodded, AnnaClaire added, ''And this is Innis Maguire.''

Dunstan glanced from them to AnnaClaire and then back again in puzzlement. ''Now that you are free, why would you willingly associate with your captor's family?''

''To know us is to love us,'' Conor said with a grin.

Beside him, Innis snorted with laughter.

Before they could continue, the gentleman in gold and scarlet entered the room to announce the queen. At once the crowd fell silent. When Elizabeth entered, the men bowed and the women curtsied. No one straightened until the queen had ascended her throne.

Elizabeth wore a gown of royal purple, with a girdle encrusted with jewels. At her neck was a starched jeweled ruff and a long triple rope of pearls that hung to her waist. There were more jewels glittering in her hair. She was an imposing presence. One accustomed to holding her subjects spellbound.

The queen was surrounded by her counsellors, who took seats to her right and left. Behind them stood a cluster of soldiers, who formed a half circle, their swords lifted in salute. Standing in a position of honor, directly in the center of the ring of soldiers, was the one known as Tilden.

AnnaClaire glanced at Innis, who had caught her hand and was gripping it so hard she had to bite back a cry. His eyes were huge, his mouth open. She turned to Conor, who had gone pale.

"The bastard," Conor whispered under his breath. "If I had my sword, I'd kill him where he stands."

AnnaClaire touched a hand to his arm. "You have a better weapon, Conor. The truth will set Rory free and strip Tilden of any shred of honor."

Though she spoke bravely enough, she was relieved that both Conor and Innis had ordered to relinquish their weapons. After seeing what his brother had suffered, she had no doubt that Conor would have leapt into battle, ending any chance they had of saving Rory's life. As for Innis, there was no way of knowing how the lad would have reacted.

For several hours they were forced to watch and listen as the queen settled one matter after another. Some were sad or tragic, as in the case of a midwife who had told a weeping young mother that her infant was stillborn, only to deliver the baby to a friend who was barren. Elizabeth electrified the crowd by ordering the midwife to relinquish her own child into bondage to the young mother for one year.

Some of the cases brought before the queen were silly, such as the tavern owner who incurred the wrath of a bride whose husband returned home too drunk to bed her. The queen's laughter faded when the tavern owner admitted that he had also taken a good part of the bride's dowry in payment for the ale. He was not only ordered to make restitution, but was ordered to share the profits of his tavern for a fortnight.

With each case brought before her, Elizabeth became more snappish. It was plain that the lateness of the hour and the endless misery of so many of the petitioners were beginning to take their toll upon their monarch.

Suddenly they heard the queen's counsellor announce, "In the matter of the arrest of the Irish outlaw, Rory O'Neil, known as the Blackhearted O'Neil, his brother, Conor O'Neil, has petitioned to address Your Majesty and to have his brother brought before this court."

There was a loud murmur among the onlookers, and AnnaClaire could overhear enough of the words to know that the people were angry and outraged that the brother of such an infamous outlaw would dare to approach the queen.

When Rory was brought before them in shackles, the crowd erupted in shouting and cursing. Many of the women, seeing his bruised and battered face, had to hold handkerchiefs to their noses to keep from fainting.

Tilden, standing behind the queen, scowled as his hand tightened on the hilt of his sword.

AnnaClaire blinked furiously to keep from weeping. She would not disgrace herself by giving in to tears. But her heart ached at the sight of the man she loved shackled like a common criminal.

Rory stared around the room until his gaze settled

on AnnaClaire. A hint of a smile touched his lips. Seeing it, Dunstan placed an arm around her shoulder and drew her close to whisper in her ear. Though she tried to draw away, he held her firmly, then turned to Rory with a knowing smile. He was pleased to see Rory's hands clench into fists at his sides.

"It appears," Dunstan whispered, "the Blackhearted O'Neil has been shorn of his power, my lady. He'll not lay a hand on you again."

AnnaClaire, pale and shaken, pushed away. But it was too late. Rory had already turned his head, refusing to look her way again.

Elizabeth could hardly bring herself to look at the prisoner. "It is obvious that this man has been tortured."

Tilden took a step out of the circle. "With your permission, Majesty, I can explain."

She waved a hand imperiously. "You have my permission to speak."

"This prisoner, the Blackhearted O'Neil was, like many of the Irish peasants, so belligerent, so dangerous, so thick-headed—" He glanced at the crowd of nobles and saw many of them nodding in agreement "—that the only way to subdue him was to beat him senseless. My men and I were loath to inflict such punishment, but he gave us no choice."

"I understand." Elizabeth waved him aside. "It is the price one must pay for protecting queen and country." She glanced around. "Who speaks for the prisoner?"

"Majesty." Conor stepped forward and bowed before the woman on the throne.

Elizabeth turned away from the bloodied prisoner, finding the sight of him too much for her delicate sensibilities. Instead, she watched Conor closely, as did every other man and woman in the room. There was a grace about him, a charm, a poise that commanded attention.

"I am Conor O'Neil, brother of Rory, and son of Gavin and Moira O'Neil. My home is Ballinarin, of the Hidden Kingdom in Ireland."

"And why is your home called the Hidden Kingdom?" Elizabeth asked imperiously.

"Because for centuries our enemies could not find their way in or out of Ballinarin. We believe it is watched over by spirits. And all who dwell therein are blessed by those same spirits."

"Spirits, you say?" Elizabeth couldn't help smiling. This was more like it. A lively exchange was just what she enjoyed. Besides, not only was this man easy to look at, but his cultured voice was deep and strong. She sat back, prepared to enjoy herself. "What do you ask of this court?"

Conor took a step closer, so that their glances could lock. It was a calculated risk. He was aware that Elizabeth held herself above all her subjects. But she was a woman. And he was a man who knew exactly how to look at a woman and make her feel special. "I ask only a chance to be heard. I know that I will receive a fair hearing from Your Majesty, for your reputation for fairness is known throughout the land."

Her smile deepened. Not just lively, but flattering. A man after her own heart. "It is so. Speak then, Conor O'Neil. You will receive what you request. Justice. Nothing more."

"I am most grateful, Majesty."

Again Elizabeth found herself pleasantly surprised. Instead of the stilted argument she was expecting,

Conor tossed his cloak rakishly off his shoulder and began to speak of his home and his family. He told of a special day, a wedding day, when his brother prepared to meet his bride.

AnnaClaire looked around. The crowd had gone completely silent, hanging on his every word. When he described the scene of carnage and the pain his brother had endured, several women were seen to wipe tears from their eyes. Even the queen seemed moved.

She held up a hand. "What you have described is an outrage. Are you suggesting such things were done at my command?"

"The soldiers who commited these crimes have spread the word that they do the bidding of their queen. But I and many of my countrymen do not believe the Queen of England would order her soldiers to slay innocent women and children on their way to chapel."

"Nor would I ever issue such a command, Conor O'Neil. If this terrible act was committed by soldiers of the Crown, they were not acting on my orders, but on their own cruel whims."

"Aye, Majesty. I believe that to be the case. You are a kind and benevolent monarch, who would not tolerate such cruelty."

"Your queen thanks you for your trust, Conor O'Neil. But such fine words do not absolve your brother of his crimes." She pointed a finger, and everyone in the room turned to stare at the man in chains. "It is said that Rory O'Neil, the Blackhearted O'Neil, has killed many an innocent Englishman in the name of vengeance. If that be true, he is no better than a wild dog that must forfeit its life for the good of mankind."

"Majesty, if what you say about my brother be true, I must agree with you."

This brought a loud murmur from the crowd.

"But what if the only ones killed by my brother are English soldiers?" Conor lowered his voice, so that the crowd was forced to grow silent once more in order to hear. "The same English soldiers who have brutalized innocent women and children. The same English soldiers who have burned the huts of hard working, God-fearing farmers. The same English soldiers who slaughtered their herds and looted their crops."

"If that be true, and it can be proved to the satisfaction of this court, such a man would be hailed a hero, and the soldiers involved would be sent to Fleet in his place." The queen leaned forward, so that her eyes were level with Conor's. "But this court would demand witnesses, who would swear to such horrors."

"Majesty, if I were given enough time, I could produce such witnesses." Conor saw Tilden relax his hold on his sword, before his scowl turned into a smug smile. In his youth, Conor had done enough fishing with Fiola the cook to know when to give the fish more line, and when to reel it in. He decided to give Tilden just a bit more line.

"I suppose you have witnesses who will testify against my brother and swear to all manner of brutal acts which they will swear he committed?"

The queen nodded. "The soldier who captured the Blackhearted O'Neil has detailed your brother's crimes. Crimes, I might add, against helpless women and children. For his courage in ridding the kingdom of such a mad dog, this soldier will be honored by his queen." She signalled to Tilden, who stepped forward smartly. "This man will become an officer in the Queen's Guards, and will be directly responsible for the safety of my person."

There was a smattering of applause, and Tilden flushed with pride.

"It was this man, then, who gave witness against my brother? This man who will now enjoy a hero's reward, Majesty?"

She nodded.

"Was it his testimony alone which has condemned my brother?"

Elizabeth was growing weary of the questions. She leaned back, tapping a finger on the arm of her throne. "Aye, Conor O'Neil. This man's word against the Blackhearted O'Neil."

"If then, this court accepts the word of one man, an English soldier, as proof of my brother's crimes, I would suppose this court would also accept the word of one witness against that same English soldier."

Elizabeth couldn't hide her annoyance. "It would. But you said you had no time to produce such witnesses."

"Aye, Majesty. There are countless men, women and children in my country who would gladly come forth to testify against the cruelty of this soldier. Alas, there is no time to send for them. But I do have one witness here at Court. And since you require only one, that will suffice."

Again the room erupted with murmurs and cries of outrage.

The queen held up a hand for silence.

A hush fell over the crowd.

"If you can produce such a witness, let him speak."

Conor turned to Innis. The boy stood quaking, his hand clutching AnnaClaire's so hard, the knuckles had gone white.

She knelt down and stared deeply into his eyes. "You must do this, Innis."

He shook his head. "Speak to the queen herself? I…cannot. Give me back my knife, and I'll cut out the heart of the bastard, Tilden. But I cannot speak in front of this company."

"You must. You must do it for Rory. And for yourself and your family. Don't you see, Innis? This is how you can avenge their deaths. This is how you will fight. Not with sword and knife, like Rory. But you will fight all the same. Like Conor. With words. With the truth."

She gave him a gentle shove.

Conor took his hand and led him before the queen. "Majesty, this is Innis Maguire."

The queen crooked a finger, beckoning the lad closer. "Come, Innis Maguire. Tell us what you know."

"I…" He swallowed several times, and cleared his throat. Seeing a blur of movement behind the queen, he looked up to see Tilden holding his sword at the ready. How he yearned for his knife. For the courage it would give him. But there was no weapon, save one.

He swallowed back his fear, clenched his hands at his sides and tried again. "I watched the soldiers kill my mum and da, my grandda and grandma, my aunts and uncles and cousins. They even killed the babies who had fallen to the ground from their mothers' arms. And all the while they were killing, they were laughing, and jeering."

The queen was visibly moved. "You truly witnessed this?"

He nodded.

"And you alone survived?"

"Aye." He swallowed. "Aye, Majesty."

"How is it that you survived while all the others died?"

"My da shielded me with his body. He died saving me."

Elizabeth paused for a moment, studying the solemn lad before her. "And you saw the men who did this?"

"I did. The leader had yellow hair, and a scar that ran from the corner of his brow to his chin."

The crowd was already murmuring and pointing at the soldier who stood behind the throne, but the queen lifted a hand in an imperious gesture. "Go on, boy. Do you know this soldier?"

"Aye, Majesty. He stands behind you now. The soldiers with him called him by name. Tilden."

The once-orderly crowd erupted into chaos. Men were shouting, swearing. Women were shrieking.

Elizabeth lifted a hand for silence. To Innis she said, "These are powerful words you have spoken, boy. Because of them, I will consider carefully."

Pointing a finger at Rory she said, "Return the prisoner to Fleet until such time as I can determine his fate."

"But Majesty…" Conor's words were cut off by an imperious look from the queen.

"My soldiers will accompany Officer Tilden to his quarters and await my decision as well."

As Tilden marched past Rory he shot him a look of triumph and leaned close to whisper, "This time, O'Neil, the beatings won't end until you're dead."

Overhearing him, AnnaClaire rushed forward and fell on her knees before the queen. "Please, Majesty." She knew her voice was trembling. "I beg you not to return Rory O'Neil to prison."

Elizabeth turned to Lord Thompson. "What is the meaning of this? Is this not your daughter?"

He got to his feet. "Aye, Majesty. My daughter, AnnaClaire."

"The one who was kidnapped by this very outlaw?"

"Aye, Majesty. The same."

"Take this impertinent young woman to my chambers. At once," the queen added with a note of righteous anger. "Before I give her a taste of my temper."

Chapter Twenty

"AnnaClaire, my dear, I beg of you." Lord Thompson kept his spine stiff, his smile pasted on his face as he walked with his daughter to the queen's withdrawing room. "I have learned to gauge Elizabeth's many moods. She has reached the end of her patience, my girl. Hold your tongue, or you will pay a terrible price. Do you understand?"

AnnaClaire nodded. "Aye, Father. But I must let her know what I overheard. Tilden…"

"Not one word, do you hear…?" His whispered warning died in his throat as the queen charged into the room, followed by her advisors.

AnnaClaire's heart sank when she saw that Lord Dunstan was among those surrounding the queen.

Elizabeth accepted a tankard of ale from a liveried servant and sipped. Then she sank into a chair and regarded the young woman in silence. As the seconds ticked by, AnnaClaire could feel her frantic pulse pounding in her temples.

At last the queen spoke.

"Lynley Lord Dunstan has told me that you were taken from your home, against your will, by that Irish outlaw. How is it that you now join his brother in pleading for his life?''

''Because I have learned that he is a good man, Majesty. A man from a fine and noble family, who suffered the loss of the woman he...'' Her voice wavered before she finally managed to say, ''...the woman he loved.''

Elizabeth's gaze pinned her. More seconds ticked by as she watched AnnaClaire with a puzzled frown. Without warning she waved a hand at the others. ''Leave us. I wish to speak to this lady alone.''

The men glanced at one another in surprise, then slowly took their leave one by one. Lord Thompson and Dunstan were the last to go, though each took long moments to look from AnnaClaire to the queen before closing the door.

When the two women were alone, Elizabeth stood and walked to the fireplace. For long moments she kept her back to AnnaClaire, while she stared into the flames.

''So. You love this Irish peasant.'' It wasn't a question. It was a statement, uttered as calmly as though she were discussing the weather.

Stunned, AnnaClaire cleared her throat before saying softly, ''Aye, Majesty.''

Elizabeth turned. Her eyes glittered with a strange light. ''It isn't always easy being a woman. There are times when our foolish hearts betray us. At such times we become weak. Vulnerable. At such times, we need someone to be strong for us. Someone who will keep us from making mistakes.''

''Majesty...''

''You do not have my permission to speak.'' Her words were clipped.

AnnaClaire bit her lip and lowered her head.

"I have lost my heart a time or two. But I have been wise enough to know that nothing could come of it. It is enough to indulge my passion and move on. There are many who urge me to wed." Her tone was ripe with sarcasm. "They would have me share the Throne. Dilute my power. Acquiesce to the wishes of a husband. But they do not know me." Her head lifted. "I am Elizabeth, Queen of England, Scotland and Ireland. And no man. No man," she repeated fiercely, "will bend me to his will."

"But Majesty…"

Those regal eyes flashed fire, silencing AnnaClaire's protest. "You may suffer for a little while, but one day you will bless my name in gratitude for the strength of my resolve. I intend to save you from your own foolish heart. There will be no more talk of loving the Blackhearted O'Neil. He is unworthy of an English noblewoman. Now." She set down the empty tankard and reached for a bell pull. "I will discuss this Irish problem with my trusted advisors. And then I will meet again with Conor O'Neil, that handsome, charming rogue with the silver tongue." Almost to herself she added, "I believe I shall keep him here at Court, so long as he amuses me."

While AnnaClaire stood rigid with shock, the door opened and Lord Dunstan and the others filed in. James Thompson took one look at his daughter's face and realized that she had just received the most painful of all news.

He took her cold hands in his. "My dear, are you all right?"

Elizabeth waved an imperious hand. "Your daughter is fine, Lord Thompson. Just fine. She will return home with you like a dutiful daughter. Is that not so, AnnaClaire?''

"Aye, Majesty.''

"Go then. You are excused.''

Fighting tears, AnnaClaire fled.

As she took her leave she heard the queen say to a servant, "Fetch Conor O'Neil. I will meet with him in my chambers when I have finished here with my advisors.''

"What is it, my lady?'' Innis, waiting alone in the hallway, caught AnnaClaire's hand when she turned away to hide her tears. She was too distraught to realize that he had ceased calling her Englishwoman. And that the note of contempt had been wiped from his tone, to be replaced with genuine concern.

"Oh, Innis. I've made such a mess of things.''

"Nay, my lady. Conor thinks he will still be able to persuade the queen to free Rory. He said the queen likes him. And women who like Conor have always given him whatever he wanted.''

"But it will be too late. You heard Tilden.''

"Aye. If I'd had my dagger, I could have given it to Rory for protection.''

She shook her head. "Already Rory has been returned to Fleet. He's in the hands of guards who will show no mercy.''

"Then it is up to us to free him.''

For a full minute AnnaClaire merely stared at him. He was nothing more than a child. She had no right to even consider the words he had spoken so simply. But it was the only thing that made any sense. Child or not, she had to agree.

Wiping her tears, she nodded. "Aye, Innis. It is up

to us. And we must not fail him now, when we've come so far." She caught his hand and began to race toward the door.

"Do you have a plan, my lady?"

"Nay, Innis." She was already breathless. And afraid. But she dare not stop now. "But I'm sure something will come to us by the time we reach Fleet Prison."

"Why did you buy these pastries from the vendor, my lady?"

AnnaClaire carefully wrapped the pastries in a linen square. "I intend to distract the jailer." She gave a wry smile. "I'm not certain my feminine wiles are enough."

"What are feminine wiles?"

"I'll tell you another time." Her smile faded at the sight of the stone fortress before them. What had she been thinking? How could she face this daunting place again?

She swallowed, and forced herself to move.

Once inside she prayed she could remember all the twists and turns that led to Rory's cell. As they descended the steps, slick with blood and excrement, she felt Innis clutch at her arm.

"I'm...afraid."

"As am I," she muttered. "But remember, if we should fail, Rory will forfeit his life. You remember our plan? Do you think you can do as I asked?"

"Aye, my lady. I'll...try." The boy bit down hard on his fear and moved by her side.

A deep voice stopped them. "'Ey there. Where d'ye think ye're goin?"

AnnaClaire and Innis froze, then slowly turned. The

burly jailer grinned, revealing blackened teeth. "Why, ye'r that lady who paid me the gold."

"Aye. And there's more for you today. But first we must visit the same prisoner as before."

He glanced at the boy, then at the woman. Two easy marks, he figured. Especially without the man to protect them this time. "Right you are. What's in the parcel?"

AnnaClaire swallowed. "Food. For the prisoner."

"Well now. I'll just have some of that." He held out his hand. When AnnaClaire took a step back he said sharply, "If you want my help, ye'd best hand it over."

"Aye. Of course." AnnaClaire unwrapped the pastries and watched as the jailer popped one into his mouth, then a second, then a third.

Innis tapped at his back. "If you keep that up, there soon won't be any left for our friend in the cell."

"Watch it, lad. Keep yer hands off me." He jerked away. "Yer friend won't mind. 'E'll still get to look at the female 'ere. That should be reward enough." He ate another pastry, then for good measure, ate the last as well. He belched loudly, then called, "Follow me."

He led them deeper into the prison, steering them along darkened corridors, far from the other guards.

"This isn't the way we came last time," AnnaClaire muttered as she slipped and steadied herself against the wall.

"I'm takin' ye along a different route this time." He chuckled to himself. "So's none of the other jailers happen upon us. Watch where ye walk. There's all sorts of…unpleasant things underfoot. Including rats."

He'd expected to hear a yelp from the female, and was disappointed when she spoke not a word. With a

soft chuckle he continued leading them ever deeper
into the depths of the prison. When he was certain they
were far enough away that he could do as he pleased
with them, he turned, only to find himself alone.
Swearing fiercely, he began to retrace his steps.

"Are you sure this is the way, my lady?"

"Aye. I recognize that cell." AnnaClaire shuddered
at the sight of the men in chains. The sounds of their
moans and cries sent fresh shivers along her spine.

She was nearly running now, in her haste to find
Rory before the jailer discovered their little trick.

"Here." She turned a darkened corner and Innis followed.

In the darkness she paused, listened, then pointed
toward the keyhole in a rusty door. "This is it."

Innis held up the key he'd picked from the jailer's
ring. When he turned the key in the lock, nothing happened.

"Rory," AnnaClaire called.

She heard a muffled reply.

"Rory." Without a torch, it was impossible to see
inside the cell. She prayed she wasn't making a terrible
mistake. "Rory. We've unlocked the door. But it's
stuck. You'll have to put your shoulder to it. Hurry.
Please."

She turned to Innis as a shuffling sound could be
heard from within. Just then, she saw the light from a
torch heading toward them. Though it wavered and
flickered, she could tell it was coming closer.

"The jailer. Rory, the jailer is coming. Hurry. Oh
hurry. Please."

She heard the curses as the jailer spotted them.
Heard the sound of his footsteps as he began to run

toward them. Then she heard the scrape of the door as it was forced open.

"So. Ye thought ye could trick old Colby, did ye?" The jailer swung the torch like a club.

Rory ducked, then, with a single blow, sent the man tumbling backward. The torch flew out of his hands and landed several feet away, where it sputtered in a pool of murky blood.

"Hurry, Rory," AnnaClaire called as she caught Innis by the hand. "We must get out of here before Tilden finds us."

"Did someone mention my name?"

They turned to find Tilden, sword already unsheathed, stalking toward them.

"I see you planned to spoil my fun." He glowered at AnnaClaire. "Now you're going to pay for this."

"Let the woman and boy go." Rory's voice was deadly calm.

"Why should I?" Tilden asked with a sneer.

"Because, if you do, I won't fight you."

Tilden threw back his head and roared. "What are you going to fight me with, O'Neil? Do you think your bare hands can win over my sword?"

"I'll manage to inflict a few blows before you end my life. But I give you my word. If you let the woman and boy go free, I won't defend myself."

"How noble. But this time, I have no intention of allowing any witnesses to survive. I'll start with you, O'Neil. Then the boy. And I may allow the woman to live long enough to…pleasure me. After that, you can have her for eternity."

He ran a hand over the blade of his sword and smiled at the thought of what he was about to do. Then he thrust it menacingly.

Rory danced to one side, and the blade sang against the stone wall. With a muttered oath Tilden turned and attacked. Rory ducked, then brought his knee up as hard as he could. With a grunt of pain Tilden doubled over. But when Rory brought his fist down, Tilden shifted, deflecting the blow. He straightened, thrust the blade, and gave a laugh of satisfaction when fresh blood flowed from Rory's already wounded shoulder.

"How much pain can an Irish peasant endure?" he called.

"More than an English bastard." Rory stepped back, avoiding another thrust, then managed to land a blow to Tilden's nose that sent blood gushing down the front of his tunic.

"You'll pay for that, O'Neil." He cupped a hand to his nose, then charged forward with all the fury of a wounded bull.

Rory managed to avoid the first thrust, but the next one caught him in the thigh. He was startled when his leg refused to hold him. Sinking to his knees, he watched helplessly as Tilden lifted his sword and towered over him.

"I didn't know it was your woman I'd killed that day, O'Neil." The soldier's eyes glittered with madness. "My men and I were just out for a little pleasure. But she was a pretty enough piece. Now the lad's mother, there was even more enjoyment. She cried and begged and pleaded for the sake of her babies. That just made it so much better."

From behind him came a strangled cry of pain and rage. "Rory was right. You're nothing but an animal, Tilden. You don't deserve to live."

At the sound of Innis' tear-choked voice, Tilden's head came up. He saw the boy lift something from the waist of the jailer. Saw something shiny streak through the air and land with a quiet thud in his chest. Felt the pain, hot and cold at the same time. And watched in disbelief as fresh blood began to ooze through his tunic.

He turned, intent upon striking down the lad. Before he could, the sword was knocked from his hand. With a cry of rage he turned toward Rory. And realized, too late, that his own weapon was now in Rory's hand.

"At last. Do you know how long I've waited for this moment?" Rory plunged the sword deeply into Tilden's chest, and watched as the soldier crashed to the stone floor and lay, writhing and twisting in pain. "May you burn in hell for all time, Tilden."

They stood, shocked into silence, as the soldier's life slowly slipped away.

Too weak to continue standing, Rory draped an arm around AnnaClaire's shoulders, and nearly fell. It took all the strength that AnnaClaire and Innis could manage to drag him, stumbling and falling, out of the prison and into the sunlight.

"We must take him to your father's home, my lady." Innis knelt beside Rory, who had collapsed in the lane.

To hide him from view, they rolled his unconscious body beneath a hedge.

"Nay, Innis. That will be the first place they'll search for us."

"But he'll soon bleed to death."

AnnaClaire watched as carriages rolled past just a few feet from where Rory lay. It was so unfair to have come so far, only to have freedom snatched from their grasp. There had to be a way.

"Stay here," she called.

Lifting her skirts, she began to walk along the street, hoping no one would notice the blood that stained her gown. Seeing a farmers' market crowded with vendors and shoppers, she strolled closer. There were several carts and carriages parked in a cluster. A quick glance told her that their owners were too busy to notice her.

She chose a vendor's small pony cart littered with sacks of fruits and vegetables. Grabbing the reins she led the pony until they were out of sight. Then she climbed up to the seat and cracked the whip. Pony and cart took off with a clatter. When she heard a commotion behind her, she urged the animal into a run.

"My lady." Innis looked up when she rolled to a stop. "You stole this?"

"Aye, Innis." She leapt down, and together they struggled to help Rory into the back of the cart. As she covered him with the sacks she muttered, "I know it's wrong, but right now I'm desperate to save Rory."

As she climbed to the seat and took up the reins, Innis said, "If we can't take him to your home, where will we hide him, my lady?"

She peered over her shoulder as the horse and cart started through the streets of London. "I've thought of a place. I know it sounds like madness, but it's the only place they'll never think of looking for Rory."

"Where is that, my lady?"

"In the queen's own home. My father has a suite of rooms in Greenwich Castle."

"Ah. Conor O'Neil." Elizabeth turned from the looking glass, then waved her maid away.

When they were alone in her chambers, she pointed to a silver tray on which rested a decanter of ale and two silver chalices. "I'll have some ale. You may join me."

"Thank you, Majesty. You are too kind." Conor filled the chalices, then handed one to the queen.

She crossed the room and sat. Pointing to the chair beside hers she said, "Come. Sit. Tell me about yourself and your family. I want to hear more of this hidden kingdom, Ballinarin. Such a lovely, musical name."

He sat down and gave her a smile guaranteed to melt her heart. "You would love it, Majesty. There is something wild and free about my home. A sky so blue, it would rival the blue of your eyes. A land greener than the emeralds at your throat."

"So." She touched a hand to her necklace. "You appreciate fine jewels."

"Aye. And beautiful women."

She could actually feel herself blushing. This Irish rogue did have a way about him. "Do you live like barbarians?"

He merely smiled. "Our keep at Ballinarin is not so fine as Greenwich. But our cook can make salmon taste like heaven. Her beef and kidney pie is a thing of beauty. And her pastries melt in your mouth." He stretched out his long legs, enjoying the fire, the ale and his regal hostess. "Besides that, our servants are loyal. Our tenant farmers are industrious. And our people are good, God-fearing men and women who want nothing more than to live and love and serve their God and their queen."

She shook her head and found herself laughing like a schoolgirl. "All this just rolls off your tongue like honey, Conor O'Neil." She sat back and studied him for several moments, noting the steadiness of his gaze, the slight flicker of amusement around the lips. Oh, he was a handsome devil.

She shook her head, as though not quite believing what she was about to say.

"What is it, Majesty? What has you looking so perplexed?"

She drained her glass and set it aside. "I'm not sure why, Conor O'Neil. Perhaps it is your charm. Perhaps it is my own foolish heart. But I have decided to have your brother brought before me once more. If he can persuade me of his truthfulness…" She shrugged. "We shall see."

As Elizabeth rang for her maid, Conor drained his ale in one long swallow. It was too soon to hope. But he couldn't help thinking about the trust his family had placed in him. And how desperately he longed to take his brother far from this vile place.

This would be their last, and perhaps their best, chance for freedom.

Chapter Twenty-One

"What do you mean, the prisoner is gone?"

The soldier who had been elected to deliver the news to the queen blanched at her explosion of fury. "I know only that when his cell was checked, it was empty." He stared at the toes of his boots, wishing he could flee. Or at least fall through a crack in the floor and disappear. "There is more, Majesty."

"More? What else? Has Fleet been emptied of prisoners? Did an army of Irish peasants storm the prison demanding the freedom of their hero?"

"Nay, Majesty. But…it was reported that the prisoner escaped with the help of a beautiful young woman and a small lad."

"A woman and lad? That is all it took? The fool guards couldn't stop one lovesick woman and a small boy? Fools. All of them. Heads will roll for this."

Elizabeth unleashed her wrath on her servant, who had just poured an elegant French wine into two crystal goblets. With a sweep of her hand the queen sent the goblets flying, sending a geyser of wine and shards of crystal spilling across the snowy linens. "Send for James Lord Thompson at once."

When the servant departed, the queen glowered at her handsome, sophisticated dinner partner. "What do you know of this, Conor O'Neil?"

"Not a thing, Majesty." Conor was feeling suddenly ill. All that fine food and wine, which, until a moment ago had been so delightful, were now congealed like a rock in his stomach.

He pushed away from the table and began to pace. "I should have expected something like this. Should have taken pains to see that they were watched." He looked up to see the queen staring holes through him. "Forgive me, Majesty. AnnaClaire and Innis are devoted to my brother, Rory. I knew they were desperate to save him. But I never dreamed they would try such a dangerous, foolish thing all by themselves."

"Not only did they attempt it, they succeeded. Now we must discover where they have taken him." Her stare had his heart stopping. "No one will be permitted to make me play the part of a fool. Do you hear?"

"Aye, Majesty." He was mopping his brow when a knock sounded on the door of the queen's chambers.

A moment later Lord Thompson entered, looking pale and shaken.

"I received word of your Majesty's...problem."

"Nay, James. It is not my problem. It is yours. O'Neil has escaped from Fleet." Elizabeth narrowed her eyes. "With the help of a woman and young lad. Where is your daughter?"

He glanced at Conor, then away. "I checked with my housekeeper. She did not return home."

"Where would she hide?"

His mind raced. "I know not, Majesty. It is too far to our country estates. In Rory O'Neil's condition, they would have to seek shelter here in London."

"You had best pray that you find her before I do, James. For when I find that headstrong daughter of yours, she will rue the day she defied her queen."

"Aye, Majesty."

Lord Thompson was about to depart when a servant entered. Seeing him she bowed slightly and gave him a smile. "I hope you enjoyed your bread and broth, my lord."

He arched a brow. "Bread and broth?"

"Aye. Three bowls of broth, in fact. And a loaf of bread and some cheese. I delivered it myself less than an hour ago to your chambers. Your daughter thanked me and said you were resting comfortably."

The queen's head came up. "Did I say she was headstrong, James? I should have said brazen. She has brought him here to Greenwich, flaunting him under my very nose." She turned to the servant. "Send for my advisors. Tell them to meet me at Lord Thompson's chambers. At once."

Elizabeth strode out the door, leaving James and Conor to trail in her wake as she stormed down the hall.

"I'm feeling almost human again." Rory emerged from the sleeping chamber, where he had bathed and dressed. AnnaClaire had applied a balm to his wounds, and had bound them with clean linen. She had even managed to provide him with a pair of her father's clean breeches and a fresh tunic, which had proved a bit too small for his muscular shoulders.

He glanced at the boy, asleep on the chaise. "He was so brave." He caught AnnaClaire's hand, brought it to his lips. "And you. What would I have done without you, my love? You gave me back my hope. My

life. My dreams for a future." He led her toward the
warmth of the fire. "How in heaven's name did you
ever manage to get me past all the guards and into these
quarters?"

"We stole a pony cart."

"You stole…?"

She placed a finger over his lips. "I know. It is very
wrong. And I'll make restitution. But desperate times
call for desperate measures, my love."

He merely grinned at her. He couldn't quite believe
what he was hearing. When had this prim and proper
woman become so clever and cunning?

"When we reached Greenwich, I told the guards we
were delivering fresh fruits and vegetables for the
queen's own supper. Outside the scullery Innis found
a small wheeled cart, and we simply loaded you inside
and covered you with sacks. No one questioned a
woman and little boy delivering food to the queen's
kitchen. Once inside, it was a simple matter to wait
until the servants were otherwise occupied to bring you
to my father's chambers."

"How very devious you are." The queen's voice
was high-pitched with anger as she yanked open the
door and stormed inside, followed by James and Conor.

At once Innis sat up, rubbing his eyes.

At the sight of the scowling monarch, Rory set
AnnaClaire behind him.

"Stand away, Irishman. I would speak to this de-
ceitful young woman." The queen crossed the room to
confront AnnaClaire.

When Rory started to speak Conor shook his head.
This was no time for heroics. Seeing the warning, Rory
stepped aside, but kept AnnaClaire's hand clasped in
his.

"You took it upon yourself to set a prisoner of the Crown free." Elizabeth's voice shook with righteous anger.

"Aye, Majesty. Please forgive me. But I overheard Tilden say he would have Rory beaten. And this time, he vowed, there would be no mistake. He intended to see that Rory would be dead, so there was no chance of escape."

"How can Tilden be a threat? I have ordered him held until his day at Court."

Innis ran to AnnaClaire and stood beside her, determined to protect her from the queen's wrath.

AnnaClaire glanced down at him, then said, "Perhaps he bribed his way to freedom. Or perhaps he broke free by force. However the method, Tilden arrived at Fleet, intending to kill not only Rory, but the two of us as well, so there would be no witnesses."

"I simply cannot believe anything you tell me, woman." Elizabeth glanced at the lad. "Is this true, boy?"

"Aye, Majesty."

"You would not speak an untruth to your queen?"

Innis shook his head vehemently.

"And where is Tilden now?"

Before the other two could speak Rory said, "He lies dead upon the cold stones of Fleet Prison. His death is on my hands, and mine alone."

AnnaClaire glanced at her father, seeing the shock and sadness in his eyes. Then she glanced at Conor, and could see only quiet relief that their adversary was dead. And a flicker of fear at what was to come.

Behind them, the queen's advisors filed into the room. Among them was Lord Dunstan, who watched and listened in stunned surprise.

Elizabeth's voice was lower now. Less frantic. More resigned. "And are you saying that you had no choice but to kill one of the Queen's own soldiers?"

"Aye, Majesty. But I do not regret what I did."

"I did not ask you how you felt about it, Irishman. I asked only if it was necessary."

"It was his life or ours."

She studied this arrogant rogue, who had caused such discord. For too long now, talk of the Blackhearted O'Neil had dominated drawing room conversations all across England. Now that he had washed away the blood and grime, she could see why. He was indeed a commanding presence, despite the ill-fitting clothes.

She turned. "Perhaps, Lord Dunstan, you were wrong in your assumption that these people could be easily subdued. Perhaps, instead of stirring their rebellious hearts, their queen should try another approach."

She folded her arms and walked the length of the room, then back. She stopped in front of Rory and pointed a finger. "I have decided to grant you your freedom, Irishman."

For the space of several seconds Rory couldn't speak. At last, finding his voice, he bowed his head. "Thank you, Majesty. I am in your debt."

"Indeed you are." She turned to Conor, enjoying the look of amazement on his handsome face. "And you, Conor O'Neil, interest me. I desire your presence here with me."

"Here? With you? In England?"

She smiled for the first time. "Aye. By my side. You will teach me about your country and its people. You will be my advisor on the Irish problem. And you will work closely with Lord Dunstan." Out of the corner of her eye she saw Dunstan's head come up. He would not be pleased by this turn of events, but he would learn to accept it.

"But first, Conor O'Neil, you will return home with your brother, to settle your affairs and prepare for a life at Court."

Conor bowed. "As you wish, Majesty." He could imagine his father's reaction when he gave him the news. It had been Gavin O'Neil's lifelong dream that his people have their own representative at Court. But for Conor it would mean leaving behind all that was comfortable and familiar, for a life among people like Dunstan, who would do all in their power to undermine his relationship with the queen.

As he brushed his lips over the queen's outstretched hand, he had another thought. This monarch would use him only as long as he amused her. When her interest waned, she would discard him without a thought.

The queen smiled her pleasure at Conor, then turned to AnnaClaire. "And now there is the problem of this headstrong young woman."

AnnaClaire flushed.

"What am I to do with you?" Elizabeth tapped a slim finger against her lips as she regarded her. "You have convinced me that you are indeed blinded by some silly notion of romance." Her eyes narrowed. "Would you deny it?"

"Nay, Majesty." AnnaClaire's heart had begun to beat faster. Could it be? Was it possible that the queen was about to grant her fondest wish? A dreamy, far-away look came into her eyes as she began to imagine herself sailing back to Ballinarin with Rory at her side. They would nurture young Innis, helping him grow into a fine young man. And perhaps, if they were truly blessed, there would even be babies of their own some day. Oh, how she longed to hear her queen give her blessing to her dream.

"I have told you how I feel about the marriage arrangement. But I suppose, in some cases it is best. In your case, I do believe that what is needed is a strong hand to guide you. It is the only thing that will save you from yourself. So." Elizabeth paused for dramatic emphasis. "I will grant you permission to wed."

"Oh, Majesty." AnnaClaire dropped a curtsy and caught Elizabeth's hands, kissing each of them. "From the bottom of my heart I thank you."

The queen waved a lofty dismissal. "It is settled then." She turned to AnnaClaire's father. "James, you will settle the terms of your daughter's dowry. Her intended has expressed an interest in your estate in Ireland. Clay Court, I believe it is called."

James Thompson nodded. "Clay Court is indeed part of AnnaClaire's dower estate. I will assign it upon her formal betrothal."

"Then, as your queen, I formally pronounce the betrothal of Lady AnnaClaire Thompson." The queen paused for dramatic effect. "To Lynley Lord Dunstan."

"Lord Dunstan?" Rory went very still. A frightening hardness came into his eyes. "If I but had a sword."

Innis, following Rory's lead, muttered, "If I but had my knife."

Conor, pale and ashen, whispered, "If I but had the words."

Seeing and hearing them, AnnaClaire fought for control, for she could feel herself dangerously close to the edge of hysteria.

At the sight of AnnaClaire's stricken face, Elizabeth added dryly, ''I thought you knew. Dunstan has spoken for you. And as your queen, I have consented.''

''But I...'' AnnaClaire couldn't speak. She made another valiant effort. ''I thought...''

''I know what you thought,'' Elizabeth said sternly. ''But I told you it was out of the question. It is enough that I have spared the Blackhearted O'Neil from the gallows. In return for that favor, you will abide by your queen's decision. Is that clear?''

AnnaClaire could feel her eyes filling. She blinked furiously and bit her trembling lip until she tasted blood. This time, there were no weapons, no words, that could save her. But if this were the price she must pay for Rory's life, so be it. She managed to whisper, ''Aye, Majesty.''

''Good. Now you and Dunstan will come with me. We have arrangements to make.'' She turned to Conor. ''You and your brother will leave at first light.''

Conor refused to even look at Rory, knowing the murderous look he would see. ''As you wish, Majesty.''

The men bowed as the queen swept from the room, followed by AnnaClaire and Dunstan.

At the door AnnaClaire turned for a last glimpse of Rory and Innis. But Dunstan closed a hand over her wrist and pulled her aside, closing the door behind him.

For long moments no one spoke. No one moved.

Then Rory swore. Loudly. Fiercely. And slammed a fist into the wall with such force, the candles on the mantel toppled.

He welcomed the pain. It gave him something to focus on besides his shattered heart.

After two long years of hardship and misery, he had

triumphed over his enemy. Had won his freedom. And had thought that all his dreams were finally within reach. But there was no sweet taste of victory. Instead, there was only the bitterness of defeat.

In one hideous moment, he had lost everything that had ever mattered to him. And the pain was almost more than he could bear.

Epilogue

"Briana." Moira was already seated in her splendid carriage, with her husband Gavin beside her. The promise of spring had given way to the glow of summer. The day was warm; the breezes gentle. "Where is Rory?"

"In his chambers." The girl pulled herself up to the carriage seat beside her parents. "He's sulking, as usual."

Moira cast a worried look at her husband.

Gavin shrugged. "It's all he's done since his return from London."

Moira sighed. "Did you tell him we were leaving for town?"

"He said he wasn't going."

"It's Velia's wedding day." Moira turned to her son. "Conor, speak to your brother. You've always had a way with words. Explain to Rory that Velia will be hurt if the whole family doesn't attend."

"Mother, stop poking and prodding at him." Conor pulled himself into the saddle of a magnificent stallion. "A festive wedding is the last place Rory wants to be. Let's just go or we'll be late for chapel."

"We can't leave yet. Innis isn't here."

"Innis isn't coming either." Briana carefully cradled the basket of rose petals that she would toss at the bride and groom after the ceremony. "He's gone to the field again. It's all he does now. Sit out there, looking at the place where they all died, and wallow in his fits of sadness. He said he'd dreamed of the Englishwoman being his mother. And now it's as though he's lost his mother all over again."

Moira gave another sigh as the carriage started off down the lane. All she had wanted was her family together again. But now that her prayers had been granted, she felt more frightened, more confused, than when they'd been apart.

Rory kept to his room, pacing like a caged animal. And Innis had returned more angry, more silent than ever. They were both wounded, and she was at a loss to know how to help them heal.

She glanced at her son, Conor, so splendid in his satin breeches and tunic, topped off with a cloak bearing the family crest. Soon he would leave them for a kingdom across the sea. It might be years before he would return.

And there was Briana, feeling lost and confused because her brothers had put a distance between themselves and her. She was growing up so quickly. Too quickly. Moira had seen the lass returning the looks of the bolder lads in the village. There was a difference now in the way Briana walked, as though aware of herself in a way she hadn't been before.

Moira shivered. It was as though the sun had been snatched from Ballinarin. And all that was left was a cold, barren wasteland. And all the dreams she'd had for her family had blown away on a bleak, chill wind.

* * *

Rory leaned a hip against the windowsill and watched as his family headed to town. The thought of Velia's wedding, of anyone's wedding, was too painful to endure.

How was he going to get through the days, the weeks, the endless years, without AnnaClaire? He knew it was possible to live with a broken heart. Hadn't he managed before? But then he'd had a goal to focus on. A burning need for vengeance had become his beacon, his reason for living. Now he had nothing. No reason to wake. No reason to dress. He touched a hand to the dark stubble at his chin. No reason to shave.

His life had become empty. Meaningless.

He knew it was the same for Innis. The boy had become a stranger to them all, spending long hours at the place where his family had met their death. Some nights he slept there, under the stars, returning only when hunger drove him. Always, when he returned, his eyes wore a haunted, desperate look.

Rory knew it would help if he and Innis could leave Ballinarin. The thought teased and tempted him. But it was an impossible dream. He'd been gone long enough as it was. With Conor going to England, their aging parents needed his help here.

Rory sighed and forced himself away from the window. So he would stay. And every day he would see her. In the gardens. In every room of this house. And miss her. Every day of his miserable life.

He walked down the hall to the room where she had stayed. He hadn't been able to bring himself in here since he'd returned to Ballinarin. It was too painful. He paused beside the bed, remembering how they had lain together, and laughed, and loved.

Without a thought to what he was doing, he snatched up the bed linens and breathed deeply, inhaling the fragrance of her that lingered still.

This was madness. He turned away, annoyed at his weakness. Why was he torturing himself this way? He could almost smell her here. Hear her footsteps. See her.

At a sound he turned and had to rub his eyes at the vision in the doorway. The vision didn't fade. Didn't disappear. In fact, the vision smiled, before speaking.

"I looked all through the keep. Where has everyone gone?"

He stayed where he was, afraid to move, for fear of frightening away the vision. She wore a hooded traveling cloak of russet velvet. Her cheeks were high with color, as though she'd been in the sun.

"Are you real? I haven't dreamed you?"

"Aye, Rory. I'm real. I'm no dream."

"But you must be a vision. I heard the queen order you to wed Dunstan."

"So she did. And it was quite a challenge to find a way to…persuade her to change her mind."

"You?" He took one step toward her, then halted. He was slowly going mad. But it was a sweet madness. Much better than hard, cold sanity. "Did you steal again, my lady?"

She shook her head and lowered her hood, revealing the familiar tumble of honey curls. "That theft shames me. I did make restitution to the vendor. I returned his pony and cart with a sack filled with gold. He told me I had his permission to steal his cart any time I pleased."

He nearly smiled. "So. You didn't steal. What did you do?"

"Something much worse, I fear. I begged, and pleaded, and wept copious tears. And when none of that would touch the queen's heart, I resorted to a lie."

"A lie?" He took another step, and another, until he was standing before her. He itched to touch her. But he held back, still afraid. "Was it a big lie?"

She nodded. "A very big lie. I told her I was carrying your baby."

"My...baby." He took a step back. "Are you?"

She smiled. "Nay."

He didn't know whether to laugh or weep. The thought of what she'd suggested was so enticing.

"We both know the queen doesn't trust me. She could have ordered her physicians to examine me. But I think she had already grown weary of the fight. And so she agreed to release me of my promise, if Dunstan would agree as well."

"How did you get Dunstan to agree to such a thing?"

"He was much easier to persuade. He doesn't love me, though he did want to use me to hurt you." She saw Rory's hand close into a fist at his side. "But what he coveted more than anything else was Clay Court. So I gave it to him."

He blinked. "You gave Dunstan your mother's home?"

"Aye."

"But it's been in your family for generations. And you love it so."

"I do. But not as much as I love your home here at Ballinarin. And your family. And Innis. I'd hoped that we could be the parents he yearns for."

"Is that all you love? My home? My family? Innis?"

She shook her head. "I do love them all. Desperately. But not nearly as much as I love you, Rory."

He did touch her then. Just a hand to her hair. She was warm. And real. And so very very soft. "Say that again."

"I said I don't love…"

"Not that part. The last of it."

She smiled. That wonderful radiant smile that rivaled the sun. And then she touched a hand to his cheek in a gesture so achingly sweet, he felt all the warmth, all the sunlight that had been missing from Ballinarin for so long.

"I love you, Rory O'Neil."

He framed her face with his hands and stared deeply into her eyes. "One more time, please."

She placed a hand to his chest and felt the wild, erratic rhythm of his heartbeat. "I love you, Rory O'Neil. Only you. But if you decide to have me, you must know that I've come with no dowry. Though my father has given his reluctant permission, there are no estates. No jewels. No gold. All I have are these clothes."

"Is that all? I'm not certain 'twill be enough." He thought a moment, then brushed his lips over her eyelids. "Will your eyes always see only me?"

"Aye." She said it on a sigh.

He continued brushing kisses over her cheek, the corner of her mouth. "Will your lips always kiss only me?"

She could barely speak now for the pounding of her heart. "Aye."

"Then I have all I'll ever want or need, my love."

"Oh, Rory." She wrapped her arms around his neck and returned his kisses. "I was so afraid I'd lost you.

So afraid you'd be gone when I got here. It took me so long. So long. And I'm truly sorry about the lie.''

"Ah yes. That lie.'' He took the kiss deeper, feeling the heat begin to spread, melting his heart, sending his blood surging through his veins once more. "What are we to do about that lie?''

"I don't know. My father believes he will be coming for a visit in the spring, to see his firstborn grandchild. Though he has cut me off without a piece of gold, he intends to lavish his entire fortune on our children. But I feel guilty that I bring you nothing.''

"Nothing?'' He rained kisses over her face, her throat. "AnnaClaire, you're real. You're here with me. Here to stay. I've found my reason to live again.'' He slipped the cloak from her shoulders and reached for the buttons of her gown.

She lifted a hand to stop him. "Shouldn't we wait? To tell your family? And Innis?''

"Aye. In an hour. Or two. Or three. But for now, just let me love you, AnnaClaire. It's been so long. So long.'' He ran hot wet kisses along her neck, making her sigh with pleasure.

As they tumbled to the bed he murmured, "Besides, if we work very hard at it, we might be able to turn your lie into the truth.''

"You mean…?'' She gave a low, throaty laugh as she realized his intention. "Oh Rory. Rory O'Neil. My wild, blackhearted rogue. I do love you so.''

"And I love you, my fine noble English lady. With all my heart. With all my being. For all time.''

And then there was no need for words. They showed each other, as lovers have from the beginning of time, just how much love they had stored in their hearts.

* * * * *

Author's Note

Ireland has such a rich history. Bloody battles.
Fierce loyalties and religious differences that
have existed for centuries and continue today. A
land that has nurtured poets and pirates,
warriors and lovers.

The hidden kingdom of Ballinarin exists only
in my imagination. But if you should travel to
Ireland, you'll find such places. Wild and
savage, cool and restful, and different from any
other place on earth. But it is the people who
are truly Ireland. Strong-willed, independent,
solid.

There is something about the lovely, green,
mist-shrouded island of my ancestors that
touches a chord deep in me. I hope the O'Neil
Saga will touch my readers as well.

If you enjoyed what you just read,
then we've got an offer you can't resist!

Take 2 bestselling love stories FREE!

Plus get a FREE surprise gift!

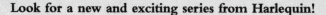

COMING NEXT MONTH FROM

HARLEQUIN HISTORICALS

- **THE WELSHMAN'S BRIDE**
  by **Margaret Moore,** author of A WARRIOR'S PASSION
  In the latest addition to the WARRIOR SERIES, a fun-loving
  nobleman and a demure chatelaine learn to appreciate their
  personality differences and ultimately fall in love.
  HH #459 ISBN# 29059-4 $4.99 U.S./$5.99 CAN.

- **HUNTER OF MY HEART**
  by **Janet Kendall**
  Two Scottish nobles are bribed into marrying to protect
  their past secrets in this emotional tale from a sensational
  new author.
  HH #460 ISBN# 29060-8 $4.99 U.S./$5.99 CAN.

- **MAGGIE AND THE MAVERICK**
  by **Laurie Grant**
  Wounded in the Civil War, the cantankerous Garrick Devlin
  finally learns to love again in the final story involving the tall,
  dark and handsome Devlin brothers.
  HH #461 ISBN# 29061-6 $4.99 U.S./$5.99 CAN.

- **THE UNLIKELY WIFE**
  by **Cassandra Austin,** author of FLINT HILLS BRIDE
  A handsome lieutenant falls for his commanding officer's
  flirtatious daughter during a journey to an army fort.
  HH #462 ISBN# 29062-4 $4.99 U.S./$5.99 CAN.

DON'T MISS THESE FOUR GREAT TITLES
AVAILABLE NOW:

HH #455 ROBBER BRIDE
Deborah Simmons

HH #456 THE TENDER STRANGER
Carolyn Davidson

HH #457 RORY
Ruth Langan

HH #458 FATHER FOR KEEPS
Ana Seymour